NOTES FROM TEXAS:
ON WRITING
IN THE LONE STAR STATE

Notes from Texas:
On Writing in the Lone Star State

Edited by W.C. Jameson

TCU Press
Fort Worth, Texas

Library of Congress Cataloging-in-Publication Data

Notes from Texas : on writing in the lone star state / edited by W.C. Jameson.
p. cm.
Includes bibliographical references and index.
ISBN 978-0-87565-358-7 (alk. paper)
1. American literature--Texas--History and criticism--Theory, etc. 2. Authors, American--Homes and haunts--Texas. 3. Authorship. 4. Texas--In literature. I. Jameson, W. C., 1942-

PS266.T4N68 2008
810.9'9764--dc22

2007038161

TCU Press
P. O. Box 298300
Fort Worth, TX 76129
817.257.7822
http://www.prs.tcu.edu

To order books: 800.826.8911

Design and Illustration by
Barbara M. Whitehead

To Texas writers and literature
Past, present, and future

W.C. Jameson

CONTENTS

INTRODUCTION

W. C. JAMESON

GROWING UP in West Texas yielded one adventure after another. I still remember standing on the north bank of the Rio Grande and staring southward into Mexico. I wondered what lay beyond my vision, what sort of people and landscapes could be found. Tentatively, I forded the shallow river and visited small pueblos on the other side where burros were more common than automobiles and the residents friendly and welcoming.

In my own neighborhood, Tejano and ranchera music rang loud and clear, live and recorded, and the air was often filled with the aromas of cooking meat and fresh corn tortillas. My young life was filled with such interesting people as working cowboys, horse thieves, songwriters and musicians, and storytellers.

In my teens, my first encounter with the Guadalupe Mountains of West Texas yielded many glorious hours discovering Indian artifacts, remote caves, and abandoned cabins and mines. I'll never forget listening to area old timers relating tales of lost mines and buried treasures, ghosts, and the final days of the Mescalero Apaches.

My encounters with the special people, places, and things along that Texas–Mexico border generated night after night of vivid dreams. Years later, some of those young-boy dreams led to published stories, then to books, many with a decidedly Texas flavor. Even at that young age, I realized there was an epic quality to that landscape of rugged mountains rising out of the creosote-dotted lowlands, broad, challenging deserts, deep canyons, wild rivers, and compelling, diverse people. Those who have traveled and grown intimate with this unique place would never deny that it ranks among the finest works of nature. The West Texas where I grew up was a place that facilitated big dreams. One of my dreams was to become a writer.

That unique segment of the Chihuahuan Desert geographers refer to as the Trans-Pecos comprised my backyard. Here could be found the aforementioned Guadalupe Mountains, the Davis Mountains, the Chisos Mountains of the Big Bend, and lesser known but no less challenging and mysterious ranges in which Apache Indians once lived and that served as hiding places for outlaws. Endless miles of sand dunes waited to be explored. The Rio Grande cutting through the deep canyons of the Big Bend called to me. Many times I rafted rapids and cascades, adrenaline-pumping journeys that are as fresh for me today as they were decades ago. The river begged to be crossed. More times than I can count I waded to the Mexican side to search and discover.

As a nine-year-old, I entered the amazing physical and cultural world of border West Texas, reveling in its beauty, challenges, and inspirations. At the same time I was encountering the land and people firsthand, I also discovered adventure in my mother's sparse collection of tomes. As I thumbed through works by Churchill, Tolstoy, Costain, and others, I marveled at descriptions of the countryside, of the characterizations of people, the lives they led, the obstacles they faced. Though too young to understand much of the content, I knew there was a special magic on those pages.

I vividly recall a day in the fifth grade. The teacher led the students out of the classroom and into the parking lot. She introduced us to a new and most wonderful concept—the bookmobile. I stepped into the sanctum of that big, boxy vehicle and the smell of the books shelved within assailed me, an intoxicating aroma that enchanted, a bewitching from which I have never recovered. I cannot enter a library, a used bookstore, or someone's book-lined study without reliving that moment.

Timidly, I walked up and down the interior of that clunky van peering at titles. As if guided by some spirit, I pulled down a copy of *A Vaquero of the Brush Country* by J. Frank Dobie. Following instructions from my teacher, I received a library card and checked out the book.

That evening I lay on my bed completely lost in the tales. After a few pages I realized I was reading about another part of Texas, its history and lore related by a Texan. I read the book twice before returning it the following week. I located and checked out another Dobie book, *Coronado's Children*. In this volume I was reading about places near where I lived, and it thrilled me. The familiar textures and aromas of the West Texas deserts and mountains revisited me, the entire landscape came alive under the skillful rendering of the author. At that moment, the seed was planted for me to become a writer.

Every week until school ended for summer vacation, I checked out a different J. Frank Dobie book. I grew curious about the other volumes shelved in that charmed vehicle. On a whim, I checked out *Tarzan the Untamed*. I knew of Tarzan from the dreadful movies, but I was attracted by the author's name—Edgar Rice Burroughs—and the alluring artwork that graced the dust jacket.

While Dobie led me down the road of Texas history and folklore, Burroughs thrilled me with his tales of adventure, danger, escape, and overcoming enormous odds in locations as diverse as Mars, Venus, the American Southwest, and the jungles of Africa. Burroughs' books were similar to the dreams I had. Years later I learned from reading a biography of the author that most of his stories came from his own dreams. I feared I would not be able to get through that summer without the bookmobile, so I went in search of other sources. I found the public library in downtown El Paso, an amazing repository for books relating to Texas in general and the Southwest in particular. I returned countless times throughout my high school and college years to this destination. It remains one of my favorite places today. As with the mountains and canyons of West Texas, I explored up and down the aisles between the stacks of books.

I could not get enough of Dobie and Burroughs. I discovered other authors whose words held me in thrall: C.L. Sonnichsen, Tom Lea, John Graves, John Steinbeck, and others. Many of them were Texans. What a wonderful profession this must be, but I had no clue that people could earn a living as a writer. I started writing in longhand on scraps of paper. At eighteen, I began to craft stories during lunch break at the loading docks, during idle moments on trips, or before going to bed at night.

When I completed around thirty pages, I would go back and read over what I had written with disappointment. I realized it was a long way from measuring up to the work of Dobie and Burroughs. Though the fruits of my rudimentary creativity appalled me, I kept on, not willing to give up. Then, in my mid-twenties, I read a magazine that published western history and lore. When finished, I was flushed with the feeling that I could write a better article than any of those contained in that publication. I decided to try. I labored over an article for weeks, sent it in, and received a check for $200 in the mail a month later. My first sale, and right out of the starting gate. I decided I would quit my job on the docks, write four or five articles a week, and live on easy street for the rest of my life.

In short order, I encountered rejection. The next seven pieces I sent out bounced back. I was discouraged, but some inner voice told me to stay with it. Writing became far more satisfying than unloading boxcars and trucks. Some fifteen magazine articles later a publisher called wanting to know if I had enough material for a book. I lied and said I did. I received a contract and went to work. The book came out, received positive reviews, went into multiple printings, and led to a series of twenty volumes.

With each book, I worked hard to craft my stories with the skills manifested by Dobie and others. I never had formal writing courses, either in high school or at the university. For years, I operated on instinct. As I wrote, I continued reading —as many as 150 books a year—in the hope of learning more from those I admired. New inspirations were added to my list of those to emulate. I found *The Time It Never Rained* by Elmer Kelton, and thought it the best book I ever read. I read *North to Yesterday* by Robert Flynn, an amazing trail drive novel that was released in trade paperback at the same time as Larry McMurtry's *Lonesome Dove*. Though *Lonesome Dove* won the Pulitzer and other important awards, many argued that Flynn's was the better story.

There were others: Larry L. King's spellbinding essays; James Ward Lee's humor; James Reasoner's well-crafted novels of the West; Carlton Stowers' impeccably crafted true crime books.

Over time, and with more published works added to my résumé, I found opportunities to mingle with some of these long admired folk at writers' conferences. Several became friends. Though my credentials looked good on paper, I remained awed. How did they accomplish their goals? Why did they choose the writing life? What influence did the history, lore, and culture of Texas play in their creative process?

I decided to ask. Therein lay the early genesis of this book.

TCU Press gave me the opportunity to invite iconic Texas writers to be part of a collection of essays related to their writing. The influence of Texas could include but was not limited to landscape, culture, music, weather, and historic events. The objectives were to inform and enlighten those of us who had long been inspired by their works.

I encouraged all the writers to make their essays boundless and not be confined or restricted. I wanted this to be a chance to express what they wished to share about their art and their life as a Texas writer.

We selected fourteen of Texas' best writers. Each responded with enthusiasm. Within days the essays, filled with vitality and passion, started coming in the mail. I held in my hands personal insights into the world of writing. I read about creativity, perseverance, success, joy. At my fingertips was more knowledge and discernment than one could receive in several years of formal instruction.

Author Judy Alter is a transplant who, as a child, thought Texas was a foreign country. She wanted to be a writer when she arrived, but didn't know what to write about. She soon became fascinated with the state's history. "Texas gave me the stories," she wrote, and "gave me the body of my writing." Some sixty books later, Alter continues to be inspired by the Lone Star State, the land, and the people. As the director of TCU Press, she has had a prominent role in publishing many noted Texas writers, among them Robert Flynn, Elmer Kelton, and Larry L. King.

Robert Flynn's earliest ambition was "to have something to say." He credits a professor at Baylor University who told him that, indeed, he had something to say and that he could write. Flynn discovered the reward for writing was the writing itself and that it provided for the occasional discovery of some insight or idea. Flynn describes his childhood in Chillicothe in Hardeman County and, via his writing, realized many new and change-inducing concepts. "I was in a wilderness," he says, and he writes almost every day trying to find a way out.

Don Graham may be best known to many Texans from his well-crafted columns on Texas books and films that appeared in *Texas Monthly* magazine. Graham discusses the excitement he felt when he learned to write his name, "the elation of seeing the words one wrote, made public." Known for both his nonfiction and fiction, Graham discusses his desire to write and how he "wants to tell the truth about the way we lived then and the way we live now."

Rolando Hinojosa-Smith recalls his first writing at a young age as one remembers a "first love, date, or kiss." Hinojosa-Smith writes about "the many lives led by Mexican Americans, particularly Texas Mexicans, in their native land [and their] experiences in the military." Hinojosa-Smith expresses his loyalty to small presses and university presses as outlets for his work and explains why.

Paulette Jiles, the author of the best selling *Enemy Women,* lives on a small ranch in the Texas Hill Country. She writes with the heart and soul of a poet and speaks about the variety of Texas landscapes and how they seem to "carry stories well."

Elmer Kelton, one of Texas' most beloved writers, was descended from generations of cowboys. He said he wasn't supposed to be a writer; he was supposed to be a cowboy. He discusses things that happened along the way to point him in the direction of writing. Kelton grew up knowing men who lived during the times of trail drives, men who hunted buffalo, and listened to their stories. Thus, he gained a fascination for Texas history. Known for his well-researched historical novels of Texas and the West, Kelton writes about the land and the people as one who has experienced it firsthand.

I first encountered the work of Larry L. King during the 1980s via his book *None But a Blockhead: On Being a Writer.* Captivated by King's prose and attitude, I searched out other writings by this Putnam native. I came to the conclusion, as others have, that he is one of the best essayists in America. King, never without a highly developed sense of humor, writes of his beginnings as an author, of his persistence and tenacity, which kept him from being dissuaded from becoming a writer by teachers and others.

My first introduction to James Ward Lee was at a meeting of the Texas Folklore Society many years ago. His banquet speech was gut-holding, roll-on-the-floor hilarious, and I have never forgotten it. Lee maintains he is not a writer, but his essays and books have delighted readers for years. Known for his insight on matters of Texas cuisine and culture, Lee confesses the origin of his vision.

Born and raised in Texas, James Reasoner, as a six-year-old, scripted out pretend gunfights with his playmates, assigning roles and generating plots. Reasoner says he was influenced by another Texas writer, the late Robert E. Howard from Cross Plains, "not because of what he wrote but because of how he wrote." To paraphrase James Reasoner, the myths, culture, history, and landscape of Texas are an inescapable and enduring part of the Lone Star writer. Some write about other places, he says, but more often than not they come home.

Clay Reynolds claims that in order to understand a place well enough to write about it, it becomes necessary to leave—physically, geographically, and spiritually. He points out that it is not the distance or the destination that is important but the journey. Reynolds adeptly writes of this and other ironies, the "raw material of character, the fountainhead of fiction."

Joyce Gibson Roach, acclaimed as an authentic Texas voice, draws on her West Texas ranch upbringing, which she says provides the strength and flavor that characterizes her award-winning writings.

Poet and songwriter Red Steagall walked and rode across much of the Texas landscape, absorbing every inch, every nuance, of the place and its people. He attributes his success "to the childhood experiences that let my imagination run wild and have prepared me to write about the people that I admire the most."

Carlton Stowers writes true crime better than anyone. The well of Texas topics that he pursues runs deep, and he says "the boundaries I've limited myself to stretch farther than the eye could ever hope to see."

Having founded and directed two successful and important presses, Fran Vick is a leading figure in the world of Texas letters. With a sharp eye and a keen appreciation for Texas writers and writing, she has been instrumental in getting important works into print.

During the process of compiling and organizing these essays, I read them many times. With each reading, I gained new insight or encountered some elusive revelation that had escaped me during my four decades as a professional writer. I absorbed additional bits of information or new observations. From these contributors, I learned what might make me a better writer. Even after fifty published books and some 1,500 articles and essays, I still consider myself the student. As such,

I greet the knowledge and observations provided by these inspiring teachers with ardor and appreciation. I invite the reader to do the same.

NOTES FROM TEXAS

Olan Mills

JUDY ALTER

JUDY ALTER is the author of nearly sixty books, fiction and nonfiction for both adults and young readers. Her latest books for children are *John Barclay Armstrong: Texas Ranger*, *Martin DeLeon: Tejano Empresario*, and *Souvenirs from Space*. Her latest adult title is the collection of short stories, *Sue Ellen Learns to Dance*. She is a recipient of the Owen Wister Award for Lifetime Achievement from the Western Writers of America, Inc, and her books have won awards from The Texas Institute of Letters, WWA, and the National Cowboy Hall of Fame. Judy holds a PhD. in English from Texas Christian University. She has been the director of TCU Press since 1987.

NOTES FROM AN OUTSIDER

I HAVE LONG envied native Texans. Elmer Kelton, Joyce Roach, Bob Flynn, Fran Vick, and others speak a language I can only imitate. Joyce Roach once said something to me about the perspective I, as an outsider, bring to Texas fiction. I am astonished to think that after forty years in the state, I'm still a Johnny-come-lately, an interloper, even a damn yankee. But whether or not you were born in Texas is important to a lot of people. Most of us remember the group that set up booths in malls during the seventies to seek out those born in Texas. If you could qualify, you received a membership and a certificate—Born in Texas. I think I bought memberships for my four children and hungered for one for myself.

I was born in Chicago, where my father was a physician and college president. He was a very British man who grew roses in his free time. When we talk in western fiction about the relationship between a man and his land, I don't think roses are what we have in mind. If my father ever rode a horse, I don't know about it. And when Texans of my generation were riding horses, I was riding a bike. I rode a horse as a child once, in a stable in Chicago, and hated it. I've not been on a horse again to this day, though I've written a lot about young girls and grown women and their relationships to horses.

Growing up, I thought Texas was a foreign country. When my brother was stationed at the Corpus Christi Naval Air Station, my parents came to Texas to see him. They came back with descriptions of what sounded almost like semi-tropical land—not at all what any of us expected of Texas.

Then when I was in graduate school, the man I would marry went to West Texas—Turkey, to be specific—to a funeral and came back describing a vast, barren brown land. More my expectation of Texas!

On our first trip to Texas together—for him to investigate a surgical residency and me to find out about the English doctoral program at TCU—we drove across Oklahoma in April. The fields were lush and green, and I remember particularly the plum thickets were in full bloom. But Joel kept saying, "Just wait till we get to Texas, Judith, it will all change." I began to wonder if a great curtain would drop at the Red River and we would instantly cross from green to brown. Of course, we came to North Central Texas, which is usually beautiful in April, as it was that year. I was surprised though that it reached the eighties during the day! So hot, I thought. (Little did I know!)

Long before I moved to Texas, I knew I wanted to write. I remember summers when I rode my bike to the public library each morning, brought home two or three books, spent the day on the front porch reading them, and went back the next day for a new supply. It did not make me popular with the neighborhood kids, but I think those library summers shaped me as a storyteller and writer. I wrote my first short stories at about the age of ten. They were about a nineteenth-century spinster named Miss Shufflebaum and her cocker spaniel, Taffy (that's because I desperately wanted a cocker spaniel). In high school I sent a short story to *Seventeen,* then the bible of high school girls. It came back immediately of course, but I tried. When I went to college, I majored in English because I liked to read—I had no thought of a career because I was going to get married and some man would take care of me. (Oh, was I ever the typical child of the fifties!)

So I knew I wanted to write—but I didn't know what to write. I used to sit at my desk and think I'd write if I knew what to write. Once a calligrapher friend and I collaborated on a Texas ABC book—there are lots of them today but there weren't back in the early 1980s. It was twenty-six pages of brief introductions to important points in Texas history, one for each letter of the alphabet—A is for Alamo, B for bluebonnet, and so on. (I had to stretch for Y and came up with "Y'all come back" for Texas hospitality.) When someone suggested I do similar books for other states and start with my home state, I thought only briefly about Illinois and realized there wasn't a whole alphabet of history there. Illinois, I'll have you know, is not a lackluster state. We gave the country Lincoln, after all, and even if you still call it the War of Northern Aggression, you have to admit his greatness. And Chicago—that city has a great sprawling history, highlighted by Mrs. O'Leary and her cow. But somehow it pales in the face of Texas history.

Over the years I've tried to write about Chicago. Once I wrote a young-adult mystery based on an actual stalker who threatened the all-female household of a high school friend of mine to the point that my parents forbade me to stay overnight there. I tried to catch the ambience of being in high school on Chicago's South Side in the 1950s, but I couldn't find a home for the manuscript. And I labored long over a novel about the Chicago World Exposition of 1893 and Mrs. Potter Palmer, who was president of the Board of Lady Managers and was the first woman to combine the concepts of wealth and philanthropy. I loved writing it, loved the research—I grew up in the neighborhood of the exposition—but every agent that read it said it read like a young-adult to them. To this day I'm not sure if it really does or if I was just pigeon-holed in their minds. But we all have unpublished manuscripts, and that's one of mine.

No, it was Texas that gave me the stories I wanted to write about. When we first moved here, Joel was in that residency, and I was in graduate school on a fellowship; we were dirt poor. We did what was free, and we frequently went to the Amon Carter Museum in Fort Worth, which then had its original name of The Amon Carter Museum of Western Art. We were both captivated by the paintings and sculpture of Charles M. Russell and Frederic Remington—I don't suppose I knew about either one before. But today I trace my interest in things western to that exposure to art. I did much of the research for my dissertation, "The Western Myth in American Literature and Painting in the Late Nineteenth and Early Twentieth Centuries," at the Amon Carter.

In the years since, I have studied hard and tried to write like a native Texan. Even so, after all these years, I have strong handicaps as an author and a nonnative. I hope that I write about horses and western women with authenticity. But if I do, it's because I have friends who are real westerners, and I am shameless about picking their brains. When I wanted to write a novel based on the life of Wild West roper Lucille Mulhall, I called Joyce Roach for information about roping. She was so thorough and I worked so much of the material into the novel that she finally said, "Quit with the roping and get on with the novel, Judith."

In the mid-1970s, an older friend gave me her mother's memoir about being a child in a small East Texas town around the turn of the century. It contained wonderful details of daily life and an exciting story. The child's father, a deputy sheriff, arrested a man for drunkenness on Christmas Eve. When the man got out of jail, he shot the deputy for disgracing him. Because I was fairly new to Texas and didn't yet know its stories, I didn't realize what a violent history East Texas has. My reaction was "That's really unusual, because after all, this wasn't the Wild West with shootouts in the streets." But later I learned that it was. Still at the time I didn't know what to do with this jewel. After all I didn't write fiction. As a PhD. candidate, I was trained to support, defend, criticize, do anything but give in to my imagination. So I put the manuscript on that huge stock of "I-don't-know-what-to-do-with-these things" every writer had. Then, almost coincidentally, I read two or three novels with young girls as the protagonist, and I suddenly realized I could do that. I could make that little girl fourteen instead of four and write a novel about her and the effect of her father's death on her and her family. The result was *After Pa Was Shot,* though I titled it *A Year with No Summer* and still like that better than the publisher's title.

Although later for several years I spent as many free weekends as I could on a friend's guest ranch near Tyler, I'd never been to East Texas at that time except to drive from Fort Worth to visit my family, who by then lived in North Carolina. So as I wrote, I called two friends and asked them such questions as, "If you were a child in East Texas in 1904, what would you do to kill idle time?" One of the answers was, "Chunk rocks in the stock tank," so Ellsbeth, the central figure, spends a lot of time chunking rocks. Another question was, "If you were going to a funeral, what food would you take?" The answer was dried fruit pies.

When I wrote *After Pa Was Shot,* I didn't know I was writing a young-adult novel. I simply told the story, in the first person, as it came to me and using the details in the memoir. By happenstance I met a New York agent who read the manuscript, liked it, and marketed it as a young-adult, probably based both on content and length. When it was published, I was categorized as a young-adult novelist and still am today, even though I've written almost as much adult fiction (and way more young-adult nonfiction than anything else).

In Texas, I've found the stories that have given me the body of my writing. Unlike most of my native Texan friends, I am less apt to find inspiration in or to write about the land, perhaps because I don't know it instinctively in the way Elmer Kelton, for instance, does. Instead, I find inspiration in the stories, the people, and the history.

On a trip to that ranch in Van Zandt County, I read a small county history and one paragraph about the Van Zandt County War leapt out at me. It seems when General Phil Sheridan was in charge of reconstruction in Texas, Van Zandt County posted announcements that it was withdrawing from Texas and the Union. Sheridan, who once said if he owned Texas and Hell, he'd rent out Texas and live in Hell, would not tolerate rebellion. He marched his troops to Van Zandt County, but the farmers hid in the trees and took potshots at the soldiers who marched up the road in formation. It was the sort of tactic the Americans used during the Revolutionary War. The army retreated, and the farmers went into town to celebrate with a huge bonfire and the little brown jug. Of course after nightfall, the army came, surrounded and arrested the celebrating "victors." The men were kept all winter in a stockade on the edge of town. When the spring rains came, they discovered they could push the posts far enough apart to walk out. One by one the men of Van Zandt County walked off into the night. Some never returned. Now who could resist turning that into fiction? *Luke and the Van Zandt County War,* my second young-adult novel, is complete with the Ku Klux Klan, a lynching, and Civil War feuding.

Much more recently, I was at a luncheon where Steve Harrigan was one of the main speakers. He had just published *The Gates of the Alamo,* his blockbuster novel. After lunch a woman came up to him and said she wanted to tell him about her friend whose great-great-(I forget how many greats) grandmother had as a young girl ridden across South Texas, urging settlers in Austin's Colony to join Sam Houston's army after the fall of the Alamo. Steve was polite. I was fascinated. I carried that story around in my head for a long time, even talked to the descendant—she had a clipping about it but didn't know where it was, which absolutely appalled me. How do you lose something that important? Anyway, the young-adult novel, *Sam Houston Is My Hero,* grew out of that brief lunchtime encounter. And I loved writing it, because I learned so much about the Runaway Scrape and the Battle of San Jacinto, things I had only vaguely understood before.

But even as I became comfortable with Texas materials, I still made mistakes and needed my friends to rescue me. In *So Far From Paradise,* an early novel commissioned by the *Fort Worth Star-Telegram* as a Sesquicentennial project, I wanted to have the central figure take a shotgun from a desperate and dangerous man. The setting was Decatur in North Central Texas, and the time was late in the Civil War, when there were hangings of so-called northern sympathizers by frustrated southerners. I called the late Don Worcester to ask how you would break a rifle if you wanted to disarm an enemy. I had planned to have the central figure slam the shotgun against a wooden stockade-like wall, but Don explained that the shotgun probably would have fired, and I would have lost my central figure right there. He suggested another solution—breaking it over the knee, I think, which sounded painful to me, but I took his word.

If true stories and historical accuracy make regional literature authentic, so too does voice. Over the years, both as author and editor, I've become more and more interested in the importance of voice in fiction, and I frequently cite Elmer Kelton as a novelist with a strong, clear, and believable voice.

If someone handed me one page of one of Elmer's novel, with no heading, no identification, I'd recognize his voice. Reading his fiction is like listening to him talk. He is a West Texan, the product of ranch country, and he sounds like it. I suspect you can make the same case for Jane Austen or William Faulkner or any number of novelists—and it might make an interesting paper. But before I moved to Texas, my voice was a Midwestern twang. After I'd lived here about a year, local people were still teasing me about my northern accent, but family and friends back home laughed aloud at my southern drawl. And even today my kids say that my voice changes—and my pronunciation—when I talk about things western.

But speaking voice and fictional voice are different, and if I have a fictional voice—and it seems presumptuous to suppose that—it's as a woman in the American West of the past. Beyond my early fascination with the Amon Carter Museum, I can't exactly tell you why my voice is western. The fiction of my contemporaries—Carolyn Osborn or Shelby Hearon or Beverly Lowry—about slick, bright, slightly disengaged contemporary women doesn't have a particularly western voice, though Shelby especially is adept at capturing the feel and details of place in Texas. Just read *Hug Dancing* and you'll be transported to Waco, for better or worse. But I write almost exclusively about women of the past. And I don't think my writing voice is a feminist statement, though I can't support that either. I just know that I'm at my best as a writer when I put myself inside the head of a Texas woman of the past and tell her story in the first person.

The first person voice is important to me. The conventional wisdom is that if an author writes a first book in the first person, he or she then graduates to the third-person voice. But I've never graduated. The few times I've tried to write in third person have been clearly unsuccessful, as though the voice were off key. Once, worried about that, I asked Larry Swindell, then book editor of the *Fort Worth Star-Telegram,* what would happen if I never graduated. He assured me it wouldn't be bad if I always wrote in the first person in a feminine voice.

In the 1990s I was asked to write the second chapter of the collaborative novel *Legend*. Elmer started the central figure out in a homestead on the Texas plains, where his family is massacred by Indians. I believe Elmer left him a bounty hunter (I would never have thought of that.) But then I wrote the only chapter in the entire novel told from a female point of view, that of a young eastern woman, come to Fort Worth to stay with her pregnant (and difficult) sister. The young woman, Melanie Beaufort, falls in love with Lyle Speaks, the bounty hunter. I wrote in Melanie's voice because I had no idea how to write about a bounty hunter. More recently I wrote the second chapter of a collaborative novel called *Noah's Ride,* again following Elmer. The novel was about a runaway slave in Mississippi who makes it to Texas and the Union Army. I worried long and hard about whether or not I could see the world from the viewpoint of a male slave, but I did write the chapter in third person from Noah's point of view. I found it hard.

My own experience and my work with other authors have led me to believe that an author grows into both voice and subject. Once you find the combination where your creativity seems to flow best, you'd best stick with it. But it's not something you always have control over. I'm reminded of Dorothy Johnson, best known for short stories that gave birth to the movies *A Man Called Horse* and *The Hanging Tree.* Late in her life, Dorothy worked on a novel she called *The Unbombed,* about New York City during World War II when the city was constantly at full alert for a bombing attack that never came. One day she wrote to me that she'd had a horrible shock: she'd just found out that the man she thought was going to come back and marry the heroine was going to be killed in the war. Since Dorothy once told me she could not write if her muse was not talking to her, I presume her muse gave her that shocking bit of news. That muse often has more control over fiction than the author. Maybe it's just another name for instinct.

My instincts about plot are not very good, so I tend to write fiction based on actual history. One of my sons said, "Mom writes historical fiction because she's so poor at plotting," and though I corrected his language, he was right. In the 1980s, Western Writers of America formed a committee to do a collection of pieces about significant women in the American West. Because I had grown up a doctor's daughter, working in hospitals and osteopathic medical schools as a teenager and college student, I elected to write about Georgia Arbuckle Fix, a pioneer physician in western Nebraska in the late nineteenth century. I was intrigued by her life—among other things, she married badly and divorced. The stories of her riding across the prairie and her care of various patients—like the man with a hole in his head that she closed with a silver dollar—were fascinating. It cried out to be a novel, so I turned it into *Mattie.* Most reviews were good, but one gave me a sound drubbing because, according to the reviewer, Mari Sandoz had done a much more authentic job with Fix's life. I have no doubt that Sandoz, an icon among western women writers, did do a better job, but my novel won a Spur Award from WWA, and I was exceedingly happy.

There followed four longer novels about women of the West. The first was *Libbie,* about Elizabeth Bacon Custer and her life on the frontier with George Custer. I wrote with Libbie's books and some of George's spread out before me, carefully following the chronology of their life together and yet telling it in Libbie's voice, as I imagined she felt about it, from the early tumultuous physical attraction to the hijinx he played on her constantly and finally to the moment when she knew, before being told, that he was dead and took her shawl from the peg on the wall to go to the other wives in his company. I loved the research, and I loved recreating the story. I think the novel is pretty much true to history.

Then came *Jessie,* the story of Jessie Benton Frémont, married to John Charles Frémont, the explorer. (At that point my editor said to me, "No more men who were failures, Judy!" I didn't think there was anything Freudian there, except that I liked those strong women and their stories.) And then *Cherokee Rose,* based on the life of Lucille Mulhall, the first Wild West cowgirl, a roper. And, finally, then in 2002, *Sundance, Butch, and Me,* the story of the Hole-in-the-Wall Gang told from Etta Place's point of view.

I loved researching all those novels, really getting into the women's lives, but I knew they took me away from Texas. All along I was writing short stories set in Texas—as most writers know, short story collections are hard to sell these days, and I was delighted to find Panther Creek Press, a small press that would publish *Sue Ellen Learns to Dance and Other Stories.*

But the market for the kind of longer novels I wrote seems to have disappeared, and I spent several years writing young-adult nonfiction on assignment, books about everything from the state of Montana to the life of Andrew Jackson or Harry Truman. It was income, and it was writing, but it wasn't Texas.

I am glad to say I'm back in Texas, writing fourth-grade biographies of "second-tier" Texans, men and women who are on the state-mandated test for fourth graders. I didn't even know that Gail Borden, inventor of evaporated milk, had anything to do with Texas, but it turns out he was a prominent figure during the Texas Revolution. I write a column about Texas books and writers for the *Dallas Morning News*, and I write historical pieces about Texans for *Texas Co-op Magazine*. The most important thing to me is that I have writing projects—I don't think I'd know how to live my life if I weren't writing. I'd feel lost, without an anchor. I'd wake up in the morning and wonder, "Whatever can I do with this day?"

But fiction lingers in my mind. I'm an avid reader of mysteries, some set in Texas but most not. And I've always longed to write a mystery. So now I'm trying it—set not only in Texas, but in the neighborhood that's less than a mile from my house. It's still distinctly Texan, but it's contemporary, not historical. It's the world that I live in every day, and the story is told in third person. We'll see.

There's a whole different side to Texas' influence on my career. In 1982, I went to work for TCU Press as an editor; in 1986, the director moved on, and in 1987 I was officially named director. Our standard line (especially, gulp! in rejection letters) is that we publish books about Texas and the American West—so don't send us that manuscript about European history! Over these happy years, doing a job that I love, I've gotten to know Texas authors, Texas subjects, Texas history. I used to have a canned speech that I gave on occasion titled, "Wearing Two Hats in the Publishing World." I do just that, I love both my hats, and I think they compliment each other perfectly.

I also love living in Fort Worth. There was a time in my life, not too many years ago, when I wanted almost desperately to move to Santa Fe, but I'm over that now, helped by my oldest daughter, Megan, who said, "Mom, you wouldn't live in Santa Fe, would you, unless you could live every day the way we do on vacation?" A sobering thought.

But Fort Worth is home. I have a comfortable house and garden, the house even much older than I am. My dog and cat and I have our routine. My youngest daughter and her husband live about twenty minutes away, and I see six-month-old Jacob frequently. I have a wonderful network of friends and, of course, a job that I love. I eat out a lot, entertain a lot, and have a good life. But lately I sometimes find my mind going back to Chicago, and once, a few years ago, someone at Megan's house in Austin asked me where I lived. "Chicago," I replied without thinking, and my daughter shrieked, "Mom!"

I don't want to live in Chicago. I don't even necessarily want to go back there. I want to be a Texan and write about Texas, but maybe a part of me will always be an outsider.

Robert Darden, the Whittenburg Door

ROBERT FLYNN

ROBERT FLYNN is a native of Chillicothe, Texas, a town so small, he says, that one has to travel to nearby Quanah to have a coincidence. According to Flynn, Chillicothe is fairly bursting with truth, and at an early age he set out to find it, despatching along the way seven novels: *North to Yesterday; In the House of the Lord; The Sounds of Rescue, The Signs of Hope; Wanderer Springs; The Last Klick; The Devil's Tiger* (co-authored with the late Dan Klepper); and *Tie-Fast Country.* Flynn is also responsible for a dramatic adaptation of Faulkner's *As I Lay Dying; A Cowboy Legacy* (a two-part documentary for ABC-TV); the nonfiction narrative, *A Personal War in Vietnam;* an oral history, *When I Was Just Your Age;* and three story collections: *Seasonal Rain, Living With the Hyenas,* and *Slouching Toward Zion.* Flynn also published a collection of essays titled *Growing Up a Sullen Baptist.* Flynn describes his life and work as "The Search for Morals, Ethics, and Religion, or at least a good story in Texas and lesser known parts of the world."

SOMETHING TO SAY

I'M A BAPTIST.

I confess to no one but God. Writing this essay is to-the-barn-and-back too much like a confessional where others can see my soul and decide my penance. Others seem to know more about my writing than I. A friend pointed out that all of my novels have a preacher in them. I wasn't aware of that. I haven't wanted to explore the writing portion of my psyche because, if I understand it, I won't need to have something to say.

My earliest ambition, at least the earliest ambition I can remember, was to have something to say. I don't know where it came from. Maybe it was because I was the youngest child. Maybe I needed to have something to say before anyone would listen.

When I was six months old, my father started to town in the truck. Unknown to him, I had crawled to the vehicle, pulled myself up by the running board, and caught the hinge that was on the outside of the door. When Dad closed the door, the thumb and two fingers of my right hand were caught inside the hinge and crushed. I was rushed to the doctor, who taped the fingers together but doubted they would ever recover. Because I was so young, however, the bones didn't shatter and the fingers did grow back, and I had to be held all the time so that I didn't try to crawl and pull them loose. Maybe I got used to that attention and needed something to say to regain it. If so, there was a bonus. The nail bed of my thumb grew only half the length of my thumbnail because of scarring. I could pull my thumbnail halfway back, which was wonderful for making girls scream and teachers glare. I managed to receive a lot of attention for this until another kid found that, like a horned toad shooting blood, he could blow air out of his eye socket.

Wanting to have something to say stubbed its toe on wanting to be heard. I needed a bent thumbnail to get their attention before I frightened or annoyed them. There weren't a lot of choices for those who wanted to be heard. Teacher or preacher. I didn't know it was possible to be from Chillicothe, Texas, and be a writer. In time, I became all three, sometimes at the same time.

Chillicothe was the kind of place where it took a village to have an idea. For a good idea, it took a village and a year. For a really bad idea, it took a fourteen-year-old boy and fifteen seconds. My idea was to be a foreign missionary. Africa appealed to me because of the elephants, but also China because it was exotic. They would listen because I was white and American. I have traveled to foreign countries and some of my books have been translated into other languages, so perhaps I did become a foreign missionary of sorts. I like to think so. But, I didn't export American culture. I was noticed, but I learned far more than I taught.

I also dreamed that my gift as a football player would be recognized without any demonstration on my part and that being a star who brought glory to Chillicothe and then to

Baylor would give me the stature I needed to be heard. But the lack of talent I showed at Wednesday practice was the same I manifested Friday night sitting on the bench.

I also played basketball, because if you were a male in Chillicothe High School, you played sports. I had even less talent at basketball, something I blamed on Midway, the first school I attended, which happened to be midway between Tolbert and Chillicothe. Midway, a two-room school, had a dirt basketball court, the boundary scratched on the ground with a stick. The only school we played that had an indoor court was Farmers Valley. My only memory of playing Farmers Valley was that I made a rare basket, even rarer because it was at the opponent's end of the court. My brother, Jim, two years older than I, played there wearing basketball shorts over his longhandles. That brought him more distinction than I ever got.

Incredibly, without anything of my own to say, I did speak to groups. Mostly, I said that I wanted us to be better: my church, my school, my community, my country. I expected more of my church and more of my country than I expected of others. If I expected more of some other place, why wouldn't I go there? Most didn't hear me, and those who did didn't like what I said. But all of that came from home. I couldn't criticize someone else and exempt myself and my faults. That notion was later reinforced by the marines, where you demanded your unit be the best and expected it to get better—and later in Baylor professor Paul Baker's drama department, where every faculty member saw every show before it opened and pointed out what was good and what needed improvement. Your opinion might be wrong, but it was valued. It was time-consuming for the faculty, but it gave value to the show.

At Baylor, I was lost in a sea of other voices that wanted to be heard. Luckily, North Korea invaded South Korea, and when it became obvious that we weren't going to severely whup up on the aggressors in a couple of weeks, I dropped out of college to join the marines. It turned out to be one of the best decisions I ever made. It took me beyond the packaged world of ready-to-use answers offered by church and school, facile definitions of good and evil. I'd smoke some gooks, pick up some medals, and return to Baylor as a man with a message and a story that needed attention.

I was once on a panel with a religious and conservative journalist who said that his dreams before going to sleep were about women and money. I didn't tell anyone about my dreams because they were about women and killing people. They were people who needed killing and, in my dreams, killing them was a good thing, and I was good at it. I was saving my country, or someone else's country, or something. Only in the past couple of years have I been able to confess, even to myself, that one of the reasons I enlisted was for the license to kill. The drill instructor reinforced that notion repeatedly. "You are a professional killer," he said. "Your government pays you to kill the enemy." There was no doubt what the marines were for.

The government didn't pay much to kill the enemy, but I didn't have to worry about food that might be cold C-rations, clothing, a rifle, pack, or helmet. I had a place to sleep, even though it might be a hole in the ground. The money was trivial. The reward for being a marine was being a marine, wearing the eagle, globe, and anchor, being part of a historic and faithful tradition, discovering things about yourself that you would otherwise not know, and a dozen other things that aren't taxed. I didn't like the routine—standing in formation, marching to chow, junk-on-the-bunk inspections. By contrast, I did see the appeal of religious orders where you didn't have to worry about mundane and essential matters.

When I mentioned "professional killer" in a letter home, my mother went beyond the place that passes understanding. What did she think marines did? Where do dreams of women and killing come from? I knew where dreams about women came from. Much of the dreams of killing came from movies where good men and sometimes women were good at killing bad men. The Bible was full of stories of those killing machines, Samson and King David. Some of it came from my father who had fought in World War I and had been forever scarred by being a survivor of a company that suffered so many casualties in the first thirty minutes of The Big Push that an officer had to be sent from another unit to lead the handful of survivors in the continuing assault. He was thirty years old, not a good age for slogging through a bog intersected by shellfire and machine gun bullets. I wanted to know whether I could go forward in the face of such disaster.

The source of some of the dreams came from church, where my country's enemies were God's enemies. Killing a commie for Christ was not a joke to us; it was a duty. But, I didn't go to Korea.

I left the marines as naked as when I enlisted. No medals, no story, no reason to be heard. I returned to Baylor to enroll in summer school before going home. After enrolling, I felt so good that, while passing in front of Baylor University's Brooks Hall, I jumped a hedge. Well, almost jumped a hedge. Unbeknownst to me, there was a wire across the top of the hedge to guide the hedge cutter. A toe caught the wire, I crashed onto the sidewalk, and went home with a limp. Not only did I have to express my shame that I didn't go to Korea,

I had to explain why I was limping when I wasn't a wounded hero.

I wasn't quite naked. I always knew what my father expected of me, but he rarely asked me to do something. He did, however, ask me to keep a journal while I was in the marines. He had not graduated from grade school but kept a diary while in the trenches of France during World War I. Every night before going to sleep, I examined and recorded the day. It became a habit.

I spoke more often before larger groups, usually at church. I enjoyed writing sermons more than preaching them. It must seem strange in today's world of blogs, MySpace, and YouTube, but I thought one had to be struck by lightning, or at least a great light, to be a writer. Then, a professor named Paul Baker told me that I could write. He didn't say I could write well, but he thought I had something to say.

I think being pastor of a small church and being able to minister to every member must be the most satisfying job on earth. It took one year of seminary to convince me that I would not likely be a pastor. I was tired of discussing drinking, dancing, divorce, along with impolite and offensive words when materialism, greed, and prejudice toward women, African Americans, and homosexuals was destroying not only the church but the country. I didn't want to spend my life reassuring the craven that God loved them, their church, and their country above all others and that faith and goodness would protect them from poverty, divorce, disease, disaster, and death.

My interest in the Bible was related to understanding how the writers came to have the revelations that they gave to the world. Did it come through meditation? From prayer and fasting? From a life of pain and sorrow? From a life of rapture?

My interest in theology was in studying the great spiritual minds of the past: Jeremiah and Jesus; Tillich, Fosdick, and the Niebuhrs; Whitman, Milton, Blake, and T.S. Eliot; Berdyaev and Bernard of Clairvaux; Chesterton, Donne, Dostoevsky, Tolstoy, Melville; Rumi, Rilke, Ramakrishna, and Ghandi. My interest in communication was not in reaffirming what others wanted to believe but in examining those beliefs, affirming the right to know more, and preaching the need to know better. If I could find, or help others find, the way to the kind of insights that prophets had into their souls or the soul of their religion or country, now that would be a life.

I returned to Baylor to teach, and my destiny seemed set. I loved Baylor both as a student and as a professor. I worked in an atmosphere of respect, collegiality, generosity, and mutual support I haven't known since. I worked with Paul Baker, my inspiration, and Eugene McKinney, my mentor. Professor Baker secured for me the rights to adapt Faulkner's *As I Lay Dying* for the stage. I was able to write scenes and have students stage them to see if they could be made to work before we cast the play and Baker began shaping it for presentation. The play had a great cast and received good reviews, including one from the *Saturday Review of Literature.*

In addition to all that, I received a check. What would I do with the money? There is nothing of lasting worth that money can buy. Diamonds may be forever, but while the value of your late grandmother's wedding ring has increased, its worth has diminished. Jean, my wife, suggested the money go into our bank account that paid for necessities, but I didn't want to spend it on bread or rent or soap. I had to work for money because most Americans, even Christian Americans, don't know of another reward or another measurement of success. I never wanted to work for money because it's hard to imagine something less fulfilling.

Writing isn't easy, and I especially did not want to write for money. I think Dr. Samuel Johnson intended irony when he said that only a blockhead wrote for money. When you write for money, you write for someone else and not to them, something only a blockhead would do. The reward in writing is writing and occasionally finding a well-wrought sentence beneath your pen, sometimes discovering an insight or idea.

I continued writing plays, sometimes using my background in dishonest ways and sometimes using pretentious symbols and grandiose language to express something I didn't understand. Baylor students directed and performed in them so that I could see how pretentious they were.

In the summer of 1962, Professor Baker secured houses for us at the Wurlitzer Foundation in Taos, New Mexico, and the entire faculty traveled there for two weeks to plan future goals and the means of reaching them. We were going to be better, and we were going to make Baylor a better place to learn. We spent long, tiring, but exhilarating hours talking of the future and the heights we dreamed of reaching. I had begun writing stories of ideas that didn't work as plays, and while I was in Taos, Jean called to tell me that *Story* magazine had accepted my first submission. Ironically, it all came to naught. The magazine folded before my piece was published, and our dreamed-of future was fated to remain a dream.

Because of Professor Baker's reputation, Baylor became the first nonprofessional theater to get the rights to stage Eugene O'Neill's play, *Long Day's Journey into Night.* John Newport, former Baylor professor and later professor at Southwest Baptist Theological Seminary, wrote in a Baptist student publication that *Long Day's Journey into Night* was a great religious play. President Abner McCall, a lawyer, who signed the contract with O'Neill's widow stipulating that the play could not be cut, ordered the performance closed.

Professor McKinney and Mary Sue Jones were at the Dallas Theater Center because Dugald McArthur, director of the play, was on a much needed break. McKinney called and asked me to tell the cast before the show that evening that it would be their last performance. He also told me not to permit reporters to interview the student actors. When he returned to the campus, McKinney asked the students to allow the department and the administration to work things out. Temporarily dismissing our plans for the future, we tried to determine how far we would have to retreat into the past in order to continue.

It was not to be. McCall was held in suspicion by some Baptist leaders because he was not a preacher, and he chose to strengthen his position with them by demonizing us. We believed, he wrote, that we thought academic freedom gave us the right to shout obscenities at children. It was a successful strategy, for suspicion passed from him to us. Some colleagues shunned us on campus, others avoided us altogether. Some fellow church members scorned us. It was one of the darkest moments of my life as those I wanted to serve decided I was unworthy to be one of them. After a fatal meeting with McCall, in which he stated that he would not express confidence in the department, we knew the future we had dreamed of at Baylor was a relic of the past. A university that would not accept enrollment from African Americans, enforced a curfew on female but not male students, expelled students because of their sexual orientation, and thought manners were more important than morals, lost a department faculty because of words in a play, all of them present in the King James Bible.

Baker was offered many prestigious positions but refused to accept one unless the entire Baylor department was taken. James Laurie, president of Trinity University, agreed to do so.

My wife, children, and I thought of Baylor as a home we were leaving, never to return.

That summer I began writing a play about the frontier. I had read about the frontier, and my father had lived there. My father was born in 1887, three years after Ben Thompson and King Fisher died in an ambush in San Antonio. He was six months old when Luke Short shot Long Hair Jim Courtright in Fort Worth and eight years old when John Wesley Hardin was shot in the back in El Paso by John Selman, who claimed self-defense. He was eighteen years old when President Theodore Roosevelt visited the nearby Waggoner Ranch for a wolf hunt.

My father was born in a Pullman car at the end of the track, the first child born in Chillicothe. The Pullman was outfitted as a home for his father, who was the section boss of the Fort Worth and Denver Railroad. This was the line that had the crews leave their laundry in Quanah, claiming residence, and voted to have the county seat moved from Margaret when Dad was three. He and his brothers hid when Comanches from the reservation across the Red River peered into their windows out of curiosity as they followed the train tracks to Medicine Mound. He was six years old when Ranger Bill McDonald killed Sheriff Matthews of Childress in a shootout in downtown Quanah. McDonald cocked his pistol with his teeth after Matthews shot off his thumb. Dad was nine years old when his father was shot in the back of the head and robbed. The murderer escaped hanging because his family swore he was only sixteen but was sent to prison. Dad kept track of the murderer for the rest of his life, intending to kill him when he got out of the pen. His last words to Jean were to tell her where the man was and asked her not to tell me.

I had read fiction as well as nonfiction about my father's childhood world, but it never seemed real to me. My first idea for the play was about a Homeric cowboy/knight who went about righting wrongs by killing people, but it evolved into a cattle drive. The cows and horses would be offstage, like Fortinbras' army, and the campfire scenes would be theatrical with dialog and action broken with songs. I wanted to show the dust, the unbathed sweat, hard work, chiggers, ticks, skunks, grass burrs, cockleburs, goat heads, prickly pear, mesquite, wild cows, and half-wild horses that my father knew.

Eventually, the play became a novel. I kept the dust and grime, but the story didn't come alive until after several drafts where the leg of a steer protruded through the roof of a dugout and the nester saw it as a gift from God. I found the voice and the heart of the story and had to do two more drafts to make the voice and tone consistent.

Like every beginning writer, I turned to *Writer's Market* to find a place to send the manuscript and selected the publishing company Alfred Knopf. Knopf said they did not publish westerns, but I thought the story was antiwestern. The horses disappeared early in the tale, the cowboys had to milk cows, and the only man with a gun was unable to shoot a sheep. I wrote a cover letter saying that the book was no more a western than Don Quixote was a western and mailed them the manuscript. And waited.

I so feared that my story would fail or that it would succeed that I began my next two novels before I even heard from Knopf. After six months, an editor wrote that the manuscript had received some favorable attention and was being sent on to another editor. In the meantime, the Dallas Theater Center had been invited as the U.S. representative at the Theater of Nations in Paris. Professor Baker, Director of the DTC, selected *As I Lay Dying* as the play to take to France, and then to Belgium and Germany. I had an agent, Robert Friedman, to represent the play and sent him a copy of the manuscript I had mailed to Knopf. Friedman represented only dramatic works, so he passed it on to Robert Lescher. Lescher called Knopf, and in a short time they offered me a contract for *North to Yesterday.*

As if all of that weren't exciting enough, I received a transatlantic telephone call from the U.S. Ambassador to France who said that when the French saw *As I Lay Dying* on billboards they would think of the late President Kennedy dying in Dallas. This was 1964, one year after the assassination.

Telephones were scary to me. We didn't have a telephone on the farm. At Midway, when pupils moved to the room for fifth through eighth grade, Mrs. D.T. Wilson took the fifth graders to her home in Chillicothe, showed them her house, her china, her crystal, and a real bathtub. She also allowed them to speak on the telephone to the operator. For most of us, it was our first telephone conversation. Telephones, for most of us at the time, meant that someone in the family had died or was about to die. A disembodied voice speaking in my ear frightened me. On the transatlantic telephone call from the ambassador, I changed the name of *As I Lay Dying* to *Journey to Jefferson.*

The Dallas Theater Center won a Special Jury Award for *Journey to Jefferson,* the highest award the United States had received at the Theater of Nations. They had won the same award a few years earlier with the Broadway revival of Thornton Wilder's *The Skin of Our Teeth* with Helen Hayes, Frederic March, and Mary Martin. Despite that success and my wish to write another play, the ideas that now came to me arrived in narrative form.

Long Days Journey into Night and *North to Yesterday* proved to me that I could not write what was given to me to write and accept censors. I found myself between flood and fire. Would my father believe what I wrote and would my mother accept it? Dad had died, but I always had his approval. I disappointed him sometimes. I imagine there were times when, like George H.W. Bush, he must have wondered, "Whose kid is this?" I think my dad would believe what I wrote.

I was always on trial with my mother. She liked the attention I received as a writer, but she worried about what others thought of my writing. She liked happy stories about pretty people who were never confused, never riddled with doubt, never lusted after gold, fame, adventure, or others. Life was ugly enough without dwelling on it. Her wish was that I write for *Guideposts*.

My father was a storyteller, and he and his friends loved the "hurrah," beginning a story with a real situation and expanding it so that the listener had to suspend more and more disbelief until the last listener realized he had been "hurrahed" and was the butt of the joke. The point wasn't to convince anyone to believe something that wasn't true. The hurrah wasn't over until everyone understood that the truth at some point blended into fiction, that reality became imagination.

My mother's world was a literal world. Every mother in every story I ever wrote was a criticism of her. Everything that happened in a story was something that literally happened to me. Everything I wrote about was something I knew about, and much of it wasn't fit to know, much less to tell.

During panels I am on I'm asked, "If you were on a desert island and could have only one book, which one would you choose?" My answer has always been the Bible, and probably the King James version, not because of its accuracy but because of its imagery. Sadly, the King James Bible that gives us some of the greatest poetry is often read and taught literally, thus robbing it not only of its beauty but of its meaning. To read and understand Genesis the same as Leviticus is to remain biblically illiterate. Literal is to truth what fact is to poetry.

The book world has changed. Newspaper book review sections shrank to book review pages. Magazines ran plots of best sellers. Major publishers that once developed stables of writers, taking chances on new ones because they saw glimpses of promise, were swallowed by corporations interested only in profit.

North to Yesterday received a great deal of attention, the next two books less so. *The Sounds of Rescue, the Signs of Hope* was the beloved child that others viewed with doubt, the outside child, the strange one. The book had always been special to me because in writing it I lived vicariously through what I would experience shortly after its publication. For a long time I had been nagged by the question: How could God let six million Jews be murdered? This was followed by: How could God let African Americans be enslaved? The question of how God could let Native Americans be exterminated came later. In *Sounds of Rescue* I discovered that faith or goodness was not an insurance policy that guaranteed protection.

In a few months, my wife would be diagnosed with multiple sclerosis, I would go to Vietnam, and our youngest daughter would die. Our world was altered forever. Our past had changed, even more so our future. Plans, dreams, and thoughts of tomorrow were gone. We were deep in a well of merciless today. Our own pain was so great it was difficult to reach out to each other, to reach out to our surviving daughter. My rope out of the well was *Sounds of Rescue*. The only rescue from life was death. The death of Jews by poison. The death of Native Americans by smallpox. The death of prophets, heretics, and witches by torture. All of this was horrible, but that was not God's wish; it was man's will. Nevertheless, they were rescued by death.

Lazarus was resuscitated, but he still had to die. Death was the Rescue God. And that was the God I had believed in from the beginning, the God who rescued me from sin and death, through death to eternal life, whatever that meant.

That insight, or misunderstanding, didn't come out instantaneously, but why bad things happen to good people seemed to me a silly question, as though faith and/or goodness was a rabbit's foot. The question was: Why do good people do bad things to good people for good reasons? I didn't like the answer, but the answer given to me was that God loved the Christian German prison guards as much as he loved the Jews, that he loved the Christian slave owners as much as he loved the Christian slaves, that he loved the lynch mob as much as he loved those being lynched, that he loves those who pronounce the death penalty as much as those suffering from it, that he loves Christian soldiers as much as he loves the Christian, Muslim, Jewish, fascist, communist, and atheist soldiers they kill. God doesn't love evil, but he offers evil-doers the same forgiveness in the same manner He offers it to me. It is not a truth my mother would accept, but it is one my father would believe.

I was in a wilderness for sixteen years before I published another book, but I wrote almost every day trying to find the way out. I worked simultaneously on what would become *Wanderer Springs, A Personal War in Vietnam, The Last Klick,* and *Seasonal Rain*. Now, I am working on the book that was the reason I went to Vietnam to conduct research. I don't know whether that's a circle or a path through a swamp.

The vision of the book has changed many times, but it has always been about the images, monuments, and lies that we worship, that shape us and our country into a people who are loved, because of our generous spirit, and feared, because of our arrogance that we are God's country, that our enemies are God's enemies, and that we serve God when we deliver death, even to the innocent among them.

I have never heard anyone "blame America first." I have heard many say "Don't blame us." We can't be held accountable for anything that happens as a result of our policies or practices because we meant well, and poverty, slavery, and death are just collateral damage. I have heard many claim that we are exempt from the rules we require of other countries because we are not only the richest and most powerful country the world has ever known, we are the best. That's a level of immaturity that will never rise to patriotism.

I hope the book will be published because I believe it will have something to say, and that is more important than being heard. The reward will be what I have learned writing the book. And yes, there is a preacher in it. In fact, there are two of them.

Bridget Scott

DON GRAHAM

Don Graham graduated from North Texas State University with a BA and MA and took a doctorate at the University of Texas in Austin where he currently serves as the J. Frank Dobie Regents Professor of American and English Literature. Among his works are *Cowboys and Cadillacs: How Hollywood Looks at Texas* (1983) and *Texas: A Literary Portrait* (1985). In 1989 Graham published the highly regarded biography, *No Name on the Bullet: A Biography of Audie Murphy.* In 1998, *Giant Country: Essays on Texas* won a Violet Crown Award from the Austin Writers League. In 2003, his *Kings of Texas* won the Carr P. Collins Prize for Best Nonfiction Book of the Year, awarded by the

Texas Institute of Letters. His most recent work is *Literary Austin,* published in 2007 by TCU Press. Graham is past-president of the Texas Institute of Letters and has won important awards for criticism and teaching. A writer-at-large for *Texas Monthly* magazine, he lives in Austin.

NINE BALL, CORNER POCKET

THE DAY I learned to write my name, in the first grade, I wrote it all over the windowsill and wall at the back of the one-room schoolhouse where eight grades, one per row, studied grammar, history, spelling, geography, and rudimentary social manners. I don't know why I scribbled my name a hundred times or more in that place, at that time. Perhaps this was the first sign of future authorial ego, or perhaps it was just the elation of seeing the words one wrote made public. In any event the teacher did not view my exercise in first-person assertiveness with the same delight that I did, and I had to stay after school to wash the penciled markings from the white paint.

This previously unrecorded event took place in Lucas, Texas, a small community in Collin County, about eight miles east of Allen. Not much has been written about Lucas. Founded in 1870, the site does not even appear on several maps in histories written a century later. In the 1940s, the time I defaced public property, Lucas consisted of two stores, two churches (one Baptist, one Methodist), one cotton gin, and one schoolhouse, which with its softball/baseball field, was the center of the community. The main business of Lucas and its surrounds was raising cotton, the old staple of southern economy. It involved a lot of stoop labor, followed by lulls and long hot days of those endless Texas summers, and then, at cotton-picking time, great excitement and anxiety. An untimely, prolonged rain could destroy a year's work, just as the absence of rain could, and the vagaries of market conditions were always a worry. Wars, incidentally, were excellent stimulants for higher profits. Armies needed cotton for everything—ammunition, uniforms, and hospitals.

One year I recall, when the cotton was all picked and packed loosely into a trailer pulled by a tractor, I was placed on the top of the heap by my father and rode high up there, regally, king of the cotton, to the gin which was less than a mile away. The gin was a strange and somewhat uncomfortable place. My father worked there from time to time, moving the huge bales around with a dolly as though they were feather pillows. There was a pond rife with snakes, and the old men who lolled around the gin would always embarrass me by asking if I slumbered in bed.

The culture was entirely southern. The men dressed in overalls or khaki pants and shirts, and if anybody had walked around in a pair of cowboy boots he would have been laughed out of the county for putting on airs, for being a drugstore cowboy. There were more mules in the county than horses. The significance of the mule in my father's life was made clear to me once when he told about the first John Deere tractor he ever owned. He bought it a few years before I was born. Curious about it—this was later, when I had begun to develop a historical consciousness—I asked him how he acquired that tractor. (We had the tractor the whole time I was a child. At age five my job was to drive it, very slowly, down the rows of our cornfield while my parents, walking behind, pulled and tossed the ripened ears of corn into a trailer.) He said he traded for it. I said traded what? He said he had traded his two mules, Tojo and Stud. (The names are interesting. Tojo has its historical resonance, and Stud shows a taste for irony.) I asked who he'd traded the mules to. He said he went to the John Deere dealership and traded the mules directly to the dealer.

Of reading I do not remember very much from those days. My mother quite possibly read to me some children's stories; in any event, they did not stick, and I find that my knowledge of children's stories is very sparse and my interest in same entirely negligible. Of much more import, as imaginative sources for future writing and thinking, were the countless westerns on display at the movie houses in the county seat of McKinney, northwest of Lucas, and Plano to the south. At that time, in the late 1940s, McKinney had three theaters. All the big westerns—*Red River, Broken Arrow*—played at the Ritz, and they were family films and families saw them. The Texan, located off the square where the courthouse with its segregated drinking fountains enforced the unofficial Jim Crow law of the land, ran westerns for children mainly. These included the Republic products and all the films of Gene Autry, Roy Rogers, Johnny Mack Brown, and Lash Larue, along with serials, and some now largely forgotten "eastern" westerns, as I think of them today, films based on the novels of James Fennimore Cooper and starring George Montgomery as Hawkeye. These were moccasin-and-canoe westerns, and I loved them; they seemed so exotic.

Many of the "western" westerns were ostensibly set in Texas, and from my blackland prairie cotton-field perspective, they dramatized a vision of Texas that set one's pulse a-throbbing. It was the same Texas that I glimpsed later in the novels of Zane Grey. In both, the West was a far more romantic and exciting place than where I lived. Both film and fiction told me that the West, Texas included, was an expanse of vast, endless vistas of desert and prairie populated by cattle and cowboys and desperadoes of nasty mien and short life span. Some of the cowboys were excellent singers and everything always worked out for the best. There were Indians all over the lot, and although some of them were noble, most weren't, and in any event they had as transitory a shelf life as the desperadoes. They died on screen before we had a chance to see them as anything other than other.

Texas, I was made to understand, consisted of men on horseback performing heroic deeds in golden deserts outside towns named Abilene and Amarillo and Galveston that were surrounded, always, by gorgeous, snow-capped mountains. It was an irresistible dreamscape. The lesson I took away with me, the imprint, was that where I lived, in southern-striated Texas, with its cotton fields, mules, stoop labor, overalls, and so on, did not really count. What counted was West Texas, out where the deer and the antelope played, and where never was heard a discouraging word. There must have been some pretty discouraging words heard in Collin County kitchens in those days as families left the farms and moved to towns like McKinney—which we did—where there were better economic prospects. Children never know that they are part of a historical process, but what in fact was happening in my childhood was that the small family farm was receding into history, and post-World War II Texas was entering a period of urbanization that was the wave of the future.

Moving to McKinney put me in easy walking distance of those theaters where the westerns rolled on. And it took me out of cotton fields forever, I thought. But then we moved closer to Dallas, to Carrollton, at that time a small outlying town, and suddenly, that first summer, needing a job, I found myself, at my dad's behest, hired to chop cotton on a nearby farm (doubtless the home of a mall now). We started at early light, and by noon I was done. I had one of those cotton field conversions that marked, I would later realize, the lives of three famous Texas writers: Walter P. Webb, Roy Bedichek, and J. Frank Dobie. All three—even Dobie, who was born in ranching country in South Texas—experienced crucial moments in cotton fields when they vowed that whatever else might happen in their lives, they planned to have nothing more to do with raising cotton.

That day was equally decisive for me; I left the field at noon and the next day hired on as a caddy at a new country club that had just opened east of Carrollton. The very idea of a country club offered a glimpse of another way of life. The caddies were composed of white and black boys who wanted to make some money. One bag for eighteen holes was three dollars; a double was five dollars. The system was instructively democratic. Black and white competed equally, and the first to arrive in the morning, long before sun-up, received the first assignment. The days were long and hot, and the boys spent hours together talking about everything. Nearby was a swimming pool where the daughters of the rich sunbathed or swam in sumptuous idleness. It was the American Dream all down the line, except, of course, for the young blacks who at day's end returned home to a separate and unequal existence.

In high school I began to read widely and extensively. The school library was small and stocked with just about every boy's sports book that had ever been published. A friend of mine and I made it our unannounced goal to read every sports book in the library—*Stover of Yale,* that sort of thing, and all the Tom Swift books—and it was in this way that I came to read *The Catcher in the Rye,* because one day my buddy slid it over the checkout counter to me, and said, "Read this, you'll like it, it's dirty." I read it and I liked it. He had stumbled upon it, thinking it was a baseball novel, and found that, like me, he couldn't put it down.

In our English classes we had to write "book reports" on a book we'd read, every six weeks, and when those mornings came round, most of the basketball team came to me and asked me to tell them about one of the many books I had read, and I did. I always kept the best one for myself, and those boys, who hadn't read a word, got the same grade on their book reports that I did.

But my real reading education was taking place elsewhere and in another venue. I was an avid, compulsive consumer of paperbacks. The more lurid the cover and the more realistic the content, the better I liked them. I could not get enough of *The Naked and the Dead, From Here to Eternity,* and *The Young Lions,* and other, mostly forgotten, ones such as *A Helmet for My Pillow* (who could resist such a title?) and John Horne Burns' great *The Gallery;* I read and reread all of these plus scores of WWII novels that I can't recall. I also read with great intensity the most sensational novel of that era, *Peyton Place.* So when I got to college and took a course in "Realism," I couldn't understand what all the fuss over the nineteenth century was about. You want realism, I wanted to say, check out the local drugstore racks. Here was where a real revolution in the word was taking place, and I felt like I was in the vanguard of truth in fiction. These novels put to shame the books one of my aunts bought through a book club, novels by Thomas B. Costain, which I considered unreadable, and equally boring stuff by Pearl Buck and a host of other sincere hacks whose names I have forgotten.

It would seem, I suppose, that upon going to college I would naturally major in English, but in the world I grew up in boys didn't major in English. Boys didn't read either, and though I lettered four years in baseball and two years in basketball, I was basically a closet reader and kept quiet about how much reading I actually did.

And thus it was, in my freshman year at TCU, I majored in business. I was also in Honors English, and the writing I did there, along with some modest success that I achieved in the annual writing contests (a third place and a couple of honorable mentions), coupled with the absolute boredom of business (plus a lack of aptitude in same) led me to change my major to English and to transfer to a more affordable college, North Texas State University, which, as it turned out, happened to have an extraordinarily good Department of English. At NTSU I took English courses with professors such as Martin Shockley and James Brown, each brilliant in his own way, and in philosophy I took a class with a young graduate student named Grover Lewis, who would go on to a distinguished career at *Rolling Stone* magazine. It was in Lewis' class in ethics that we read, along with classical philosophers, that classic from high school days, *The Catcher in the Rye*.

I received a first-rate education in English and American literature and in linguistics. This happened almost by accident because the classes I most wanted—in modern fiction—were always closed, so I found myself in courses that I would never have taken—Victorian fiction, Romantic poetry, and so on. All of this enforced serendipity turned out to be of long lasting value.

I also remember seeing actual writers in action. Billy Lee Brammer, whose novel *The Gay Place* was published while I was at North Texas and who himself had graduated from

North Texas a decade earlier, came, but all I remember of Brammer is a man in a suit and a razor thin tie of that era. The other writer I remember much more vividly from that time is the poet John Ciardi. We were using his poetry book in a class, and Ciardi came and gave a dynamic reading. He had written a book of poems for children, based on a restricted vocabulary list, and I remember his saying that he struggled to describe rain until this line came to him: "The rain came down like strings of wet." I thought that was about the greatest description I had ever heard.

But the real local star of that period was Larry McMurtry. He had graduated from NTSU the year I finished high school. His novel *Horseman, Pass By* appeared to much fanfare in Texas, and several of my professors had taught McMurtry in their classes. One of them, whose specialty was modern literature, said to me once that it was unfortunate that Larry used so many four-letter words, like the one that rhymes with hiss for example. Since this same professor had recommended *Lady Chatterley's Lover* to us, I considered his pecksniffery regarding Larry's language rather odd.

I thought that McMurtry was so in tune with adolescent culture that the book was simply wonderful; it was so good in fact, so true to the spirit of the age, which I was already learning to call the zeitgeist, that it discouraged me from attempting to write fiction. I thought that I could work at writing fiction for years and never produce anything the equal of *Horseman, Pass By* (let alone *The Catcher in the Rye*). McMurtry's book, Brammer's (which I did not read until much later), and John Graves' *Goodbye to a River,* published the year before, in 1960, were certainly key to my nascent understanding that a place like Texas could produce excellent writing. But that was about the extent of any interest in regionalism on my part at that time.

Without really knowing what I was going to do for a living, I enrolled in graduate school and attended the University of Maryland for one year, then returned to finish at NTSU with the MA. My thesis was on E. A. Robinson, and both then and later, in my PhD. studies at the University of Texas, I concentrated on mainstream American literature. At UT from 1965–1971, I took courses in American and British Literature (while at the same time teaching full time for five of those years at Southwest Texas State University, where the course load was three sections of freshman English and one of sophomore). When I announced, back home, that I would be writing on Frank Norris, and before I could explain who he was, my mom was very enthusiastic, as she thought the Frank Norris I referred to was the flamboyant (and infamous) preacher of the same name, from Fort Worth, who had once shot a man to death and got away with it.

I wrote my dissertation just before the critical earth shifted and everything was channeled into this theory or that theory. I wrote it in English, not in any theoretically clotted, jargon-laden diction and syntax that would dominate English studies for the next forty years and counting. And, amazingly, I got a job in the Ivy League, at the University of Pennsylvania. There I was, a Texas boy, a southerner, amidst some of the (retired) giants of the field—Robert Spiller, Albert C. Baugh, Tristram Coffin—and some still active: Daniel Hoffman, and my chairman, R. M. Lumiansky. A young novelist named Philip Roth came down from New York to teach on Tuesdays and Thursdays. It was pretty heady company.

But there was a marked sociological phenomenon that was occurring as well. Some of the oldest professors were basically dollar-a-year men with private incomes. One owned an island. They considered the teaching of literature and philology a gentleman's game. They could not imagine anyone actually living on a professor's salary. They could not imagine the professionalization that was beginning to take hold in the formerly gentleman's profession of teaching at university. They had a rather innocent belief in literature. They didn't know that literary criticism was about to become a deadly competitive game of careerism; they didn't know that history, philology, biography, and bibliography were about to be thrown on the scrap-heap of what was thought to be a useless, outmoded, outdated, and hopelessly reactionary ideology.

Among the junior faculty, things were changing fast. Assistant profs with degrees from the best universities seemed not to have read anything. The beautiful thing about theory is that you didn't have to read widely; all you had to do, with theory, was reread the same seven or eight Victorian novels over and over again in an attempt to decode the obvious and reveal the hidden, or what they wanted us to believe was hidden. Novels were no longer novels; they were texts; and indeed there was nothing that was not a text; suddenly *Ozzie & Harriet* was equal to *Hamlet* and as worthy of study. (Now the word "text" itself is passé, replaced by "cultural productions.") At the time I believed that all of this theorizing was relatively harmless. I didn't know that it was part of a political agenda; I didn't know that it was, often, a form of academic Marxism, but I certainly did know that almost all of its practitioners were merely the newest specimens of the petit-bourgeois, and that they wanted, beneath everything, to have the goods and services that society could provide. In their hearts they were no different from the middle class capitalists they despised.

At Penn I was asked to teach a course in western movies, something I would never have thought of on my own. The department wanted to build up its enrollments in English and turned to film as a means of doing so. A course in detective/crime film (essentially film noir) was created, and there were numerous faculty prepared to offer this course. But the department also wanted a course in the western, and as there was only one "cowboy" on site, the course fell to me. So I began to take westerns seriously, in a way that I had not before; I began to see westerns as "texts," and I read extensively in the burgeoning field of popular culture as it related to westerns. I also began to attend conferences—in the West! —to read papers as preambles to publishing articles about westerns, so there opened up a whole new field of study that simultaneously propelled me back, in my mind, to Texas, to Collin County. My first year at Penn, 1971, *The Last Picture Show* was released, and seeing the bleak little town, the big sky (even in black and white it looked like a Texas sky), I felt a sharp nostalgia for the wide open spaces of Texas as compared to the rabbit hutch feeling of much of Philadelphia.

The second thing that happened is that the chair of the Department of English from the University of Texas, Roger Abrahams, a noted folklorist, came to Penn (his alma mater) to give a talk, and at a luncheon for him that I attended, he asked me what I was doing in Philadelphia and said I belonged in Texas. I didn't think much more about it until 1975 when a job opened up at UT for someone to take over the course that had been invented and made famous by J. Frank Dobie—Life and Literature of the Southwest. And so it was that I came back to Texas the next year, and the first thing they wanted me to do was what I'd done at Penn, to teach a course in western movies and build up the enrollments.

I got in just before the theory crowd was beginning to take over at UT. In the late '70s something called deconstruction fetched up on Texas shores, and everybody was excited about it. Interestingly, Derrida's translator, Gayatri Spivak, was at Texas at that time, and now and then I'd pick up a copy of

Of Grammatology, a book by Derrida which she had translated, but I could never get past the first paragraph. Under the sign of deconstruction a text meant everything except what it appeared to be saying.

Our department's attraction to theory led to huge blunders, I thought. In the 1980s, Hugh Kenner, a distinguished Johns Hopkins professor and author of the classic *The Pound Era,* was not permitted to teach a graduate course because his work was considered old-fashioned and he insufficiently theoretical. Never mind that he was brilliant, erudite, witty, charming, and far more knowledgeable than anybody on the graduate committee that turned down his proposal (he was visiting the Humanities Research Center at UT for a year at the time). The African American poet Harryette Mullen is another case in point. A UT undergraduate, she earned her doctorate at a prestigious university back east, but was judged "sufficiently untheoretized" (a phrase I shall never forget) even to be accorded a campus visit to UT when she was on the job market. In any event she went to UCLA (a large university on the West Coast) and in the intervening years has become an important postmodern poet. From 1976 to the present, theory has ruled virtually every professional aspect of English at UT and around the country. Like Ishmael, I alone escaped to tell thee.

Once back in Texas, I finished the revision of my dissertation on Frank Norris and published that all-important "tenure" book in 1978. Two edited collections, one on Norris, and one on westerns (with Tom Pilkington), appeared in successive years, and then, in 1982, I received, again out of the blue, a contract to write a book on Texas in the movies. Published in 1983 under the title *Cowboys and Cadillacs: How Hollywood Looks at Texas* (Texas Monthly Press), this work marked a decisive moment in my writing. The editor,

Barbara Rodriguez, wanted me to write the book in my own voice, and I was only too happy to do so. I pursued autobiographical and narrative lines of exposition. For the first time, I drew upon my upbringing in the unromantic part of Texas that was Collin County. I played off of the nationwide enchantment with Texas afoot in those days, chiefly in the vast popularity of the TV show *Dallas,* which I tirelessly pointed out to anybody who would listen, was set in Collin County. The other big Texas hit of the day, *Urban Cowboy,* offered further opportunities to comment ironically on the brief, intense interest in cowboy duds, dancing, and country-western kitsch that defined the Lone Star state at home and abroad.

At some point in the mid 1980s I felt that I had exhausted the western genre—from a teaching standpoint anyway—and so I turned my attention to the literature of Texas, which had become a consuming interest. One of the outgrowths of this focus was the editing of several anthologies, including two in the 1980s and two recent ones: *Lone Star Literature: A Texas Anthology* (W.W. Norton, 2003) and *Literary Austin* (TCU Press, 2007).

From *Cowboys and Cadillacs* on, most of my critical writing was, for better or worse, in a recognizable "voice": a vernacular idiom laced with learning and leavened with humor and carried along by a certain narrative line of development that is often grounded in autobiographical experience. I had always wanted to write for a larger audience than an academic one, and I have always had a strong interest in the ground of personal experience as a starting point. The last thing I wanted to write was static, analytical essays tethered in theory and directed at an audience of seventy-three academics. And I have not done so. The best instances in print of my work in vernacular criticism can be seen in the collection *Giant Country: Essays on Texas* (TCU Press, 1998) and in columns appearing in *Texas Monthly* from the late 1990s through 2005.

But there was another kind of writing that I wanted to do, all along, and that was narrative nonfiction. In 1986 I secured a contract from Viking—with an advance, one of my favorite words in the English language—to write a biography. Biography offered the perfect opportunity for a fully developed nonfiction narrative, and the result was *No Name on the Bullet,* a life of Audie Murphy, the Texan soldier/actor who had been born and raised in the same blackland prairie cotton culture that I had grown up in. Murphy was from Hunt County, adjacent to Collin, and the sign over Lee Street in Greenville, the county seat, was known the world over:

GREENVILLE
WELCOME
THE BLACKEST LAND
THE WHITEST PEOPLE.

It was out of this impoverished dead-end of the sharecropper way of life that Murphy had emerged. The Murphy project, which led to many trips to Los Angeles to interview directors and actors in the movie industry such as John Huston and Budd Boetticher, was tremendous fun from beginning to end.

In the early 1990s I spent some time in France and Australia, and during this period two influences upon my writing life led me towards writing fiction. One was my wife, Betsy Berry, who writes poetry and fiction. I learned a lot from her. We collaborated on a story called "Giant Country," which dealt with a couple named Harry and Jamie, autobiographical projections, admittedly, who had adventures together on a trip to the border and West Texas. Later I wrote stories of my own using the Harry and Jamie characters, and I intend to write some more.

The second influence, Michael Wilding, a major figure in modern Australian writing, became a great friend while we were on exchange at the University of Sydney. In many of his stories Wilding writes with a striking immediacy influenced, in part, by Jack Kerouac's spontaneous prose. According to Wilding, reading Kerouac made him want to write. In my case, reading Wilding made me want to write fiction. In one of his best stories, "Bye Bye Jack. See You Soon," Wilding describes the method as "instant experience." One story that I wrote directly under Wilding's influence was a story about Australia, featuring Harry, titled "The Voice on the Verandah." It appeared in a collection of stories published in Australia, and the only other American in the volume was Jack London. This is one of the high points of my life in writing.

I continue to write fiction about Harry and Jamie under the sign of Betsy Berry and Michael Wilding. I wish I had started sooner, but there were other things to write. Among them, a recent book, *Kings of Texas: The 150-Year Saga of an American Ranching Empire* (John Wiley, 2003). This book, too, came about by accident, or at least not from an idea originating with me but from my agent, Jim Hornfischer. And so it was that I turned to another big Texas project, the storied King Ranch, and found myself plunged into another fascinating period of research into the past heightened by a vital connection with the present. As with the book on Audie Murphy, this one involved creating a narrative flow and bringing to life the living and the dead. This book convinced me, that in terms of history, the only place left in Texas where history really matters is South Texas. Down there, the old ranches are haunted by living ghosts, and stories of stolen land are the stuff of dinner table conversations.

All of my adult working life has been spent in classrooms and in writing. Teaching continues to hold my interest, and today there seems a greater urgency than ever. The Texas I knew is disappearing over the horizon or already has slipped out of sight for most of the Houston or suburban-born students who enroll in Life and Literature of the Southwest. A year ago, I realized with considerable shock, that in a passage I was reading aloud from Roy Bedichek, the students did not have a clue as to what the author meant when he referred to "chopping cotton." They thought he was talking about cutting down the cotton (instead of the weeds). Then later, in their essays about *Horseman, Pass By,* they confused the terms "farm" and "ranch." So now I find it useful to put this simple equation on the board: farm=cotton; ranch=cattle.

As a child in Lucas, I wanted to write (at least this is how I interpret the windowsill episode), and today I still want to. In the classroom and in print I want to tell the truth about the way we lived then and the way we live now.

Marsha Miller

ROLANDO HINOJOSA-SMITH

ROLANDO HINOJOSA-SMITH serves as the Ellen Clayton Garwood Professor in the English department at the University of Texas at Austin. Aside from his English and Spanish novels, parts of his works have been translated into Dutch, French, German, and Italian. He is a member of the Texas Institute of Letters and the Texas Literary Hall of Fame. He earned a baccalaureate degree from the University of Texas, a master's from New Mexico Highlands University, and a PhD. from the University of Illinois, which awarded him its prestigious Alumni Achievement Award in 1998. His work *The Klail City Death Trip Series* consists of fourteen novels.

WHY I WRITE

I COME FROM a family of readers; my parents read to each other and, as the youngest of five, I also saw my older brothers and sisters reading individually or as a group. Until I was ten or so, I thought most people read and that they did so for pleasure or amusement. I certainly did until high school when my oldest sister showed me how to read as a writer: how and when the writer introduced a character or the setting, how the story was moved by using adverbs of place and time, how a character behaved or what the character did, how this created what she called an attitude in the reader's mind. This was a revelation, and although she wasn't a writer, she knew how writing worked. She and my other older sister became teachers as did an older brother. I did not give one thought to teaching when I was in high school. My interests lay in sports, reading, and girls. I was a normal enough adolescent, I suppose, although I had given some thought to being a journalist. My reading continued as did my interest in all manners of reading: humor, mostly, from James Thurber, Dorothy Parker, S. J. Perelman, Corey Ford, Robert Benchley, and a now-forgotten writer, H. C. Witwer, who wrote, primarily, boxing novels with humor and a turn of phrase which any fifteen- or sixteen-year-old would appreciate. I also read the popular writers of the time: J. P. Marquand, Lloyd Douglas, and others of their contemporaries. I was introduced to Mark Twain and Matthew Arnold by my sophomore English teacher, Miss Merle Blankenship, and to a wider reading of American and British literature by Miss Amy Cornish. This was the extent of my reading in English along with books on African adventures of Frank "Bring 'em Back Alive" Buck, a Texan, and Clyde Beatty.

And so, I read whatever fell into my hands as well as the assigned material, Matthew Arnold's *Sohrab and Rustum,* for one, and as many detective novels as I could get my hands on; in this regard, I was fortunate that my hometown, Mercedes, down in the Valley, was equipped with a well-stocked library. At one point, in the lower grades, I was appointed librarian when someone donated a four-tiered bookcase full of books to the school.

Prior to this, at age five or six, I taught myself to read Spanish by learning the alphabet; it wasn't difficult. I was a sickly child, and my father would bring me books in Spanish: comic books as well as books on history with a focus on the Mexican Revolution of 1910. I also read *The Brownsville Herald* and the Spanish-language daily, *La Prensa,* published in San Antonio and shipped by rail all over the state; the newspaper was of a conservative bent, and although my father disagreed with it, he read it assiduously, and later, I delivered it in and around the neighborhood.

Ours was a quiet household, and although I missed school for days and weeks due to rheumatic fever and other ailments, childhood asthma, for one, I kept up my schooling because my mother, a former schoolteacher, saw to it that I didn't lag behind. This was so to such an extent that I skipped a couple of grades in elementary school and later graduated from high school at age seventeen.

The two English teachers I've mentioned were most helpful, and Miss Cornish was in charge of a writing program called Creative Bits. Juniors and seniors were encouraged to write, and I did so. Evidence of my writing is available at the Mercedes High library. To claim I was influenced by this writer or that writer would be an exaggeration. What I did was try to imitate the writers I'd read, the humorists in particular.

The one serious piece I wrote at that time was in Spanish, and it dealt with a levy intent on impressing farmhands into military service. I wrote it in the course of the first of three summers during World War II that I spent in Arteaga, a village of 1,200 souls, which lies fifteen kilometers from Saltillo, the capital of Coahuila. I also attended classes there at the Ateneo Fuente and met many youngsters my age whose names, such as Buenrostro and Malacara, I use in my writing.

I lost that piece, but I remember it still, as I imagine one remembers one's first love, date, or kiss. How I came to write it, I can't remember, but I do remember sitting down and using the surrounding farmlands and the irrigation ditch (la acequia) where the farm hands were apprehended.

The piece ends violently. One farmhand's arm is hacked off with a machete, and his body falls into the irrigation ditch. The blood then runs down the mountainside. I had no idea of symbolism at the time. I just thought it would be a natural thing for the blood to spread all over México much like it did during the Revolution.

Upon my return to Mercedes for the fall term, I began to write with the idea of submitting a piece to Creative Bits. I won an honorable mention in my senior year, and this was most gratifying. The typing was done by other students, and still another group of students presented the bound volume to the principal during the Monday afternoon assemblies. It was a small school, and our graduating class numbered forty-six.

Two months after graduation, I joined the army with the parental permission required of seventeen-year-olds. One of the pleasant surprises came after basic training when I was assigned to edit the camp newspaper (I was a high school graduate and could type).

The post library was across the road from the Information and Education Office where I worked. At Carlisle Barracks, Pennsylvania, where I was later sent to school, another fine library was provided. I was home.

As usual, I perused whatever I wanted and again with no systematic reading. I would finish a book by an author, and if I liked what I'd read, I would then read whatever else was available by that writer. The first novel I read by Faulkner was something called *Mosquitoes;* I found it dull and thought I'd not read him again. This is known as irony. At the University of Texas I learned to appreciate what he did, how he did it, and what he was up to. On occasion, phrases from Faulkner pop out: "Mule in the yard. . . them sons-of-bitches."

It was the same with Hemingway's short stories and with Steinbeck's novels, which struck me as accurate since I was raised in a farming community. Sinclair Lewis, whom I read when I was in my thirties, I found dated, particularly his short stories. The novels, though, were something else: they were eye openers. F. Scott Fitzgerald's *The Great Gatsby* was another revelation, and I proceeded to memorize the last paragraph of that fine little novel.

I read more than I wrote and then turned to translating works by American authors, but this didn't attract me at first. I knew both languages, of course, but there was something lacking; what that was at the time, though, I didn't know, and I soon returned to reading. I had no intention and, obviously, no idea of how to submit a story, but I did know I wanted to write. I worked in many different jobs, none of which had to do with creative writing.

After completing my military service I attended college at the University of Texas. It was a breeze; I earned good grades, enjoyed my undergraduate years, and worked at the reserved reading room for four years, which was like Mr. McPherson assigning Peter Rabbit to guard the lettuce patch.

Most of my friends knew where to find me: between the stacks in the university tower, which housed the books during my years in Austin. I still had no systematic reading plan. I was picking out favorites. What proved of greater value was to reread certain novels and authors. This is something I would later encourage my students to do: to reread favorite works because, by doing so, they will see what they skipped or skimmed through during the first or second reading. From this, I believe I learned to love rewriting. I wanted to write plainly, and this is where Orwell came in. I bought a used paperback edition of *Homage to Catalonia,* and from this, I went on to read his book reviews, where I learned of his wide reading, of his social and political views, but above all this, his style, which I found illuminating. It was to the point with no embellishment, no showing off, and it exhibited a love and respect for the English language.

For my college graduation my mother gave me a hundred dollars as a gift, and I bought Spanish Peninsular literature in paperback editions in Matamoros. This was in the mid-fifties, and a hundred dollars went a very long way, especially when one bought the Espasa-Calpe paperback editions. And so, this Spanish-language library, coupled with what I'd brought home from the university, settled it for me. I was going to write.

I then read Russian and German works in translation. I came across six of Proust's novels published by the Modern Library and paid a dollar per volume; much, much later I was able to buy *The Sweet Cheat Gone* from Proust's *Remembrance of Things Past.* I also read and was lost when I started *Tristram Shandy.* I had no idea what Sterne was up to, but I liked what I saw and what I read. It was daring, different from what I'd seen or read before. I believe it was a Signet edition, the same company that published and sold Greek and Roman classics at fifty and seventy-five cents a copy. Daniel DeFoe came next, and I was enchanted. I still wanted to write but had no idea how to begin.

Nine years after my undergraduate work, I earned a living in many ways; this, too, was a stroke of luck because I got to meet varied levels of our society. I taught high school for a while; I then worked for a chemical company as a laborer and was promoted to the engineering office where I edited the engineers' reports. I also worked as an office manager and later as the sales manager for a work clothing manufacturing company. I returned to high school teaching and then took a Federal Service Entrance Exam. As a veteran, I was given a number of points, and this won me a G-7 salary. I planned to work until I could save $1,800.

During the last teaching job, I had spent a summer studying at Highlands University, a small institution in Las Vegas, New Mexico. That summer did it for me. I told the university dean of my plan, and he said to let him know when I could return. I would be the graduate dorm advisor, and this assured me a room. I would teach one course and receive two meals a day at the school cafeteria. Who would want more, I asked myself? I saved $1,800 in thirteen months and wrote the dean. I began to work on my master's degree and then on the doctorate. This, I knew, would give me the opportunity to write. I would be in an environment where literature flourished. During my doctoral studies at Illinois, I told a fellow student of my plans to write after I finished my degree, and he said I would never achieve tenure. I didn't know what tenure meant and didn't pursue the matter.

Upon completion of the doctorate, I accepted a position at Trinity University and returned to Texas. Two years later, I was offered a chairmanship at what is now Texas A&M in Kingsville; before accepting the offer, I asked advice from Bruce Thomas, Trinity's vice president, and explained my situation. He encouraged me to go and gave me sound advice about the place, the type of student enrolled there, the administration, and the area.

In Kingsville in 1971, a student from the Valley came to my office. He brought a copy of *El Grito,* a literary journal, which carried the explanatory subtitle *A Journal of Contemporary Mexican American Thought.* It contained a short story by Tomás Rivera and an interview. I was much taken by the story and by what Rivera wrote. I had no idea where Rivera was from, but after rereading the short piece, I knew I'd found what I wanted to do: to write about the Valley, its people, its history, its anthropology, and its changing culture. Soon after, to my good fortune, Tomás and I met at a conference at his alma mater, Southwest Texas State University (now Texas State University), and we walked on that lovely campus for most of the day without attending a single session of the conference.

We talked about writing, and I mentioned I had a piece, "Por esas cosas que pasan," and told him what it was about, and he asked me to send it to him. I did so, and he sent it to Quinto Sol Publications, an independent press established by junior professors, undergraduates, and graduate students at the University of California, Berkeley, which had published his novel. That meeting resulted in a warm friendship. As the years went by, I won two writing awards, the Quinto Sol Prize for *Estampas del Valle y otras obras,* which had been won earlier by Tomás for his . . . *y no se lo tragó la tierra* and also by Rudolfo A. Anaya's *Bless Me, Ultima.* Then came the breakthrough prize: the Premio Casa de las Américas (1976) awarded by the Casa de las Américas. It was with that second novel, *Klail City y sus alrededores* that the idea of writing a series with recurring characters developed. This was followed by *Korean Love Songs* (1978), which I wrote in English because the book was set in Japan and Korea, and the characters' lives in the military were lived in English. With this third book, I thought the series needed a name and called it *The Klail City Death Trip Series;* the origin of the title is now known, since I've spoken of it at several universities and published its provenance in an essay or two. Of course, Google can now furnish the provenance.

I wrote from the inside about the Valley, its people, its history, its values, its successes and disappointments, and against the usually one-sided telling of Texas history by Webb and others. For example, I enjoyed and admired Steinbeck's *A Medal for Benny,* set during World War II. Benny, the medal winner, is a California Mexican, but when the film was released, none of the actors were Mexican American: J. Carrol Naish, an Irishman, Dorothy Lamour, a native of Louisiana, and Arturo de Córdova, a leading light in Mexican cinema.

In short, it stereotypes what the Anglo vision was, perhaps still is, of Mexico, Mexicans, and Mexican Americans: cute, mostly fun-loving, lazy in a charming way, and with a singsong intonation when speaking English, which became a staple of Hollywood's representation of Spanish-speaking Americans. My characters, Texas Mexicans and Texas Anglos predominantly, were not meant to be caricatures. Some would be good people, others not so; some indifferent, shallow, self-sacrificing, generous, mean, and so on, but no stereotypes. The language would be their language, it would reveal their social class and standing, it would be rough and tender, and it would reflect the changes in the language, too. Not real, no, but realism.

After *Korean Love Songs,* I decided that Mexican American literature needed to expand and not restrict itself to one theme. The novel is an elastic genre, and I would then show future writers that they didn't have to use nineteenth-century forms and structures. I realized that novels didn't have to be linear, so I proposed to exploit the genre's elasticity and write all manner of novels. Thus, *Korean Love Songs* was followed by *Rites and Witnesses,* which contains chapters in dialogue with little to no direction for the reader regarding the speakers. I believe in trusting the readers, and the careful readers more so, and they will know from the context who is speaking. The second part would be reportage, where the characters from the dialogues would explain themselves in monologues. *Rites* was followed by *Mi Querido Rafa,* an epistolary novel—an old form, of course, and one not much used in the twentieth century. The second part, again, was a series of monologues where the characters mentioned in the letters appear, and this rounded out their characterization. I continued with *Claros varones de Belken,* again in Spanish. It too was a fragmentary novel, and after this I decided to translate the first two novels, *Estampas* and *Klail City* into English. Each appeared ten years after the Spanish versions, and they continue to be taught here and abroad. My decision to translate came when I realized that the knowledge of the language did not suffice. One had to be proficient in the culture of the people of all classes, and this was the object in translation.

I then began to look at the changes in the Valley and found that a city of 60,000 housed fourteen banks in a section of the United States that is considered one of the poorest in the country. Cursory readings of the local newspapers and visits to my family in the Valley revealed an increase in violent crimes, the result of drug usage and contraband. This led me to write a detective novel, *Partners in Crime* (1985). Further changes in the culture, a decrease in church attendance, a rise in divorce among traditional Catholic families, and the increased education of women of the middle class produced *Becky and Her Friends.* I started it in Spanish as *Los Amigos de Becky,* spent some seven months on it, and hit a stone wall. I laid it aside, thought on it for a while, changed it, and decided there would be no narrator; the characters would carry the novel. Some would be in favor of Becky's decision to divorce her husband, while others disagreed. This, too, would further reveal the cultural changes in the Valley. I switched to English, and the novel sailed off. After its publication, I returned to the Spanish version and finished it as well.

It was my good fortune to buy and read and later reread Paul Fussell's *The Great War and Modern Memory.* I'd read much of nineteenth-century British literature: Dickens, Hardy, Thackeray, Austen, the Bröntes, George Eliot, and others, but with the exception of Robert Graves' *Goodbye to All That,* which I'd read several times, as well as some of Evelyn Waugh's work, twentieth-century British literature was a closed book to me. I knew but had not read much of Siegfried Sassoon, Rupert Brooke, Isaac Rosenberg, Wilfred Owen, Edmund Blunden, David Jones, and Graves, and other so-called Trench Poets, but Fussell's points about them changed whatever ideas I had of that group. Reading them anew proved an education and a revelation. Through him I also discovered Anthony Powell. *A Question of Upbringing,* the first novel in Powell's sequence, *A Dance to the Music of Time,* is set at the end of the Great War.

In The Valley, the English version of *Estampas del Valle,* I included a brief diary by one of the characters and mentioned, in the briefest of terms, the Korean War. However, the more I read, the more I wanted to write about Korea, to be rid of that time somehow. I had the characters, some of the scenes, most of the characters' names, and a good enough reading and background of that horrible war to give me a start, but I wasn't a poet by any means or stretch, and Paul Fussell's *Modern Memory* opened up that possibility. I also decided to write about Mexican Americans' experiences in the war in a full novel and wrote *The Useless Servants.*

Some thirteen years had passed since *Partners in Crime* (1985), and the Valley was now a full-blown center for drug smuggling. This called for another crime novel: *Ask a Policeman*. The novel is topical, which is usually something to avoid, but since it forms part of the series and is a mixture of historical fact and fictional-and-not-so-fictional scenes and events, it plays well with the chronology that reveals the changes in my part of the world.

I then decided to write an academic novel, something that was also lacking in Mexican American literature. I wrote *We Happy Few* (2006) aboard the *Lykes Eagle*, a freighter owned by Canadian–Pacific bound for Japan and China. This allowed me to write for thirty-five days straight with no e-mail, no radio, no committees, no students, and no telephones. For this novel, I returned to writing by hand, and this, too, was an added pleasure.

I also came up with the following: I know Peninsular poetry, how it works, how its syllables are counted, that six and eight and ten syllable stanzas are used in popular poems, that seven and eleven syllables, imported from Italy, are employed for more elevated works, such as sonnets, and that the Alexandrine's fourteen syllables with a caesura was used in epic poetry and so on. Why not write, I asked, in English but employ the Spanish syllabic form? To date, no literary critic has stumbled onto the fact that W. D. Ehrhart mentioned, in a fine piece of his, that I was no poet. I wrote him and agreed and went on to explain how Spanish syllabification works.

One reason I write is the mystery of what happens to one's works. For example, *Korean Love Songs'* first two printings (1978, 1980) were published by Justa Publications, owned by Herminio Ríos, one of the founders of *Quinto Sol*. *Korean Love Songs* lay dormant but not dead; in 1993 it was published in a German–English edition in a first-rate translation by Wolfgang Karrer from Osnabrück University. Then, ten years later, it popped up again, in full—this time in the United States Air Force Academy's literary journal, *War, Literature, and the Arts,* through the kind recommendation of W. D. Ehrhart. Parts of *Korean Love Songs* continue to be published in anthologies on war, and some three years back I gave permission for parts of it to be taught to the cadets at the United States Military Academy. A strange life for a brief novel written in narrative verse.

Because Mexican American literature formed one more addition to national literature, I proposed, as mentioned, to write in as many genres within the novel and thus show young Mexican American writers that there was more than one avenue of expression and that Rivera's work had done the best job possible regarding the migrant farm labor experience. A cursory thumbing of *The Klail City Death Trip Series* will reveal fragmentary novels, a novel in narrative verse, the use of imaginary newspaper clippings, a semblance of legal depositions, maps, brief writings, recurring characters, a diary, police fiction, and the latest one, the academic or campus novel, *We Happy Few.*

I also wanted to show that Mexican Americans, in my case, Texas Mexicans, had experienced many lives and had served this country as a good part of its workforce, had served and continue to do so in the military and in public service, and as said earlier, to show that we're neither devils nor angels, not by a long shot.

As a reward, I guess, master's and doctoral theses have been written on my work in this country and abroad. This is most pleasing, particularly because the literature is written from the inside, and I am a member of that academic society. The reader will find no excuses for the behavior or the language used by the characters at times. That is not the writer's job.

So, what started during my summer months in that village in the state of Coahuila and in the program of Creative Bits in my high school has given me the freedom to do what I wanted to do in and with my life—and has given me pause. I, too, from time to time, question why I write. And why do I?

Well, it certainly isn't the money, not that it wouldn't be welcomed. And, too, despite what I've said in public and have answered in numerous interviews (and I don't hang back or deliberate whether or not I should say this or that or whether the readers wouldn't like it or whether it would be appropriate or politic or not), it comes down to, I think and believe, wanting to leave something of me when I die. Perhaps three feet of books by me or on me in some libraries. Perhaps the idea, fixed as it is sometimes, is that it is human to want to create; why, then, do people write on tombstones? To be remembered by their family? No, not really. By strangers? That's close to the mark. By friends who see the name of someone they met, know, or heard of. That's probably closer.

As for me, I can, as I have, give reasons, and I hope I've been clear on this. There are many writers, and readers, to whom I'm indebted for what I've written, for it takes what all writers know and should admit, that it's arrogance to hold on to the belief that there are people who read and want to read what one writes.

On submission again, years ago, sitting down and hidden in some library, I read what Mencken said of himself and his work—that a writer should not submit something until one was sure (no need for the modifying adverb *absolutely*) that what had been written, worked over, edited, and judged, was ready to be submitted. And not before!

We writers differ from critics who can retract or amend what they said or wrote. We're stuck with what we have written, and I, for one, although I'm not alone, decided, as is the writer's duty, to submit when, and only when, as said, it was ready.

It doesn't do to beg. Readers have no obligation to spend their money on what one writes. Because of that, we have the obligation to do not only our best but our very best. If that falls short, that's because we lack the talent, or, not an unusual case, because we're lazy.

Paradoxically, it's also through arrogance that we develop some humility. To say or claim that one writes for oneself is a lie as big as a whale. One writes to be read by others. I want to write as clearly as I can and avoid words that stop the reader from reading: The plot, usually simple, is visible, the characters are convincing, and the setting works. Simple enough and neither new nor original, but it's important, and a writer should always keep that in mind.

Writers usually do not know who will read us; in my case, however, my reading public is composed primarily of university professors and their students. This allows me a certain latitude in subject matter in that it doesn't have to be popular writing. Someone once wrote that J. P. Marquand couldn't write a sex scene to save his life; for my part, I can't write a popular novel. Recognizing this, I don't try. I rely on the readers I have and what success I have is *succès d'estime.* And so, I write and consider myself fortunate to be able to put together words that some readers find worth their while.

Calderón reminds us that life is a dream, and I agree. Life is also short and as uncontrollable as dreams are, and sometimes life makes little to no sense at all. Writers, then, are not magicians; some are born storytellers, some are not, but we all share a gift that has been brought about by hard work, by a lifetime of living, by experiencing and witnessing everyday events, and by being able to recall some of these events and deform others; what results is a work of fiction based on some reality, as fiction always is.

In closing, I read somewhere that cryptic answers are meant to hide and to illuminate at the same time. I'm not sure I can go along with that. I think that the proposition is false and pretentious, much like those questions someone asks, after a reading, which last two or three minutes—during which time I, and the other person, I suspect, have lost track of where the question was headed. But back to the cryptic answers: Beware of writers and what we put down. It's confession time again, and I'm the one who came up with that piece about cryptic answers. Why? Because I'm a writer.

Writing remains one of the few acts where one works alone and without supervision—where one does not answer to someone else at the time of composition. There aren't many professions like that anymore. Writing also gives one a sense of independence, and that, too, is why I write.

Money. Setting aside Dr. Johnson's dictum that only blockheads do not write for money, the truth is I don't write for money. Oh, I like it and want to receive it for the work done, but it's not only for money, and this has freed me. This calls for an explanation. I don't have an agent, and I don't know how to find one, but I do know that agents negotiate for the amount a writer is to receive for an appearance or for a publication. It's in their interest, of course. I don't charge much, although I have received what I consider sizable sums. But what if it's a school district, or a community college, or a four-year school with limited resources? The agent wouldn't want to work for 10 or 15 percent of three or four or five hundred dollars. What about working for one-hundred and fifty in the case of a poorly funded independent school district? Would an agent work or be happy with 15 percent of one hundred dollars? The answer is obvious. But, then, neither would many writers, and this includes many Mexican American writers.

The same goes with publishing; some houses have paid me as much as $2,000 for a short story. To me, that's a lot of money. It is welcomed, of course, but remains a large sum. What, then, with a university press? They're nonprofit organizations, and what they offer is small, at times, infinitesimally so. But what if I wish to publish with them? No one can advise or stop me from doing so.

Have I published some of my short pieces or chapters of the novels with Heath or McMillan or any of the large publishers? Yes, but I remain loyal to the small publishers such as Arte Público Press at the University of Houston and Bilingual Review/Press at Arizona State. They're loyal to me, and I am loyal to them.

But, it's also about letting the United States, Europe, and elsewhere know of this other American literature that's been around since the mid-nineteenth century, which resurged during the turbulent sixties and continues unabated in every genre: novels, short stories, poetry, children's and young adult literature, the essay, and so on.

It's well-known that all literature begins as local, it moves on to being national, and finally universal. It has to persevere to do so.

And that, in the end, is why I write.

Mary Hughes

PAULETTE JILES

PAULETTE JILES was born in Salem, Missouri, and graduated from the University of Missouri with a BA in Romance Languages. She is the author of the best selling *Enemy Women,* a novel of the Civil War. Her latest novel, *Stormy Weather,* is set in Texas. Paulette lives on her ranch in the Hill Country west of San Antonio.

THE COUNTRY OF THE MIND

I LIVE ON A HILLTOP in the Texas Hill Country, and in all directions I can see for several miles. From the front porch I look east into the valley of the Sabinal River and the small town where the post office is, the general store, the feed store, and the steeples of the Methodist and Baptist churches lifting above the live oaks. From the back, to the west, the view is of another valley and a range of hills, and at night there is not a light to be seen in all of that stretch of country.

I think of this as the front of my mind and the back of my mind. From the front is daily business to be done and mail collected, a three-mile trip to town in the pickup, and greeting people I know. It is a social world where I sing in the Christmas cantata or attend a benefit for Tim who operates the cedar-clearing machine and who broke his leg, or maybe shattered would be a better word, so money has to be raised for a serious operation. They had some fair scratch bands playing old country and western songs in the park alongside the Sabinal River under giant live oaks, colored lights, and barbeque, and by midnight there was enough to pay the surgeon.

In the back is all that uninhabited geography; although I know there are houses far back in the folds of the hills it seems perfectly uninhabited. It is a landscape you would think of walking out into with a feeling of joy and release and imminent danger. It is a different world, like the world of writing and the telling of tales. The country of the mind, which has a tenuous and variable attachment to the daily existence in which we find ourselves, appears and disappears like rain in a dry land. Sometimes I am singing my heart out in a cantata with twenty other people, and other times I'm perfectly still here in this small house watching cloud shadows move over the hills to the west like the images and plots that occur in my head. These images and plots are ancient, mythic, but perpetually renewed. It is like a kaleidoscope, with a limited number of pieces but an infinite variety of combinations.

Like most writers I am refreshed and encouraged in my work by other writers more than anything else, because literature is its own landscape. But every story takes place somewhere, and that somewhere matters. The only thing I can compare it to is the work of the artists of Altamira who painted their Paleolithic bulls on the cave ceiling, overlaid one after the other, learning from other artists, using the stone as if it were their canvas, yet taking advantage of the convolutions and projections of the stone itself to produce bulls, horses, and reindeer that were almost in bas-relief. So when I write it is the same; I learn from other writers, my stories take place in the imagination first and foremost, yet the stone and the mountains, the rivers and the highways, the live oak and agarita and Spanish oak of a real Texas make them a bas-relief, and like the kaleidoscope of mythic forms, the combinations and variations are without end.

Every writer comes upon places and times and people that are striking, sometimes amazing, and you know you have no place for them in any story that has as yet occurred to you, but like most writers you have a sort of mini-storage place in your memory where these images will stay until needed. Maybe it is a mental cave of the treasured, hoarded images like those of Altamira. Images from the landscapes of Texas are, for me, striking, elemental. In my mental hoard, they shift and change in small ways, they are mercurial. When I have started to write of some incident or landscape from memory, and I check it against what I wrote in my journal, I find subtle changes, which must have taken place in a kind of fossilized darkness.

Which brings me to the cinnabar mine in Terlingua:

I was invited to a celebration at an odd place just outside of Terlingua, Texas, in Big Bend, by friends who lived there. It was a sort of collapsed dude ranch or tourist place, and somebody at some time had filmed a few scenes from some famous western film there. The remains of the film set consisted of a fake Spanish chapel made of two-by-fours and plaster with a fiberglass bell and old cracked plastic bottles of Deja Blue lying around in heaps. Since, at the time, I was writing a book that had a scene where my heroine was crossing a stretch of desert much like that of Big Bend during a full moon, I was happy to accept the invitation, especially since the celebration was taking place during that event, which, in the desert in far West Texas, is not to be missed. During the day the host and hostess took a group of us to visit the cinnabar mine, about a half a mile away.

Red mercury is the basic ingredient in cinnabar. This mine was a slit in the hillside, and all the rock was the color of blood, fresh blood, ancient dark purple blood, arterial blood, venous blood. It was creepy. I was unable to follow the rest of the group to the inner chambers of the mine because of this creepiness and a sudden, overwhelming claustrophobia. I was ashamed to admit that when the last shaft of daylight disappeared and the small and limited flashlight beams took over, I could not go a step further. In the strange combination of bloody darkness and the crushing walls, I froze. From far ahead, people called back to where I was, as if I was coming. I found myself grappling with a kind of disabling terror that seemed to have no clear reason, but I felt as if I were being shut up and suffocated in some kind of wounded, sinister, non-human heart.

After a moment I told myself I didn't have to do this, and I turned and walked out into the flat, brilliant desert sunlight and went back to my truck. I fed my dog and drank cold soda and was furious with myself. But there was nothing to be done about it.

That night, I made my bed in the truck and watched the full moon come up over the Chisos Mountains to the east and the moon shadows crawling westward before it. It rose over the hilly desert until it flooded everything with its peculiar and intense light where everything seemed to come alive. If not alive, then possessed of some kind of dark, silicate energy. I sat awake half the night and saw a great many things, most of which were probably not real, or at least not bodily. I wrote of this at length later on and ended up having to throw it away. I have never yet used that terrible moment in the cinnabar mine, but it's in my cave of images.

So, this is the synergy between imagined stories and real landscapes. Texas has a great many of the sort of landscapes that carry stories well, from the East Texas swamps to the oil fields to the deserts of the western part of the state and my own fossil-studded Hill Country with its limestone escarpments and the now-dry creek beds in which I find fossils of shells, palm nuts, and sometimes arrowheads. I usually write the sort of tales in which external events impinge on my characters' lives; they are forced out of their everyday routines and go wandering around in the countryside and have to get from one place to another, usually under terrible circumstances. I believe these are usually called quest stories, as opposed to the narratives about people in large cities for whom social relationships are primary and form the basic matrix of what occurs. The history of Texas is replete with people trying to get from one place to another under terrible circumstances. Not that social relationships do not figure into these stories, but the landscape of Texas lays out the groundwork, so to speak. The history of Texas is as rich with very odd, unexpected stories as the cinnabar mine was with mercury.

Since I live so much in my head and don't like to do any intellectual work other than my writing, I find the duties required of me on this small ranch to be very much needed. I am enormously fortunate in being able to devote my time to writing, in being able to support myself by writing. Most of my writing life until recently has been crowded with jobs and family and all the shopping and caring and meeting deadlines that go along with that, but at last I have all the time I need to myself, and I sometimes wonder how I got so lucky. So to balance the long hours needed for writing, I can walk down to feed my horses or work at clearing brush and clearing my head in silence. Listen to the wind, walk the drying pasture and wonder when there will be rain. I feel sunk into and part of this landscape.

To the west, looking out my back door where the world is a series of blue folding ridges of what seems to be uninhabited country, there is a layer of limestone in which I find an endless supply of fossilized Nipa palm nuts. They look like hearts and people call them heart stones. They range from the size of a walnut to that of a grapefruit. There are still Nipa palms in the world, somewhere in the South Seas. This was once a South Sea. Apparently it was a shoreline with forests of Nipa palms dropping their nuts in tons. There was no one here to eat them at the time, and when I think about it, a world without human beings at all, without stories to tell or mythic forms to contemplate, it is chilling, a kind of loneliness without bottom.

I put the nuts in a bucket with bleach to bring out their lovely creamy limestone color and stack them in baskets and then get back to my work. This means writing by hand for the most part and then later transferring it to the computer, falling into the seductiveness of research, which leads to odd places, and then giving it up for the day because I have horses to feed and a dead battery in the truck and a section of fence down, and my neighbor wants me to help her load a goat, a billy, who does not want to get into the back of her truck. So, I return to the social world, a world of people who are not imaginary but still, as in all our lives, we seem to participate in these larger, mythic forms whether we wish to or not.

After the goat loading, I asked her to lend me her battery charger. Her husband is away for fifteen days of the month because he is a tugboat captain pushing barges between Houston and Brownsville, and she, like Penelope, stays home and weaves the continuity of their lives on land. Two women and an Alpine billy, and the women won.

There is not much of a *why* in why people write, and the *hows* aren't all that interesting. It is not a spectator sport, and I can't invite the reader to sit and watch while I scribble. Even musicians and painters are more interesting to observe as to the *hows* of their work, and with them I would include mechanics and people who do steer roping, so I will pass on any description of *whying* and *howing*. I will tell you this, that it is exhausting, and after a good number of hours of work I can stand on my front porch, and if it is a cloudy night far to the southeast I can see the lights of San Antonio, and it takes a while to readjust my eyes and my mind. The distant city lights glowing on the cloud cover make a kind of overhead sea with the fossil light of stars occasionally breaking through in patterns that were once nameless.

It takes a while to get from one place to another in Texas.

When I leave the Hill Country, the distance between here and, for instance, the land of the bloody cinnabar mine and the full moon, can be counted in country music stations. I listen to them; the writers know what they are doing. They are experts in these shifting mythic forms. They are also very good at slant rhymes and developing a story in three verses, and I think "I'm Going to Hire a Wino to Decorate My Home" is some of the best comic rhyming I have ever heard. It is Dickensian.

I drive to places where things happen, or will happen when I write about it. When I get out of the truck and let the dog go for his run I am in some place where Kitty Kelsay was scalped and left for dead, where a man plotted to murder his father-in-law and throw him down the Devil's Sinkhole, where oil came crawling up out of a cratered well and slid all over the countryside in a glittering unstoppable sheet, and a small town where sweet Bonnie Parker pasted movie stars' pictures in her album. But I can't be gone too long among these startling occurrences and strange people; if I am away for more than two days I worry and fuss and imagine that my horses are starving and brush has choked out my house and that if I stay away it won't rain and if I go home it will.

Today I collected four more of the palm nut fossils. They are becoming like zucchinis—proliferating, filling up basket after basket. I give them away to friends. They make good presents. The man who shoes my horses is a Texas Ranger. He says he's got three kids to put through college, and besides, his hobby is steer roping, which takes good horses, and good horses cost money. So, he adds to his income by farrier work.

While he shoes he tells stories about steer roping. He remains reticent about his work as a Texas Ranger, which is only right. Men and horses and male cattle make up three of the more brightly colored glass pieces of the kaleidoscope, and his stories are both hair-raising and funny. I gave him one of the heart stones, and he turned it over in his hands and said, "Palm nuts. Prehistoric palm nuts. Wonder if there was anybody around to eat them."

No, we weren't there yet. The world was lonely for us. We were still only prototypes in the shallow blue oceans that surrounded this ridge, called Seco Ridge, a crystalline structure like salt present in the water, and there was as yet no mind that contained an east or a west, front or back. Texas was speechless with longing. Rudimentary mythic forms were joining together like the valves of a heart and solidifying, waiting for the storyteller.

Drawing by Barbara M. Whitehead

ELMER KELTON

ELMER KELTON of San Angelo, Texas, is the author of more than forty western and historical novels, primarily set in the Lone Star State. A native of Crane, Texas, he spent forty-two years as an agricultural journalist in tandem with his sixty-year career as a fiction writer. He grew up on the McElroy Ranch in Crane and Upton counties, where his father was a foreman and eventually general manager. He earned a journalism degree from the University of Texas at Austin.

Among his novels are *The Time It Never Rained, The Good Old Boys, The Man Who Rode Midnight, The Wolf and the*

Buffalo, and *The Day the Cowboys Quit*. He has earned seven Spur Awards from the Western Writers of America, Inc., four Western Heritage Awards from the National Cowboy Hall of Fame, and numerous other career awards. One of his novels, *The Good Old Boys*, became a television movie starring Tommy Lee Jones.

I LOVE A GOOD WESTERN

I WAS NOT SUPPOSED to become a writer. I was supposed to be a cowboy. However, neither nature nor training gave me the skills necessary to earn an honest living in the saddle, so by default I became my next best choice, a writer. I decided if I could not do it, I could at least write about it.

Writing was one of the few endeavors I found I could handle with any acceptable level of competence. It involved no heavy lifting and no being thrown from bad horses. I have managed to make a living at it now for some sixty years, albeit with lean times here and there.

By rights of inheritance I should have been a cowboy. Three generations before me followed that profession. One of my great-grandfathers was a cattleman in Oklahoma and Central Texas. Another brought a covered wagon and a string of horses out from the East Texas piney woods in the late 1870s. My grandfather and father were cowboys, but somewhere a glitch occurred in the genes, and I never managed to live up to their standards.

I spent my boyhood on the McElroy Ranch in Crane and Upton counties where my father was foreman. From the time I was old enough to take note of the world around me, I was exposed to cattle, horses, and cowboys. I grew up wanting to be part of that world but never quite mastering the requirements.

My mother had been a teacher before she married. She read stories to me before I was able to read them for myself, and she taught me to read when I was five. I immersed myself in books and magazines. I vicariously lived many lives of adventures through them. To me, a story was a magic that carried me to places I could only imagine and to times beyond my ken.

Moreover, cowboys, as a class, were good storytellers, and I was an avid listener, sitting discreetly out of notice on a front porch, at a chuck wagon campfire, or near a lively game of 42. Some of the oldest of the men had been around in the open-range era and the final days of the cattle drives. An elderly neighbor was said to have hunted buffalo. Through them I gained a fascination for history, for they had been part of it. Through them I felt a direct connection to the past. History, to me, was never dull; it was as real as those men and women I knew when I was a boy.

By the time I was eight or nine, I was making up and scribbling stories of my own. I decided even then that I wanted to become a writer, but for the most part I kept it to myself. Writing stories seemed a sissy thing to do when others were riding and roping or knocking each other around playing football. I went to school in Crane, an oil-patch town, a bit on the rough and rowdy side. I was not any better at athletics than at being a cowboy. But, I was good in English class and usually even beat the girls at spelling bees. That made me automatically suspect.

My three younger brothers were becoming good cowboys while I was always found lacking. For one thing, I was forever getting lost when we worked a pasture. I was supposed to keep my place in a broad line while we pushed the cattle before us. In brushy country, I could not see the riders on either side of me, so I was frequently falling behind the drive or getting in front of it, letting cattle slip around behind me. Not until I was in the fifth grade did an observant teacher notice that I was woefully nearsighted. Glasses helped me see much better, but by then the die had been cast. My failures were already legend, and I never outlived them.

Besides books and magazines, I loved the movies. Living nine miles from town, I never got to see films nearly as often as I wished to, but I was fascinated by stories that unfolded on the screen. As a budding artist, I drew "movies" of my own on long strips of paper, drawing them between slits in a piece of cardboard so that only one panel showed at a time. I vocalized the dialog from behind the cardboard and inflicted many an hour of boredom on my younger brothers.

Another turning point was a bout with tuberculosis, which required that I remain in bed all but a short time each day for the better part of a year. The school sent lessons out to me so I could keep up with my classmates. I had a lot of time to read and make up stories and "radio" scripts, another atrocity I dispensed to my helpless siblings.

Newspapers had appealed to me from the beginning, first because of the comics but eventually because of the stories the headlines told. The *Fort Worth Star-Telegram* came to our mailbox every day. I also discovered two grand magazines: *Boy's Life* and *The Open Road For Boys.* Each contained good fiction as well as interesting articles. I could envision myself one day writing stories for them, though I never did.

One late summer day in 1939, a new cowboy showed up

at the ranch. John Patterson had been a regular hand there for several years. His younger brother, Paul, had signed on to teach in the Crane school in the fall but came a few weeks early. To kill time and earn a few extra dollars, he joined his brother on the McElroy roundup crew. I first got to know him as cowboy Paul. School started, and suddenly he was Mister Patterson, my teacher in Spanish and journalism.

More than anyone before, other than my mother, Paul Patterson encouraged me in my writing. I credit him with giving me the idea that one way into professional writing was through newspaper work. We published a school newspaper a couple of times a month. This gave me my first real taste of printer's ink, for I had never tried before to have any of my work actually printed. Mister Patterson took several of us to a journalism workshop at the University of Texas in Austin. From that point, there was no looking back.

I had a problem, however: my cowboy father. He had long since conceded that I was never to be a cowboy, but he thought I might be able to make a living at something "practical" such as engineering, or even law. The day came when I had to tell him my plan: to go to the University of Texas, study journalism, and become a writer.

I had always assumed he would not understand, and my assumption was one hundred percent correct. He declared, "That's the way with you kids nowadays. You all want to make a living without having to work for it."

He relented, however, and I entered the university in the fall of 1942. Having started school in the third grade at age seven, and Texas schools at that time having just eleven grades, I was only a few months past my sixteenth birthday, too young yet to go into World War II. I majored in journalism with a minor in English.

I found that I learned far more about professional writing

in the journalism school than in the English creative writing courses. The latter tended to be old-fashioned, stuffy, and a bit contemptuous of anything that smacked of being "popular." In one English course we were assigned to write an essay on a subject of our own choosing. I wrote a piece about ranch life. The teacher gave me high marks on writing skill but a D for my choice of subject matter.

She wrote on my essay, "If you are ever to become a serious writer, you must learn to choose subjects of importance." Ranch life was without importance in her view. Had I written about life in an English manor or a French villa, perhaps I would have received an A. But rural America, or at least rural Texas, did not count.

On the same campus, folklorist J. Frank Dobie was teaching his course in southwestern life and literature. He considered all life to be important, wherever it was. I always wanted to study under him, but by the time I had the prerequisites for the course, he was no longer teaching. I eventually took the course under another great folklorist, Mody Boatright. It was one of the most rewarding of my university experiences.

Most of my friends were going off to war, and I felt I was falling short of my duty by not going with them. At seventeen, I volunteered for the navy, but I was rejected because of flat feet. At eighteen I went into the army. There, I wound up in the walking infantry. Evidently flat feet were considered no obstacle to carrying a rifle. The only requirement was that I have two of them.

My military service is another story for another time and place. Suffice it to say that I wound up in Germany during the last weeks of the war and was riding on top of a Sherman tank, trying to keep up with the retreat, when the tank ran into a stone wall. I saved it from damage, however, by cushioning the impact with my foot. I finished the war in a field hospital and then a military hospital in France. Later, I served in Austria, where I met a young lady named Anni, who eventually became my wife and has remained so for sixty years.

Upon discharge from the service, I still had three semesters to finish at the university. I decided it was time to get serious about writing for publication. The pulp magazines I had read as a boy were in their final years. Because teachers had always condemned them as trash writing, I thought they should be a pushover for me. I figured I could earn easy money while learning the craft, then go on to more serious stuff.

That was a gross miscalculation. I plunged in head-first, spending all my spare time pounding out stories on a portable typewriter I had bought my junior year in high school. I sent them off not only to the pulps, but also to the slick magazines such as *Post* and *Collier's.* Some of them seemed to get back from the post office before I did. I soon had a tubful of rejection slips. I also lost weight because I was spending much of my lunch money on stamps.

Not only did I learn a hard lesson in humility, but I discovered that the pulp stories, even at their most formulaic, required a far higher level of craftsmanship than I realized. I began studying writers whose work I liked, analyzing what made the stories click, studying the way a skilled writer could paint word pictures in the reader's mind. I even copied segments on the typewriter to get a feel for the rhythm, the flow of the language. I studied under some of the best teachers in the world, though they never knew it.

Finally, a lady editor, Fanny Ellsworth of *Ranch Romances,* began writing short letters instead of sending printed rejection slips. She would point out why the story was rejected and urge me to keep trying. Those letters bolstered my wounded confidence and restored hope that, frankly, I had been in some danger of losing. Mark Twain said anyone could quit smoking; he had done it dozens of times. I would get discouraged and decide to quit writing. Sometimes I would stay quit for several hours. Then a new story idea would hit me, and I was back at the typewriter.

In my last weeks at the university, I received the most beautiful check I have ever seen in my life. Mrs. Ellsworth finally bought one of my stories, "There's Always Another Chance." I was sure I was on my way to fame and fortune at last. I didn't know it would be a year before I sold another story.

By the time the story was published, I had accepted a job as agricultural reporter for the *San Angelo Standard-Times.* My ranch raising gave me a good background for that kind of work. Though I was not ranching or cowboying, I was earning a living writing about it. Initially, I fantasized that I would soon be selling fiction like a pro and that newspaper work would only be a temporary distraction, a stepping stone I could leave behind.

I did, forty-two years later. I had two parallel careers, one as a fiction writer and one as an agricultural journalist. I started with the *Standard-Times,* then edited *Sheep and Goat Raiser Magazine,* and finally spent twenty-two years as associate editor of *Livestock Weekly,* which John Erickson has called the "cowboy's *Wall Street Journal.*" I found that I enjoyed the journalism work because it kept me in constant company of the kind of people I had always known best: ranchers, farmers, and others in the agriculture industry.

I worked as a reporter by day and wrote fiction at night and on weekends. My two occupations complimented each other. The people I knew in my daily work were sometimes morphed into characters in my fiction. The writing techniques I developed in fiction improved my writing as a reporter. My job took me to locales I could use in my stories. The history I found in these places was useful to me in crafting fiction.

I have always felt fortunate that I had the advantage of working in the pulp magazines during my formative years as a writer. They taught me to set a stage, introduce my characters, tell a compact story, and get off the stage in five thousand words. These short stories imposed a discipline that longer fiction does not. Novels can move along at a more leisurely pace with more time to develop characters, interweave multiple plots, and deliver a message, if that is the writer's intention. That is good, but it can lead to dull spots and idle passages that break up the story's rhythm.

I admit that I never was as good at short stories as at novels. The pulp stories were strongly plot-driven, and plot was never my long suit. I always was more comfortable developing rounded characters and letting them lead the plot rather than have the plot lead the characters. Nevertheless, I am grateful to the pulps for what they taught me. I regret that young writers today do not have this splendid training ground that allowed me to earn while I learned.

There is relatively little demand for short stories today. The beginner must start with the full-length novel, a little like learning to swim by jumping into the deepest end of the pool. He may indeed learn to swim, but on the other hand he may drown.

Concurrent with the rapid spread of television in the early 1950s, the pulp magazines began dying out. My then-agent, August Leninger, warned that if I wanted to continue a career in fiction, I would have to begin writing full-length novels. The paperback novel was increasing in popularity even as the pulps were fading out.

With trepidation, I wrote my first novel. Unfortunately, by the time I finished it, the market had become saturated. I had no previous credits as a novelist, no name known to the reading public. My novel bounced around for about a year, unsold. Then, a second lady editor came to my rescue. Ian and Betty Ballentine, pioneers in the paperback field, were starting their own publishing company and were looking for some young and untried workers who might have staying power. Betty bought my novel, *Hot Iron*. Out of that developed an editor–writer relationship that was to last for many years. I averaged writing a book a year as a sideline to my newspaper work. The Ballantines bought more than a dozen of them. But, eventually they sold their company, and the easy rapport I had with them was gone.

I had met a Doubleday editor, Harold Kuebler, at a Western Writers of America convention. He had urged me to write something for his company's Double D Western hardcover line. Looking for a new outlet, I wrote a story that I had been thinking about for several years, a fictional account of a cowboy strike in the Texas Panhandle in 1883. It was published as *The Day the Cowboys Quit* and started an association with Doubleday that lasted about twenty years. It included what I consider my signature books, *The Time It Never Rained* and *The Good Old Boys.*

In recent years, I have been published by Tom Doherty's Forge Books, which has been good for me, not only in presenting my new work, but also in reprinting most of my fifty-year backlist.

I credit a third lady editor, Judy Alter, for helping my

career along at a time when a push was needed. Through TCU Press, she republished several of my books that had gone out of print. Suddenly and unexpectedly, I became acceptable to academia. My books attracted far more attention in their second incarnation than they did in their first.

Speaking of Western Writers of America, I must credit that beloved institution for many of the good things that have happened in my career. As a new member and kid in the outfit, I was privileged to meet and pick the brains of many old-time professionals whose work I had read for years. Some, like S. Omar Barker, gave me suggestions from which I have profited ever since. The association's aim is to support and encourage good western writing. The annual conventions give beginning writers, as well as established professionals, a chance to make new contacts and find new outlets for their work.

I am frequently asked about my writing methods, my routine, and the like. When I had a full-time job, I had to apportion my time so that I gave due attention to both careers. Since retirement from newspaper work, I have lost some of that structure and discipline, I am sorry to say. Age has slowed me down but has not stopped me.

Each writer has to find what works best for him or her. No one set of guidelines will fit everybody. For instance, I find that many writers work through their first draft as expeditiously as possible to get the basic story on paper (or disc), then go back and rewrite, revise, and polish. On the other hand, I tend to revise and rewrite and labor over the story as I go along, which means I am much slower in finishing the draft. However, when I get to the end, the story is usually in pretty good shape because of all the polishing and trimming I did as I went along. What works for me might be deadly for someone else, and vice versa.

I consider myself first and foremost a storyteller. The first function of a fiction writer is to tell a story. Often I have a message or viewpoint I am trying to convey, but if I don't tell a story interestingly enough that the reader stays with it to the end, he will never be exposed to the message.

I tell my story through characters, through their individual viewpoints. The characters have to be compelling enough to involve readers, or they will put my book down and pick up someone else's. The characters have to face problems and obstacles. The story revolves around the ways they solve these problems, or in some cases, fail to solve them. Sometimes I start with a character and decide what kind of story can build around him. Other times I start with a situation and invent characters to set upon that stage and live out the story.

Before I start to write a novel, I have to know at least something about the principal characters. My acquaintanceship will grow as I work with them. They usually take on extra dimensions I did not foresee at the beginning. Before starting to write, I need to know how the story is to open, and I have to have a vision for the end. The middle part usually takes care of itself, as the characters grow and take over the course of the story. Often, by the time I approach the end, what I had originally envisioned no longer fits the characters and the situation. Not often does a story end exactly as I envisioned when I started.

To me, a story feels more spontaneous if the author can surprise himself from time to time. If I can surprise myself, I hope I can also surprise the reader. However, the story must always remain plausible. A surprise twist does not work if it is not believable. It will look contrived.

I remember a story I wrote when I was perhaps twelve

years old. Toward the end, the villain was getting away, and the hero could not catch him. So, I invented an earthquake. The ground opened up and swallowed the villain. How glad I am that the story never saw print.

My writing is almost entirely about Texas because that is where I spent my life. In my work I have traveled extensively over the state and feel that I know it and its people. They are my people. I think I understand them. In Texas history, I can find more stories than I could write about in three lifetimes. I am never comfortable in writing about places and people I do not really know. Therefore, I leave writing about New York to Woody Allen and his contemporaries, and about the South to William Faulkner, Eudora Welty, and others who have done far better with it than I could.

I have always specialized in the western, or the western historical novel. Growing up in the atmosphere that I did, I always related to the western. It reflected my heritage. True, I read books and stories of all kinds, including the standard childhood classics of the time such as *Tom Sawyer, Huckleberry Finn, Treasure Island, Hans Brinker and the Silver Skates, The Wizard of Oz*. But I also read the fine cowboy-and-horse books by Will James, the western romances by Zane Grey, and the folklore tales of J. Frank Dobie, not to mention dozens of pulp magazines.

Some of the western stories I read struck me false, as if the writer didn't know sagebrush from mesquite. That made me want to write stories that reflected reality, at least reality as I saw it. It gave me a strong appreciation for such knowledgeable writers as S. Omar Barker, Bennett Foster, H. H. Knibbs, William McLeod Raine, and others.

As I began trying seriously to learn the craft of writing westerns, I studied works of then-contemporary genre leaders such as Ernest Haycox and Luke Short. I appreciate the literary qualities of Haycox and A. B. Guthrie, Jr., and the splendid characterizations that were a Luke Short specialty.

From the first, I recognized that the western was not granted the prestige that attached itself to other genres. The critical establishment has wrongly consigned the western to a sort of literary ghetto, automatically assuming that if the setting is in the West, the work must be juvenile. Many a splendid piece of literature has been ignored simply because it had a western label and was considered unworthy of attention by the literary elite. To some degree, this chauvinistic attitude is extended even to serious scholars who write nonfiction works about western history. Only occasionally do they receive the accolades accorded to historians who work in other fields. This is akin to my long-ago university teacher who criticized me for writing about ranch life instead of something "important."

Now and then, a piece of western literature breaks through and receives the attention it deserves, as have the works of such writers as Walter Van Tilburg Clark, Wallace Stegner, Frank Waters, and in more recent times, Larry McMurtry. But for each of these, a hundred are like flowers in the field, blooming unseen and dying unmourned.

They deserve much better. A fine novel is a fine novel regardless of its setting, so long as it deals honestly with the human condition and shows respect for the subject matter.

Many people question the western's place today, asking if it has any relevance to a modern world inasmuch as most of it goes back to the nineteenth century. The basic human emotions are universal and timeless. Any literature which reflects these realities has something to tell us, regardless of its timeframe.

The western illuminates our past, tells us what we have

saved and what we have lost. Whether or not we choose to acknowledge it, the past has formed us. If we are to understand ourselves, we must understand what has brought us to where we are and to be what we are. Literature, western and otherwise, can give us that and offer us a vision of what we can become in the future.

Austin American Statesman/Larry Kolvoord, Courtesy of Southwest Writers Collection

LARRY L. KING

LARRY L. KING grew up in Putnam, Texas. He is writing his fifteenth book, *Safe at Home: Life in World War II America*. He is also the author or co-author of seven stage plays, including the international musical hit, *The Best Little Whorehouse in Texas*, and has written four television documentaries, a dozen short stories, and more than 300 articles and essays. He is the only writer to have been nominated for a National Book Award, a TV Emmy, and a Broadway Tony. The Larry L. King Theatre in Austin, dedicated in 2006 in ceremonies at the parent Austin Playhouse, will host an annual new play festival also named after King.

King is a member of PEN, the National Writers Union, Dramatists Guild, and the Texas Institute of Letters. He lives in Washington, D.C., with his wife-lawyer-agent Barbara S. Blaine who, like her husband, grew up in Texas.

FAMOUS ARTHUR

WHEN I WAS eight years old in 1935, I told all in the vicinity of Putnam, Texas, who would listen that I intended to become a rich Famous Arthur, believing "author" to be spelled and pronounced as the given name.

Twenty miles to the west was the nearest "city," Abilene, with a population of about 25,000 in the mid-1930s. An unimaginable 159 miles to the east was Fort Worth, surely almost as big as New York City since it had tall buildings, cafés that stayed open past dark, a newspaper that came out *every day,* and a college that existed, in my mind, for the sole purpose of unleashing the mighty Texas Christian Horned Frogs on such sorry outfits as the Baylor Bears, Southern Methodist's Mustangs, the Texas Longhorns, and the Texas A&M Aggies.

In the summer of 1936, when I was seven and laid low by whooping cough, events conspired to inspire my first fantasy of becoming a "rich Famous Arthur." Mother, compensating for my having missed the Clark family reunion in Cisco, got from the library there a copy of *The Adventures of Tom Sawyer* and read it to me. It was ever so much more interesting and entertaining than the books I had read in school ("See Spot run. Run Spot. Run. See Dick and Jane chase Spot. Run Jane."). So, I asked mother if Mr. Mark Twain had written any other books. She soon provided *The Prince and the Pauper.*

Scribbling on a five-cent Big Chief tablet, I began stories titled "The Adventures of Hap Hazzard" and "The Rich Man's Son and the Poor Man's Kid." They were truncated, but the few pages I wrote persuaded me that I had found my calling. Unlike my contemporaries, I never entertained notions of becoming the next cowboy movie star, à la Tom Mix, or a war hero, or a fireman, or, a bit later, Superman. Perhaps now and again I dreamed of saving Anna Lou Williams from a fire-snorting dragon, but such dangers were in short supply locally. When I wrote Anna Lou a mash note, she crumpled it and threw it in my face. It was my first rejection slip, even though the poem I wrote Anna Lou was not original with me: "Tell me quick/Before I faint/Is you mine/Or is you ain't?"

Few were safe from my dispatches. I read to the unwary, ambushed on the school playground, in the town square, or in Uncle George Gaskin's Piggly Wiggly grocery store. I wrote that any number of "white hopes" could defeat Joe Louis, the Brown Bomber and current heavyweight champion. I wrote that Louis won because he paid off the referees, just as did our natural enemies eleven miles to the west, the loathsome Baird High School Bears. I also "proved" that Franklin D. Roosevelt was the best president we ever had, that Texas was not only the biggest but the best state, that on the evidence of the Bible's report of winds blowing from "the four corners of the earth," the earth was most assuredly flat, that Turkey Triplett and Hooter Allen of the Putnam High School Panthers deserved to be named All-American football players, and that only girls and sissies patronized Shirley Temple movies. It was a bit more difficult to prove that my Uncle Claude, who owned the town barbershop and had been defeated for county commissioner in nine consecutive elections spanning eighteen years, should be elected governor of Texas, but I tried.

As a high school student, I discovered that not everyone wished me to become a rich Famous Arthur. The first was a typing teacher, hereafter known as Miss Killjoy, who rejected my application to join her class on the grounds that she only accepted girls. I brooded and seethed, finally approaching the principal with my sad story. He did not seem eager to get involved, but I persisted until he said he had spoken to Miss Killjoy and had strongly suggested that she take me the next year.

I should have let well enough alone, but that wouldn't have fit my character. So, all summer long, after my day as a carpenter's helper was over, I repaired to the mezzanine of the Scharbauer Hotel in Midland. There, for one dime, I could use a typewriter for one hour. I was practicing, you see, so that on the first day in typing class I could challenge Miss Killjoy to a speed test and publicly humiliate her. My reasoning was that she would be so surprised and made nervous by my dare, that she would make errors while I did not. Alas, all that happened was that Miss Killjoy said, "Don't be ridiculous!" and all the girls laughed. My challenge only cemented Miss Killjoy's low opinion of me, and though I believed I was as good as at least half of the girls, she bestowed my only F. Neither of us knew it, but she had done me a favor: by having to repeat the course, I became a much better typist, so good in fact that Miss Killjoy had no choice but to pass me.

The other "critics," my *Midland Bulldog* teammates, were more easily disposed of. On learning that I was in a typing class, a wit among us said in the locker room, "Take a letter, Miss King!" The laughter abruptly died when I parted his hair with my football helmet. The warrior–poet was teased no more.

Once each month, the *Midland Reporter-Telegram* gave *The Bulldog*, our mimeographed school paper, a full-page set in real type. Most of the stories were about school extracurricular activities—sports, plays, field trips, new school rules, or the message of some visiting speaker. I rarely got anything published, though it was not for lack of trying.

The two faculty advisors blue-penciled my efforts because I wrote "opinionated pieces, editorials rather than news stories, that represent YOUR opinion, not those of our publication." I had written complaints about cafeteria food, fussed that nowhere on campus was there a jukebox and space for lunch-hour jitterbugging, said it was stupid that smokers had to go across the street from school property to indulge their habit during the noon hour, and complained of infringements on free speech when school authorities forbade us to boo a motorcycle policeman, Opp the cop, who almost daily showed up as school turned out to check students' drivers licenses. No teachers, no adults of any kind, I complained, were so treated.

None of that saw print. Naturally, I wrote that the two faculty advisors lacked both brains and guts when they blue-penciled "anything not praising Midland High, apple pie, mom, and Jesus." Guess how happy that made them and how quickly they did not rush to print that particular personal opinion.

Perhaps it's just as well that during the summer of 1946, some three weeks before I would have become a senior at

Midland High School, I suddenly joined the U.S. Army. Believe it or not, I had a plan.

My plan was to see as much of the world as the army permitted and to assist my becoming a rich Famous Arthur. I had been to Dallas once with the MHS debate team and to El Paso to play football twice. I went to Lea County, New Mexico, which adjoins a corner of West Texas, as an oilfield worker. I traveled to Mead, Liberal, and Dodge City in Kansas to help lay a pipeline across several miles of wheat fields. I cheat a little in including Oklahoma in my travels, because I had crossed only a thin, arid, lightly inhabited strip of it, maybe twelve miles, separating the Texas Panhandle from Kansas.

The army cooperated by shipping me by rail all the way to Fort Dix, New Jersey, for basic training. Following that, I was sent to nearby Fort Monmouth to radio repairman's school. This I flunked. I could barely play a radio much less repair one. A board of officers and civilians took me to task, saying they would give me one more chance by sending me to cryptography school on the same base.

"And if you screw up there," said a grim-faced major, "you'll be sent to the Army of Occupation in Germany to pull KP in the mess hall and walk guard around warehouses."

My first thought was "Germany! Whee! Overseas! All right!"

"Sir," I said, "why don't you save us all a lot of time by shipping me to Germany now?"

I meant to explain about wanting to be a writer and learning about other places and cultures and such, but the major's faced darkened as he thundered, "Don't be a smart-ass, soldier! Stand at attention! Shoulders back! Chin up!"

He then fiercely chastised me. I was a disgrace to the uniform, he said. He wished he knew the name of the g.d.

recruiter who'd been foolish enough to enlist me, opining that if I rose as high as Private First Class it would be a higher rank than I deserved and than would benefit the army.

"Dismissed!" he shouted. I saluted and quickly retreated, uncertain what would happen next.

Within a week I was at Camp Kilmer, New Jersey, with others who were to be shipped to Germany, presumably also to peel potatoes or wash pots and pans and maybe guard warehouses full of unspecified treasures. Suddenly, a young corporal stormed into the barracks.

"King, Private Lawrence L.!" he yelled.

"Yo!" I responded.

The corporal handed me a set of orders sending me to the Signal Corps Photographic Center, 3511 35th Street, Astoria, Long Island City, New York. Among the papers was a train ticket to Manhattan along with a number to call so as to be transported to my new duty station.

First Sergeant Argast examined my pitifully thin personnel folder and said, "Your army occupational specialty is rifleman? We don't have a weapon on this base! Why'd they send you to me?"

"Damned if I know," I said.

"Well, we make movies here. Training films. Are you an actor?"

"Well, I was in the junior class play back at Midland High School," I said.

Sergeant Argast gave my acting career a one-word critique.

"Shit," he said.

Sergeant Argast used me as his company runner, or errand boy, but had trouble keeping me busy.

"King," he said, "don't hang around underfoot so damned much. Go watch 'em make movies or something.

Just check with me every morning after reveille, then again right after noon chow."

Great! I thought. I'd been wanting to do just that.

I roamed from one sound stage to another in the huge old building that once had been the headquarters of a major motion picture studio before Hollywood was Hollywood and the industry moved west. I was not bashful about asking directors, cameramen, carpenters, prop men, script girls, or whomever many questions. Only a few treated me like the dumb kid I was. One director somehow took a liking to me.

"Would you like to be part of this picture unit?" he ultimately asked.

Hail, yes! That's how I came to be a bit player in such hits as *Characteristics of Coastal Topography, Rolling of the Horse-Shoe Field Pack, Improper Wearing of the Military Uniform,* and *The American Soldier and Personal Hygiene.* In the latter, I had my big moment, saying to a stern officer inspecting the V.D. ward, "But, sir, she *looked* clean!"

Alas, it was too good to last. When our company clerk was discharged, Sergeant Argast remembered I could type—few men could in those days—and ended my movie career in favor of a clerk's job. But, it had its compensations. Since I decided who pulled KP duty, guard duty, change-of-quarters at night, and rec room attendant in the daytime, men of many ranks courted my favor.

I had no way of knowing that a change in military policy would, years later, affect my writing career. The photo center, you see, became one of a half-dozen military bases that were quietly integrated to about 50 percent black troops and 50 percent white troops. This occurred a few months before President Harry Truman officially integrated the military by executive decree. While at the photo center, I learned that word came down from the top brass to "make the thing work." Careful plans were made: Careerist old heads who complained on hearing of the upcoming policy change or used the "N" word or other racial epithets were transferred out before the first blacks arrived. One of these newcomers was a black first sergeant named Percy D. Ricks who replaced Sergeant Argast. So I, who had never known a black man personally, was suddenly working for one. Privately, I admit that I was not happy about it.

At the same time, a young first lieutenant, Kenneth W. Thomas, a white North Carolinian who had won a battlefield commission during World War II combat, arrived as our new company commander. Years later, when I visited retired Colonel Thomas, he told me that he and First Sergeant Ricks had agreed that I needed a higher rank so as to back the first sergeant's authority among the white GIs who might resent him. Consequently, I was made a corporal and a brief forty-three days later a sergeant, leading me to believe I must be one hell of a fine solider.

First Sergeant Ricks and I became close over time and remained lifelong friends. That entire experience prompted me years later to write a book called *Confessions of a White Racist.* It traced my personal evolution in matters of race and opined that most whites who had never lived in close proximity to blacks or worked closely with them were as ignorant of them as I had been. In 1971, the book was nominated for a National Book Award. Later, I wrote for *Parade* magazine a long piece about Sergeant Ricks that was published, to his glee, not long before he died.

Sometimes I shudder to think of how innocent I was in trusting the army to teach me about places and cultures other than those native to me. What would I have learned that could compare, had I been shipped to, say, Fort McClellan in Alabama or to Fort Bliss, Texas, or any place not all that different from where I grew up? I could have been sent someplace where I would not have learned about moviemaking, acting, screenplays, or the politics of racial integration in the military. Even the size of the Signal Corps Photo Center assisted me. I was ideally positioned in a small unit and had great authority there so that I was able to found the first newspaper. Naturally, I named myself editor and wrote 75 percent of the stories in it. That was, indeed, a learning experience.

Following my army discharge, I wrote for one small newspaper in New Mexico and two in West Texas, with a brief stopover as a bored student at Texas Tech University. During those five years I wrote two-and-a-half novels, all unpublished. I was not yet a good writer, but even worse, I flew in the face of the oldest advice to beginning scribes: Write what you know. *The Secret Music* was set in North Korea and was about an American serviceman who refused repatriation and opted to stay in the country where he had been a prisoner of war for several years. It was loosely based on a young soldier from Kermit, Texas. Since I covered his return home for the *Odessa American,* I saw Claude Batchelor twice for a total of maybe three hours before the army brought charges against him and took him away—not enough, by far, to get to know him or his story. And as for Korea, I never had a twitch to go there. Do you wonder why *The Secret Music* hit only sour notes?

The Back of a Bear was the first-person story of an eight-year-old boy in West Texas. I knew a fair amount about West Texas, I thought, but not all that much about the subject most on the kid's mind: nookie. I had the kid's thoughts dwell in lowly places, you see, thinking sex would sell my book. If you haven't figured out my problem, here's a clue: my ignorance of many things was appalling.

Perhaps, mercifully, I cannot recall the title of a private eye novel I wrote set in Midessa, Texas, an obvious melding of the twin prairie mini-cities of Midland and Odessa. My novel was, I fear, inspired by the success of Mickey Spillane's best-selling potboilers and what little I had learned about police procedures while covering the cop shop for the *Odessa American*. At any rate, I flung it against the wall, unfinished, on receiving one too many rejections relating to *The Back of a Bear*, none of which had offered a single word of encouragement. Most of them were preprinted forms and were brief, cold, and brutal. They said, "Sorry, not for us," or words to that effect, though they would have been more honest had they said, "Fuck you, Buddy! Stop wasting our time!"

I was then living in Washington, D.C., and working for Texas congressman J.T. Rutherford. I had supported him in his maiden race. I liked politics and had dabbled in numerous local races for years, but the main reason I went to Washington had to do with the vague notion that living in closer proximity to New York City, the world center of publishing, would somehow assist my efforts to become a Famous Arthur.

And, in time, damned if I didn't do exactly that.

I first met Billy Lee Brammer, an underling on Senator Lyndon B. Johnson's staff, and we soon became friends. At the time, Billy Lee was writing a novel that turned out to be that huge critical success, *The Gay Place.* I read a chapter at a time as he wrote it. It was good, I knew, and I studied it closely in hopes of understanding why it was good. I quickly discerned that Brammer knew his material: politics, Texas, and LBJ, who was obviously the model for Brammer's Governor Arthur Goddamn Fenstermaker.

Brammer introduced me to another writer, Warren Miller, who lived in New York City, and we hit it off.

Without reading a word of my failed manuscripts, Miller, in 1962, told a New York book editor, Bob Gutwillig, that I might be capable of writing a good book. He based his opinion on our several conversations and a couple of letters I had written him.

Gutwillig sent a letter asking if I had a manuscript he might look at. It was a bolt from the blue. I did not, of course, but I was not above lying about it. I wrote back that, yes, I had been working on a political novel for several months. Then I spun a plot in that letter, making it up as I wrote, that had to do with the integration of public schools and other facilities in a die-hard mythical southern state. I found my title, *The One-Eyed Man,* by thumbing through Bartlett's Quotations ("In the land of the blind, the one-eyed man is king") and shipped off that pack of lies within three hours of having opened Gutwillig's letter.

Very shortly, Bob Gutwillig phoned to say, "If you can write a novel that's as good as your letter, we'll both become rich and famous."

Lord have mercy, Percy! I was thrilled to the bone. The editor said I should fly my manuscript to New York as soon as possible. This would be a neat trick, since there was, of course, no manuscript. I did, however, agree to bring a portion of the nonexistent document to New York within ten days. I conveniently came down with the flu, then had it turn into strep throat, although my ills were as nonexistent as my novel. While "recovering" at home, I wrote one thirty-six page chapter and an outline for the remainder of the novel in about eight days.

Warren Miller had me come to his West Side apartment from LaGuardia Field. He took my thin manuscript into his study to read it. His wife, Jimmi, seemed as nervous as I was.

When we heard laughter escaping from the study, Jimmi said, "Is he supposed to laugh?" Is your novel *funny*?"

"I hope to God it is," I said, but my heart was sinking. I couldn't think of a word in my truncated novel that was funny!

A short time later, Warren burst from his study and said, "Get your coat on! I just called Gutwillig and told him I think you're on to something and that he should see you now rather than wait for your appointment tomorrow."

Things were happening too fast. I was in a daze and almost left the Miller's apartment without the manuscript. Warren walked me outside to hail a cab and said, "Come on. You look like you're going to the dentist! You may be on the verge of your first sale!"

Indeed. Gutwillig said he needed an hour to read it, so I went to a nearby bar. When the hour was up and I went back to see him a second time, he said, "I like it. My boss likes it. Of course, it *is* a first novel, so. . . will you take a fifteen hundred dollar advance?" I would have taken $1.98, and it was all I could do not to say so.

My promise to finish the novel within a year was sincere, but I didn't complete it until two years had passed. Then, the *New York Times* was hit by a strike, and publication was pushed back several additional months.

The first review of my book came out simultaneously in *The Washington Post Book World* and some San Francisco Sunday supplement and was—I'm not kidding—the worst review I have received in forty-one years of writing books, stage plays, hundreds of magazine articles, two screenplays, and several television documentaries. Naturally, I felt gut-shot and dead. It's hard to exaggerate how much murder lived in my heart on behalf of the reviewer, R. Z. Sheppard.

I felt much better when the Literary Guild Book Club made my novel an alternate selection and, in so doing, bestowed 10,000 front-money dollars. Good to fair reviews popped up in many newspapers and a few magazines, diluting some of the mischief Sheppard had contributed—may it rain on every parade he attends and may dogs in time water his grave.

During the writing of *The One-Eyed Man,* I had become friends with the late Willie Morris, then an underling editor at *Harper's* magazine. What I did not know, and what he could not tell, was that he was being groomed as that prestigious magazine's next editor-in-chief. Long before that happened—as soon as I quit Congress to become a full-time writer—Willie asked me to write an article for him based on stories I had told about my experiences and observations on Capitol Hill. My "Washington's Second Banana Politicians" was well-received and brought the first fan letter I ever received. It was from no less than John Kenneth Galbraith, the economist, author, and later John F. Kennedy's ambassador to India. Willie gave me other opportunities, and the more my work appeared in *Harper's,* the more other magazines solicited: *The Progressive, The Nation, Life, Saturday Evening Post, Sports Illustrated, Playboy,* you name it. To date, I have written for sixty-seven periodicals as best I can count, am working on my fifteenth book, and have written several stage plays that have been widely produced, two making it to Broadway and two others to off-Broadway.

Largely, I am happy writing. One can do it indoors, sitting down, and in the shade. Even on days when the words won't come, writing beats heavy lifting. When the words won't come is when one must press on. To say, "To hell with it," and take the day off means it will just be easier to put it off again in the future. I can't stress enough how important it is to keep one's butt in the writing chair.

I have been, I know, luckier than I once dared dream. In the past couple of years I have received what I call "One Foot in the Grave" awards. In 2004, the Texas Book Festival gave me its Bookend Award, which is a career achievement acknowledgement. And in October of 2006, Don Toner, the honcho of Austin Playhouse, who has produced all of my plays multiple times in several venues, along with *Texas Monthly* magazine and several of my old friends, raised $58,000 to refurbish and enlarge his second stage, which became, in a ceremony I attended and certainly enjoyed, the Larry L. King Theatre.

And if that doesn't make me a rich Famous Arthur, I don't know what can.

Courtesy of Jim Lee

JAMES WARD LEE

JAMES WARD LEE is emeritus professor of English and a former department chair at the University of North Texas. Born in Leeds, Alabama, he is a graduate of Middle Tennessee State University and Auburn University. Lee is the author of hundreds of articles, short stories, and reviews and is the author of *Adventures with a Texas Humanist; Texas, My Texas; William Humphrey;* and *John Braine*. He has edited or co-edited several books and is currently working on a book on Texas country singers. Lee was the founding director of the Center for Texas Studies and the University of North Texas Press and is a former president and fellow of the Texas Folklore Society.

TWO STATES OF MIND

Wandering between two worlds, one dead.
The other powerless to be born.
"Stanzas from the Grande Chartreuse"
Matthew Arnold

I AM NOT SURE the Matthew Arnold quotation really applies, but it's how I feel when I set out to talk about my writing. It seems that I am indeed wandering between two worlds—one as a teacher and one as a producer of humor, fiction, folklore, criticism, and literary journalism. I am also wandering between being a Texan and an Alabamian. I have written a great deal about Texas in the fifty years I have lived here, but I have never considered myself a writer. I was a college professor who wrote, first, as a way to promotion and pay and, second, because I wanted to. Well, I should admit that I hardly ever wanted to, but once in a while someone will put me on a program or ask me to write a piece such as this one. Then I stall. I put it off. If I used a pencil I would sharpen a dozen or so to keep from writing. But I don't use a pencil, so I run out of excuses and drag myself to the computer to confront failure. I wrote a little piece for *The Langdon Review* once that was titled, "I Am Not a Writer." I argued that writers are people like Balzac or Elmer Kelton or Larry McMurtry or the wretched Louis L'Amour or even the thrilling and tempestuous Sandra Brown. Those people wake up in the morning and can't wait to get at quill pen or Olivetti typewriter (McMurtry's implement of choice) or computer. Balzac must have written over fifty novels. Anthony Trollope wrote forty-seven big three-deckers, plus five volumes of stories, some travel books, some generalized nonfiction, and a couple of biographies. And he held down a full-time job with the British post office. Trollope was a writer. The post office was his sideline, even though he rose to be the number two person in the service. He made more money from writing than from his job. My living has never been dependent on what I wrote. In fact, the most money I ever made for a single essay was $800, and that was a "kill fee" from the *Dallas Morning News* back in 1986. I wrote a survey of Texas folklore for a special quarterly supplement they were planning for the sesquicentennial year. Then they dropped the project. I got the money and syndicated the article (for free) to some smaller papers. About that time, I heard that the average writer in America makes $5,000 a year from writing. Even then I knew I did not come up to the standard for writers.

If I am a writer, I am a Texas writer. And I am one of about three in the whole state. A.C. Greene admitted to being a Texas writer, but almost all the others that I have interviewed or served on panels with or written about, deny being Texas writers. They are practitioners of American literature like Faulkner or Willa Cather or Robert Frost. Or they shyly admit being writers for the ages like Virgil or Thucydides or Shakespeare. But except for a book I once wrote on John Braine, the British novelist, an article or two on writers like Trollope and Alan Sillitoe, I have mostly written about Texas. Well, sort of. But you will have to wait a bit before I get to my wanderings between two regional worlds.

In 1959, I read my first paper before the Texas Folklore Society, and I was hooked on Texas. I was a folklorist already. (The great thing about being a folklorist is that it does not require a license. You just declare yourself.) I had studied folklore in graduate school and was amazed to learn that I already knew all that stuff. I had learned about superstitions, customs, songs and tales and myths, about folk-say (which we all spoke back in Alabama), and folk art (which we decorated our yards with back home—scalloped tires painted pastel colors, bottle trees, and cutesy mailboxes). I was a natural, and then I learned that the Texas Folklore Society would put up with a great deal of semi-folkloristic humor. I was off and running. For years, I pleased half the audience with my stories about pie and collard greens and grease. The other half of the audience was made up of trained folklorists with advanced degrees in clog dancing and motif indexing and archetypes of this and that. They were dismayed by amateur folklorists like me and wanted the society put on a more professional basis. They never prevailed, and last year I was made a Fellow of the Texas Folklore Society. It stunned me, and it must have really stunned the "real folklorists" in the group, though I should admit that they have always been gracious to me.

Way back in 1965 or thereabouts, I persuaded the Austin publishing company, Steck-Vaughn, to let me edit a pamphlet series on Southwestern writers. I lined up a dozen or so friends from the Texas Folklore Society to write these pamphlets. Over the next several years, we produced about fifty pamphlets on Southwestern writers, mostly Texans. The series ran until Steck-Vaughn was sold to a New York company that did not see the value of regional literature. Besides, the series was not making money. It was not losing either, but Intext Publishers was not in business to break even. Here is a sidebar: the pamphlets were forty-eight pages long and sold for one dollar. The authors got seven cents a copy and I got three cents. We all got rich, which is why my Social Security check is so important to me. I still see these pamphlets at book and paper shows and rare book events, and some go for as much as $20 each. I wish I had bought all the stock when the company killed the series, but I did not. I think the authors were offered copies for a dime apiece, but all my friends were as economically savvy as I was.

In the late 1960s my friends Edwin Gaston and the late John Q. Anderson joined me in publishing a book called *Southwestern American Literature: A Bibliography.* We enlisted everyone we knew or had heard of and produced a very long bibliography of writings about the Southwest. Half the book was made up of author checklists, and we must have enlisted fifty or a hundred teachers and graduate students to do all the library digging. Doing the book taught me a great deal about Texas and the Southwest, but I had still not given up my hope of "transcending the region," if I may steal a line from some of the Texans who are not Texas writers. I won't say who they are: "No names, no pack drills," as the British soldiers say.

I looked upon my foray into Texas literature as a sideline for a long time. When I came west to Texas in 1958, my goal was to become a famous scholar/critic like Ian Watt or Maynard Mack or Cleanth Brooks. I am not sure how long I daydreamed about being a name on every graduate student's lips, a person to be Oohed and Aahed over on elevators at meetings of the Modern Language Association, the kind of dashing young critic summoned by Yale or Harvard or implored by the *New York Review of Books* to say significant things about the likes of Karl Shapiro or Norman Mailer or Maya Angelou. My phone sat silent when New York called Texas for opinions about great American writers. I think it was in 1983 that I decided to be a Texas scholar/critic/writer, to give up my dreams of wearing elbow patches and lighting and relighting briar pipes while strolling under the trees at Stanford or appearing spectrally in the wisps of fog at Berkeley.

Then an event in Austin decided my course for me. The University of Texas became one hundred years old in 1983, and they threw a big centennial event on "the Forty Acres" in Austin. I was invited. I was even given a topic—"The Old South in Texas Literature." I set to work reading all those writers who wrote out of a tradition that had nothing to do with sagebrush, sand, cattle drives, and gunplay. When the printed program for the event came out, it featured spurs, horses, and all the usual Dobie-Bedichek-Webb cultural baggage. There were no cotton bolls, no slaves toiling in the fields, no timber clear-cutters from the Big Thicket. It looked to be a celebration of Texas as a far western state. What I wrote about concerned that part of Texas east of what is now Interstate 35, the part of Texas where most people live. I read the Williams—Humphrey, Owens, and Goyen—K.A. Porter, Karle Wilson Baker, Ruth Cross, Laura Krey, Elizabeth Wheaton, Leon Hale, George Sessions Perry, Jewel Gibson, and Bill Brett. I discovered for the first time the wonderful memoir C. C. White dictated to Ada Morehead Holland. It is called *No Quittin' Sense* and narrates what it was like to be African American in East Texas early in the twentieth century. I read J. Mason Brewer's tales of slave and post-slave days on the Brazos. I was fully immersed in things Texan, or things East Texan. After the conference, the College of Liberal Arts hired Don Graham, Tom Pilkington, and me to edit a book growing out of the conference. We could reprint the papers read there, as well as write and commission new pieces that reflected the culture of Texas. The three of us jointly wrote a long introduction and a chapter called "Slouching Toward Houston: Texas Urban Fiction." The book was called *The Texas Literary Tradition: Fiction, Folklore, History.* I would like to announce that the volume sold out and was reprinted and reissued and landed on every coffee table in Texas.

Actually, after a year or so, the College of Liberal Arts divided up all the unsold copies and gave them to Don, Tom, and me. It may have sold a few copies, but I can't prove that. I gave most of mine away to students in the Life and Literature of the Southwest class that I was then teaching. It was the course invented by J. Frank Dobie way back in his glory days at the University of Texas. When I was assigned it at the University of North Texas, I was no longer the modern American and British lit guy. I was the folklore/Texlit guy. There is a real stigma attached to being the regionalist professor, but by that time, I was a tenured full professor and could let the rest of the world go by.

So I did.

The Old South story does not end with the bestseller we edited. The three of us got a grant from the Texas Committee of the Humanities to do a video, which we entitled "Texas Literature: the Southern Tradition." We went all about the state with a camera crew and interviewed authors, shot scenes of cotton fields, and filmed one scene in an abandoned cotton gin in Pilot Point. We even found a man outside Nacogdoches who plowed with a mule for our cameras. I would like to say that the film made it all the way to Hollywood—or at least got onto PBS—but alas and alack, no Oscars were forthcoming. I still show it to classes from time to time, and a few of my friends stun their students with this vivid example of videography.

I was in it for the long haul. I was a Texas writer for sure. No more trips to the Modern Language Association in New York. No more thoughts of weighty tomes on Keats or Byron or Thomas Hardy. In 1986, I was so famous as a Texas writer at the University of North Texas that I was put in charge of the University of North Texas's Sesquicentennial Committee. Part of the reason, I suspect, was that I was the only person in

Denton who could pronounce sesquicentennial on the first try, much less spell it. At first, I couldn't think of much to do about the 150 years of Texas, so I set out to write a book review a week on a Texas novel, and the Public Affairs Office started sending them to newspapers all over the state. I did not find my way into the *Dallas Morning News, Fort Worth Star-Telegram, Houston Post, Houston Chronicle, Austin American-Statesman,* or the *Abilene Reporter-News,* but I was big in the *Orange Leader* and the *Sherman Democrat.* I found a publisher willing to take all fifty-two of these reviews plus some other Texas literary stuff and put the book out in hardback. Once again, I did not get rich, but I have a bunch of extra copies—about twenty I bought at a garage sale for fifty cents apiece. Now I see it at rare book exhibitions for big bucks—maybe $20. I called it *Classics of Texas Fiction,* and at least one used book dealer in Fort Worth keeps it under the counter to guide him in pricing books. At least there is some fame to be had in his shop in North Fort Worth.

As the sesquicentennial year progressed, I had a call from Austin. The governor of the state, Mark White, wanted to celebrate things all over the state, and the University of North Texas was chosen to hold "The Governor's Conference on the Literary Arts." Since I was the local sesquicentennial guy, I was made chairman (they now say "chair"). We rounded up fifty-five famous Texas writers and had the biggest literary conference held in Texas before Laura Bush started the big Literary Festival in Austin. The governor's people promised us $25,000, and UNT was generous with its cash. The governor's office never came through with one red cent, and we wound up losing $50,000, which I heard about for a few years after that. But we had everybody I could think of: Larry Jeff McMurtry, Elmer Kelton, Horton Foote, William Owens, movie star Robert Duval, William Humphrey, Robert Flynn,

Betsy Colquitt, Don Graham, Diana Hobby, wife to the lieutenant governor, Governor Mark White, Jay Presson Allen, Rolando Hinojosa-Smith, Jim Lehrer, and many others I will now insult by not remembering.

In the sesquicentennial—and before I presided over the loss of fifty grand—the College of Arts and Sciences at UNT let me start up the Center for Texas Studies. Over the life of the Center, we published *Texas Books in Review* (which we took over from Tarleton State University), and I started up two journals, *New Texas,* which now resides at Sul Ross State University, and *Texas Studies,* an annual which lasted only two years. *New Texas* published poems and stories, and *Texas Studies* published general Texas history, geography, and general culture.

After the Center's great fiscal success of 1986, we struck again in 1991. This time I persuaded the UNT administration to let us talk to a new governor about hosting the fiftieth anniversary of Texas' entry into World War II. Once again I was chair (we had become more correct by then). I promised not to lose as much money as before, and the administration went along. We threw a big bash with Texas writers, Texas historians, and Texas heroes. We had three of the four living Texas Medal of Honor winners from WWII. We had Pearl Harbor survivors, POW survivors, the Tuskegee Airmen, and many other old vets. We even got a three-star general to come up from Fort Hood and award a Medal of Honor to the relatives of an old Indian fighter whose medal had been revoked because he was a scout and not a regular. We published a book, *1941: Texas Goes to War*, and a beautiful map of all the military bases in Texas during WWII. I edited the book and wrote Governor Ann Richards' introduction. (It was dumbed down by her press secretary, who thought he could capture her idiom better than I had.) The map came out late and had to be given away, and the book sold as well as I feared. And we lost another $50,000. The public relations woman got the administration off my back by saying we could not have got that kind of press for $100,000. I have no idea what publicity costs, but I have not been asked to produce any more extravaganzas.

Having done all the damage I could at UNT, I decided to retire. Before I left, UNT Press published my *Texas, My Texas,* a bunch of essays that I hoped were humorous, and some may even have been. People used to ask me to read one on Texas honky-tonks and one on pie, but I never got the long-expected call from the Pulitzer people, and the *New York Times* took no notice of it; however, the *Dallas News* gave it a nice review. The Mercedes I had hoped to buy from the proceeds does not grace my garage. I moved to Fort Worth, where I had been on the editorial board of TCU Press for several years and was editing their Texas Traditions Series. I took on the unpaid job as acquisitions editor for TCU Press (the letter appointing me to the staff read "Visiting Editor Without Compensation"). You can see why Social Security is my friend.

Now we come to the "two worlds" business. I have gone on and on about how Texan I have become. I even declared myself a native Texan in 1986, and nobody has questioned my Texas nativity. But here is a dirty little secret: I have smuggled a whole world of Alabama into my Texas world. All that work I did on the Old South in Texas echoed all the folklore and culture I had absorbed in Alabama. East Texas and Alabama were so alike that I was on home turf all the time I was reading the books and wandering the cotton fields of East Texas. Way back in 1967, I wrote the Southwest Writers Series pamphlet on William Humphrey, a writer who always pointed out that he was not a westerner, but was rather a southerner. The more I wrote about East Texas, the more I remembered what some call "my formative years." I lived in Alabama for a total of about seventeen years, but I will never go back there to live—remember, I am a native Texan—but "the Heart of Dixie" keeps on living in me.

Here is the first example of its rearing its head in my Texas writing. Back when I was centennialing and sesquicentennialing, someone asked me to contribute a section to a book called *A Texas Christmas.* As should be clear by now, I am always willing to show off (we called it "showing out" in Alabama), so I readily agreed. Then it occurred to me that I didn't have any old-time Texas memories. I was either going to have to decline the offer or come up with something Texan. I recalled a story told about my father's sorry attempt to make a Christmas tree stand up way back before I was born. My father was the second unhandiest man I ever knew. He comes in second because I am first. Back about 1928, he bragged to J.B. Adams, his nearest neighbor, that he was going to put up a tree after years of hanging a wreath on the door and letting it go at that. J.B. always had a tree that *Southern Living* would have loved if that magazine had been in existence in 1928. Back in days of yore, Christmas trees were usually put up on Christmas Eve, and the stores didn't start pounding out Christmas carols and putting up tinsel shortly after Labor Day the way they do now. Thinking how easy it would be to put up a tree, my father got his brother to cut him a cedar out in the woods in Shelby County, and my father hauled it home. In 1928, you couldn't go out and buy a stand; you had to cut some two-by-fours and make your own. My father knocked the skin off his knuckles with his hammer and two-by-fours and still couldn't make the tree stand. In desperation, he drove a nail into the ceiling and hung the tree just barely in time for J.B. Adams to come look at it. Well, this is an Alabama story, so I had to do some state smuggling. I had been in the navy with a guy from Bonham, and he made Bonham sound a lot like Leeds, Alabama. I drove up to Bonham, looked over some street signs, found where the post office was, located the railroad station, and moved my story to the county seat of Fannin. My father was a rural mail carrier who hauled mail to Vandiver and Bridgeton and Sterrett and Brompton, and it was not hard to have my thinly fictionalized mailman carry mail to Dodd City and Windom and Savoy. The story won no prizes, but I got my $65 and nobody was the wiser.

I was off and running after my first blistering success as a short-story writer. I wrote a number of them after that, but I quickly decided that I had better not use Bonham as a setting, for somebody in Fannin County would figure out that I didn't know the locale and was likely to get tripped up on what street ran where. (All this was assuming that anyone would ever read one of my stories.) I invented my own East Texas town, Bodark Springs, and my own county, Eastis. I set this county along the Red River somewhere near Paris and Sherman and Clarksville and Bonham. My main character was the same mail carrier I had used in the first story. I had changed his last name, but I had begun using real Leeds names for most of the characters. I could never invent names as good as the nasty-tempered Melvin Spruille or Tarp Davidson, the walking mail carrier, who was Grady Dell's buddy. I used Fonzie Noah, Red Cobb, the white twins Bunk and Banty Isbell, the black brothers Bub and Rendon Maubry, and my age mates Puddin' Pie DeShazo and his brother, Buttercup. The late Pud has gone off to glory, but Buttercup is still around—his wife calls him simply "Butter." I don't think anyone from Alabama is likely to read the stories I have written, and according to Texas law, you can't libel and slander the dead. Most of my characters are dead, all except Buttercup. My mother was named Mamie Pearl Lee, so I changed her to Mamie Pauline Dell. All it takes is a little ingenuity to steal a state and a time.

My friend from Bonham spoke the same dialect I learned back in Leeds, knew the same expressions, many of the same dirty jokes, and saw life the Alabama way. Once I started writing stories and other things about East Texas, I was half writing about Alabama. I wrote a couple of stories about backwoods honky-tonks up in my fictional county, and they were taken straight from the honky-tonks I went to as a child. (Yes, you read that right, "as a child.") My folks went honky-tonking several nights a week, and back in those days before babysitters, I was taken along. The Silver Slipper, up at Cook's Springs between Leeds and Pell City, had a playground down under the honky-tonk, which was set out on stilts over a creek. Several of us learned hillbilly songs and brushed up on our cussing from playing under the Silver Slipper. I took that honky-tonk straight into Eastis County. Another slab-sided joint called the Briar Patch, I located up at Iron Stob, Oklahoma, just across the Red River from Fannin County. (I am not sure there is a town called Iron Stob, but there is a sign pointing to it off Highway 70.) My all-time favorite honky-tonk, the Moon River Beach, located on one of the muddiest parts of the Cahaba River between Leeds and Birmingham, was the setting of a story I wrote about Grady Dell and his nephew offering to whip the entire house while the jukebox was playing Ernest Tubb's "Walking the Floor Over You."

My favorite Alabama story transported to Texas was about Jesse James, who came to the Leeds Theatre about 1938. Jesse claimed to have been in hiding since his supposed murder at the hands of Robert Ford. The old man on stage appeared to be about ninety, and he told the audience (I was about seven when I saw Jesse) all about his robbing from the rich and giving it to the poor, etc., etc. For weeks before and after that, people in Leeds wondered whether it really was Jesse. I wrote "The Return of Jesse James," and the focus in my story is on two old Confederate veterans who got into a fistfight on the courthouse lawn over whether it was Jesse. I moved all this to Texas, and those who heard me read the story and who might have read it, never knew it was an Alabama story.

The more I have thought about all this, the more I realize that my own Texas was often a transportation of Alabama —and not just in the short stories that I consciously moved across the Mississippi but in much of the folklore I was engaging in from the sixties on. Once I had figured out that many of the customs and songs and cookery of my native state were exactly the same as in Texas, I was home free. I just had to summon up the remembrance of things past. I wrote a lot of what passes for humor in *Texas, My Texas* and in a lot of other essays based on what I had seen in my childhood and adolescence. People used to kid me about the tales I spun about my cousin J. T. , who ran a little whiskey, made some rotgut in a car-radiator still that he and Taft Sheets devised, and drank a quart of white lightning or Four Roses a day. J. T. would rave and rare (an Alabama and East Texas term) and take on and talk a language that would be understood in DeKalb or Leeds or Vidor—"I God, I love a pie!" he would shout. J. T. was such a character that people spoke of him in hushed tones. Their voices would get quiet and they would say, "You know, J.T., he dranks." I'll bet the same words have been spoken about topers from Timpson to Tenaha to Bobo to Blair. (You have to remember the old Tex Ritter song to recall "Timpson,

Tenaha, Bobo, and Blair." These are towns in Panola County —or somewhere close.)

Knowing how things were cooked in Alabama put me in perfect position to write the foreword to Ernestine Linck and Joyce Roach's great award-winning *Eats: A Folk History of Texas Foods.* When Deborah Douglas, a doctor from San Antonio, put together *Stirring Prose: Cooking with Texas Authors,* I submitted three dishes from my Alabama past: collards and rape (one dish), neck bones and liver (also one dish), and fried corn. Everybody in Alabama and East Texas knows that the three best things in the world are sugar, grease, and dough, and I once wrote a whole essay on grease. I lifted the whole thing from what I had learned in my boyhood. I once wrote a paean to meat (this was before my quintuple bypass), and I became famous for the essay on pie. I would like to repeat J.T.'s famous line "I God, I love a pie!" I learned about cooking with hog meat and other kinds of grease from my Granny Lee, my Aunt Rene, and my father, the best fork cook in Alabama. He could fry meat, make gravy (red eye or sawmill), scramble eggs, stir up grits, and cook pork brains with no implement more complicated than a fork. And so can I, I am glad to say.

Lest I get carried away with my thievery, I ought to admit that after I moved to Fort Worth, Judy Alter and I edited *Literary Fort Worth,* and try as I might, I couldn't import any Alabama stories into it. And not long ago, when TCU Press came up with the idea for a collaborative novel called *Noah's Ride,* I wrote a chapter that had absolutely nothing to do with the Great State of Alabama. My chapter takes Noah Freeman, an escaped slave, on a trek from San Angelo to Fort Stockton where he runs into an Indian fight. Here I was on uncertain ground, never having written a western and not knowing much about Indian fights, but you will have to read chapter ten and judge for yourself.

And finally, a couple of years ago, I wrote and cobbled together a book of essays called *Adventures with a Texas Humanist.* I actually did some semi-research, even though I have passed into what AARP calls my Golden Years. I wrote chapters on Dobie and McMurtry and some other Texas subjects, and I reprised some essays I had published elsewhere. Then at the end of the book, in desperation, I wrote a series of personal essays. These were Alabama stories. One was about how I managed to escape from Alabama in 1945, just before I was fully fledged as a juvenile delinquent, and attended St. Andrew's School in Tennessee. Another is about my career in navy boot camp. I had joined the U. S. Navy immediately after the Korean War broke out. Wait, don't assume! I didn't join out of an excess of patriotism. I went in to get the G.I. Bill, even though it was not enacted for Korean War vets for nearly a year. I knew it would get passed as it had for WWII vets. It was, and I managed to use it almost all the way to a PhD. One story was about destroyer duty off the coast of Korea in the dead of winter and another about my trip to the bomb tests at Eniwetok and Bikini in 1952 and again in 1954. *Adventures with a Texas Humanist* (I stole the title from Roy Bedichek) did somewhat better than the book Graham, Pilkington, and I did, but I still have not heard a word from the Pulitzer committee. When the book came out, some of my friends said, "Why don't you give up the Texas stuff and write about Alabama; that is what you are good at?" Actually, I made up the "what you are good at" part, but I was steered back to the days that haunt me.

I have tried several times to blast into an Alabama book, but somehow it eludes me. I need the perfect first sentence, and then I am sure I would be home free. I tried this one: "My mother was a bastard and that counted against her all her life, but I moved to Texas and. . ." Then I tried, "I left Alabama sixty years ago, but Alabama won't go away."

Both those sentences are true, and it is also true that Alabama has influenced me as a Texas writer. Maybe the sentence above is false; after all, as I said earlier, I am not a writer. Not like Trollope or Balzac or my friend James Reasoner from Azle, Texas, who has written 200 books under various names. He hits the floor writing every morning. I only write when my back is to the wall.

Like now.

Shayna Reasoner

JAMES REASONER

A PROFESSIONAL WRITER for thirty years, James Reasoner has written more than 200 novels, including mysteries, historicals, and westerns. His work has been praised by *Publishers Weekly* and the *Los Angeles Times*, among others, and several of his books have appeared on the *USA Today* bestseller list. Reasoner is perhaps best known for his cult classic private eye novel, *Texas Wind*, which was reprinted in 2004 by Point Blank Press. Most recently, under his own name, he is the author of a contemporary crime novel entitled *Dust Devils*, published by Point Blank Press, and a western mystery, *Death's Head Crossing*, published by Pinnacle Books.

BARBARIANS, COWBOYS, AND PRIVATE EYES: HOW I BECAME A TEXAS WRITER

THE IMPACT of Texas on my writing starts with the fact that I was born and raised here and have never lived anywhere else, nor wanted to live anywhere else. And if anyone was born knowing that he wanted to be a writer, it was me. As far back as I can remember, I was making up stories. When I was six years old and "playing guns" with the other kids in my neighborhood (because in the late fifties we did things like playing guns), they were content to run around yelling and pretending to shoot each other. That wasn't good enough for me. I insisted that we determine who everyone was supposed to be ("Dusty, you're the sheriff, and Ronnie and I are outlaws . . .") and figure out why we were shooting at each other ("We robbed the bank and you're chasing us, see, and we'll go over behind the chicken coop, and you'll come around the other way and shoot us, but then . . . but then you see that we're really your long-lost brothers . . .").

I didn't say I was good at plotting back then, but that's definitely what I was doing. It's a wonder any of my friends would play with me at all.

By the time I was in fifth grade I had progressed to writing down my stories, scribbling away with a fountain pen on sheet after sheet of notebook paper. Most of my stories featured myself and my friends in the starring roles, solving mysteries that were heavily influenced by my avid reading of the

Hardy Boys books (the original ones, where Frank and Joe raced around in a roadster with their chums; I never liked the updated ones nearly as well). My friends read the stories, and thought I was crazy for spending so much time writing them, but found it borderline cool that I had turned them into fictional characters. What they didn't understand was that I wrote because it was so much blasted fun. My stories kept getting longer and longer, running over a hundred handwritten pages. I called them novels, and considering my small, cramped penmanship, some of them probably approached 40,000 words, so they almost qualified.

In the back of my mind, some small, insistent voice was already muttering, "I want to be a writer. I want to be a writer." But writers weren't real, normal people. At least, not any that I knew.

Then my cousin Richard Finley, who was considerably older than me and in college, wrote a story that was accepted and published by his college literary magazine. It was about hunting rattlesnakes along the edge of the Caprock in West Texas. I remember reading that story and being fascinated by it, not so much because it was a good story (although it was) but because it was written by someone I knew, and its setting was someplace I had been. If Richard could do it, that voice said, so could I.

Then something else happened involving an even bigger snake than the rattlers in Richard's story.

Being an avid reader, bookstores and libraries are some of my favorite places in the world. Back then, since I was still several years away from being old enough to drive, I pestered my mother into taking me to Fort Worth as often as I could so that I could visit the downtown library and a couple of bookstores that were located nearby. One of them, Barber's

Bookstore, was only a block away from where the library was located at that time.

The library has moved to the other end of downtown, and Barber's is long gone. I assume the building is still standing, although I haven't been by there for a long time. If I could get in the building, and if the interior hasn't been remodeled too much, I could take you right to the place where one of the paperback racks stood, the one that held science fiction and fantasy books. As vividly as if it were yesterday, I remember standing in front of that rack and looking down to see a paperback with a particularly striking cover. The foreground featured a muscular fellow with his back to the viewer, heavy chains attached to each wrist, drawing his arms out to the sides. Skeletons littered the floor, and some sort of vaguely-rendered monsters lurked in the background. Dominating the scene was a huge snake, its body bigger around than the body of the chained hero, who was straddling it. The snake's head was reared up and turned around to glare at him, mouth open and fangs bared. I looked at that picture and said to myself (as fourteen-year-olds sometimes will), *"Whoa!"*

The artist was Frank Frazetta. The book was the Lancer Books edition of *Conan the Usurper.* And the author was Robert E. Howard.

"The World's Greatest Fantasy-Adventure Hero," the cover proclaimed, and I couldn't buy the book fast enough in my desire to find out if that was true. I took it home, opened it to the introduction by L. Sprague de Camp, and that was when an even greater bombshell burst on my fevered teenage brain. The first line of the introduction stated that the author, Robert E. Howard, was from Cross Plains, Texas.

Cross Plains? I'd heard of it many times in my life, because both sides of my family come from nearby Brown County and Comanche County, and I'd heard my relatives in Brownwood and Blanket and Zephyr mention going up to Cross Plains or knowing somebody from Cross Plains. I struggled to wrap my brain around the idea that somebody from a little town like Cross Plains, Texas, could write a book that would have a great cover like that. Then I read the stories and fell in love with Howard's writing, a relationship that continues to this day.

I read other paperback collections of Howard's stories and learned more about his life (1906-1936). At that time, the book review editor of the *Fort Worth Star-Telegram* was Leonard Sanders, and he often wrote columns about Texas authors. One Sunday his column was about Robert E. Howard and mentioned that Howard was born in Peaster, northwest of Weatherford.

Peaster is about twenty miles in a straight line from where I lived, although you have to go through Weatherford to get there easily. Once I found out that Howard had been born that close, I had to go see Peaster for myself, so I talked my brother into driving over there one day. Then, as now, Peaster was your typical wide-place-in-the-road Texas community. There was nothing to indicate that Robert E. Howard was born there, and indeed, the current residents were probably unaware of it. But that didn't change the fact that one of my favorite authors had been born in a little Texas town even smaller than the one I lived in.

If Bob Howard could do it, I asked myself, then why couldn't I?

Many years later, I was fortunate enough to meet Leonard Sanders at the annual TCU Press book signing in Fort Worth, and I was glad I got a chance to tell him how important that long-ago newspaper column was to me. I won't say it literally changed my life. But it sure helped point me in the direction I wound up going.

. . .

I've always been a believer in the idea that to be a writer, you have to sit down and write. That's what I continued to do throughout high school and on into college. I wasn't yet to the point where I had begun to submit anything, but I wrote steadily.

The idea that someone could make a living by writing was a little too much for my family to comprehend, but it was always in the back of my mind even as I prepared for a career as a history teacher, or a librarian, or any of several other options I considered. By the early 1970s, I was at North Texas State University (now the University of North Texas) majoring in English, where I took a course called Life and Literature of the Southwest from Dr. George Hendrick. Dr. Hendrick was a well-known expert on history and folklore, and he wrote a book about western outlaws entitled *The Badman of the West.* His course was fascinating because it opened my eyes to even more that had been written about the area I called home.

One of my interests at the time was the history of the Texas Rangers, especially as it was presented (and sometimes distorted) in fiction. When I had to write a paper for Dr. Hendrick's class, my topic was an easy choice: The Texas Rangers in Fiction. Two of the novels I wrote about were *The Wonderful Country* by Tom Lea and *Captain's Rangers* by Elmer Kelton. Again, many years later I was lucky enough to meet both men and came to know Kelton well enough to call him a friend.

Another of my professors at NTSU was an older man named Dr. Key. I don't recall his first name. In one of his classes some twenty years earlier, a young Larry McMurtry had been his student. As an assignment for that class, McMurtry had written a short story that turned out to be the basis for his first novel, *Horseman, Pass By* (filmed as *Hud*). Dr. Key mentioned that in my class, and again my mind made the connection. McMurtry had gone to NTSU and taken English classes from one of the same professors as I was. He had gone on to have success as a writer. Why couldn't I do the same?

I was already aware of McMurtry's books and had read several of them. One that affected me quite a bit was *The Last Picture Show*. In the novel, the characters Sonny and Duane make a trip from Thalia (McMurtry's fictionalized version of his hometown Archer City) to Fort Worth, traveling down the Jacksboro Highway to do so.

Well, as it happens, I grew up a block away from the Jacksboro Highway where it passes through my hometown, and I remember sitting in my room reading *The Last Picture Show* and thinking about how Sonny and Duane passed by *right down there*, on the same highway I had walked across countless times.

If Larry McMurtry could write about places where I had been, why couldn't I write about places where I had been? Hadn't I already done that years earlier with my hand-scrawled stories about me and my friends running around and solving mysteries in my home town? Now I was ready to write something more serious in a setting that was familiar to me.

I was ambitious. I started what was intended to be a big, sprawling, coming-of-age novel centered around high school sports. I still recall the opening line: "They say there are only two real sports in Texas—football and spring football."

I wasn't a high school athlete, far from it, in fact, and after a few chapters my inspiration and ambition petered out. My great Texas novel wasn't meant to be. I don't know what happened to the pages I typed of that manuscript. They may be stuck in a box somewhere, but I suspect they're long gone, as well they should be.

I wasn't finished writing about Texas, though. I just hadn't found the right vehicle yet.

I mentioned reading Hardy Boys books when I was younger. Along with Texas, the Texas Rangers, and Robert E. Howard, one of my abiding interests, then and now, is mystery fiction. I read it all, from Mickey Spillane to Agatha Christie to Ian Fleming. I began to gravitate toward the more hard-boiled mystery novels, though, especially those about private detectives. While still at NTSU, I took a class in mystery literature, and naturally enough, when it came time to write a paper, I wrote about private eye fiction, focusing mostly on the works of Dashiell Hammett, Raymond Chandler, and Ross Macdonald, three of my favorite authors in that field. That started me thinking about writing some private eye fiction of my own.

One day I came across a copy of *Writer's Yearbook,* a thick annual magazine published by *Writer's Digest.* It had a listing of magazines that published short stories, gave the names and addresses of the editors, pay rates, and other information like that. As I was reading that magazine, it dawned on me that I could actually submit stories to those markets. Those editors didn't know that I was just some college kid from a small town in Texas. If the stories I sent them were good enough, they would buy them. So I began to submit. I was trying to crack the market, as the old-timers say, and achieve my dream of becoming a professional writer.

Of course, the stories weren't any good, and I sent them to all the wrong markets (yeah, suuuure *Playboy's* going to buy that amateurish little suspense story and pay you two thousand bucks for it, kid), but at least I was trying. All the stories came back very quickly with form rejection slips attached, and I allowed myself to get discouraged.

I had also fallen in love, so I graduated from college, got married, and settled down to work at a normal job. My wife, Livia, knew I wanted to write, though, so one day she gave me just about the best advice I've ever gotten: "You know, if you want to be a writer, you're going to have to work at it."

So I did. I was managing a TV and appliance repair shop at the time, and one of our customers was a retired prison warden who had written a book about his life and gotten it published. He loaned me a copy of the current *Writer's Market,* and I realized just how many places there were to try to sell short stories. I also became a regular reader of *Writer's Digest* and studied their market listings every month. In addition, I read every book I could find in the library about creative writing.

And I started writing stories again.

I wrote all kinds of things, but Texas kept cropping up. I did a mystery story I called "Comingor," set in a fictional small town I created that was modeled after Comanche, and sent it to Sam Merwin Jr., the editor of *Mike Shayne Mystery Magazine,* a digest-sized publication that featured a 20,000-word novella each month about the famous private eye Mike Shayne, who had been appearing in popular novels by Brett Halliday since 1939. The magazine also had an assortment of short stories in every issue.

I had been sending stories to Merwin for quite a while, and although he hadn't bought any of them, he always returned them with personal notes explaining why he wasn't buying them. I learned a lot from those notes that Sam scrawled out on scraps of paper. In fact, he had asked for a revision on one story and indicated that he would probably buy it if I would rewrite it. While I was working on that, I sent him "Comingor."

And he bought it. No revisions, just a note saying that he wanted it for the magazine, followed shortly thereafter by a check.

This was actually my second sale. A few weeks earlier, I had sold a story to one of the so-called "confession" magazines, a mystery yarn of sorts that was published anonymously, as all confession stories are. But "Comingor" would be coming out in a mystery magazine, with my by-line on it. I was a real writer at last. (It really hadn't been all that long, but it seemed like it at the time.)

And I did it with a story set in Texas, in a place I knew very well. That was a pattern I would come back to again and again.

To backtrack a moment, I mentioned the Mike Shayne novels by Brett Halliday. I was a fan of those books and had been reading them regularly for years. I knew by now that "Brett Halliday" was a pseudonym for an author named Davis Dresser, and I suspected that other writers were doing the Shayne stories in the magazine under that name.

Sam Merwin bought the story I revised at his request, and he began to buy almost all the stories I sent him. My by-line showed up regularly in the magazine. Then one day in a letter Sam asked me if I would like to try my hand at one of the Mike Shayne novellas. The pay, he said, was "a flat, lousy three hundred bucks."

Well, three hundred dollars didn't sound that lousy to me, and I had been a Mike Shayne fan for a long time, so of course I jumped at the chance. This was the first time I would write under a house name (a pseudonym shared by multiple authors) and the first time I would work with characters and situations created by another author. It certainly wouldn't be the last time.

Merwin was pleased with my initial Shayne story and asked me to do more of them. I wrote two or three Shaynes per year, while still doing short stories under my own name. When Merwin retired and his assistant editor, Charles E. Fritch, took over the magazine, Fritch asked me to write *all* the Shayne stories.

The idea of a regular writing job, in which I would have to come up with 20,000 publishable words each and every month, was a little daunting, but of course I took it. I had already learned the motto of the freelance writer: "Sure, I can do that."

I had also gotten the itch again to write a real novel. The Shayne novellas were good practice, but I wanted to do something bigger. I wanted to write a private eye novel of my own.

The problem was that all the private eye novels I'd read over the years were set somewhere else, like New York or Los Angeles or Chicago. The Shayne stories I'd been writing were set in Miami. I wasn't sure I could write a whole novel set in some place I'd never been and do a good enough job to sell it.

So why not write a private eye novel set in Fort Worth? Nobody else had ever done it, but that didn't mean it couldn't be done. I came up with a character: a middle-aged, hard-bitten private investigator named Cody. That's his last name, and the only one anybody ever used. To this day, I don't know what his first name is. I worked up a plot, a case for Cody to investigate, and started writing, setting most of the action in places I knew firsthand in Fort Worth. Cody's office was on Camp Bowie Boulevard, not far from the museum district, and he would often go to the Amon Carter Museum to look at Remington paintings. He drove on roads that I had driven, ate in restaurants where I had eaten. When he was jumped by some thugs and beaten up to discourage him from his investigation, they dumped him in the Fort Worth Nature Center, a place where I had been numerous times (never after a beating by gangsters, of course). During spare moments at the shop, I wrote and wrote in a spiral notebook during the fall of 1978, until I had the book finished. My wife, who was typing up the manuscript from my handwritten draft, made some suggestions for revisions. I did some polishing on the book, based on those suggestions, and there I was with a finished novel that I had titled *Texas Wind*. It was what I'd always wanted to write, a novel set in Texas, in places that I knew, and I thought it was a pretty good book.

Selling it was another story.

I had no contacts in the business other than a couple of magazine editors, no literary agent, and had never even met another fiction writer. *Texas Wind*, good or not, wound up in the slush pile at numerous New York publishing houses, and it always came back with form rejections.

I had seen some books from a paperback publisher called Manor Books, so after a while I sent the manuscript of *Texas Wind* to them. To my surprise, and joy, instead of the manuscript I got back a large envelope containing a contract from them. The advance they offered me for the book was, to put it mildly, terrible, but I didn't care. They wanted to publish the book. I was a novelist.

A Texas novelist.

Texas Wind was the proverbial foot-in-the-door, even more so than my published short stories were. Even though the distribution of Manor Books, never widespread to start with, got even worse exactly when my novel was coming out in October 1980, the book met with a good reception from most of the people who read it. I had gotten to know some other authors, and one of them put me in touch with his agent. I sent the agent a copy of *Texas Wind,* and she was willing to take me on as a client. Within a few months she sold a historical novel that my wife and I wrote together (nothing to do with Texas this time). This sale was to a bigger publisher for a much better advance. My wife and I have both gone on to lengthy careers as novelists, often collaborating on our books, and while there have certainly been peaks and valleys along the way, we've been able to make our living by writing and consider ourselves blessed to have been able to do so.

Since 1980, there have been numerous other private eye novels set in Fort Worth, but I believe *Texas Wind* was the first, and I'm proud of that. Over the years the book has acquired quite a few fans, and there were several attempts to reprint it that always fell through for some reason or other, until finally a new edition came out from Point Blank Press in 2004. I'm very pleased to have it back in print again.

My character Cody also appeared in several short stories, also set in and around Fort Worth. I've considered resurrecting him for another novel, but I doubt if it will ever happen. I haven't written anything about him for a long time, and I think he's probably best left in a well-earned retirement.

I've been busy with other things, though. And sooner or later my writing always comes back to Texas.

During the eighties and nineties, I became a specialist in western series novels, usually written under various pseudonyms and house names. As Hank Mitchum, I wrote the novels *Stagecoach Station, Pecos* and *Stagecoach Station, Panhandle.* As Matthew S. Hart, I wrote most of the novels in the series *Cody's Law,* about a Texas Ranger (back to that!) named Sam

Cody. (Yes, the character's name came from my private eye character.) In other series, I sent characters up the Brazos River in search of settlers captured by the Comanches and had others threatened by Karankawas along the Gulf Coast. I got them mixed up in the Fence Cutting War in Brown County in the 1880s. I wrote the occasional mystery story ("The Zephyr Flash") and science fiction yarn ("Season of Storms") set in Texas and sold them to various anthologies and small-press magazines. When I was a kid I used to eat at a café in an old rock building that had been standing for nearly a hundred years and had once been a saloon. The café was called the Red Top, after the color of the tiles on its roof, so a saloon called the Red Top began showing up in my books. I've studied the history of my hometown quite a bit, and I've had characters ride through there on numerous occasions. If there's a way to work in a place I know, I always do. Under my own name I wrote three novels based on the television series *Walker, Texas Ranger,* and wouldn't you know it, in one of those Walker visits my hometown. To me there's just something very special in writing about places that I know.

People sometimes ask me what my favorite of all my books is. I point them toward the novel *Under Outlaw Flags,* published under my name by Berkley Books in 1998. It's the story of one of the last old-time western outlaw gangs and how, when they're captured after a bank robbery, they're given the choice of going to prison or joining the army to fight in World War I. Other than the story itself, which I think is pretty good, there are a couple of reasons I really like it. Some of the novel is set at Camp Bowie, on the west side of Fort Worth, when the sprawling military camp that later gave the boulevard its name was located there. I was able to research the camp and present what I think is an accurate, interesting portrait of it and Fort Worth during that time period.

The other reason I like *Under Outlaw Flags* so much is that it opens with a framing sequence set in a small, central Texas town during the early 1960s. That town is based on Blanket, Texas, where many of my relatives lived, and the grocery store where the framing sequence takes place was my uncle's store. The chubby little kid eating popsicles and reading comic books? Yep, that's me.

That's not the only time I've appeared in one of my books as a character. My Stagecoach Station novel, *The Last Frontier*, closes with an epilogue set on the first day that the amusement park Six Flags Over Texas was ever open, in 1961. The little boy who wants to ride the authentic western stagecoach that was one of the early attractions at Six Flags? Me again, of course. My family was really there that day, and I rode the stagecoach. The thought that I might someday be writing a scene like that in a novel never crossed my mind, but the memory was there when I needed to use it.

Camp Bowie in Fort Worth was not the only military camp to bear that name. During World War II, there was a Camp Bowie in Brownwood. I heard a great deal about it over the years from my father. So when I started writing a novel about World War II entitled *Battle Lines* (Forge Books, 2001), where did I send my raw recruits for basic training? Camp Bowie in Brownwood, naturally. If there's a way to get my characters to Texas, I take it. I'm still writing series westerns, and every chance I get, I set them in Texas. I can write about other places, and have many times, but to me there has always been something special about this state. Write what you know, the old proverb says, and I know Texas. Not only that, but as my friend, author and critic Larry Richter recently pointed out to me, Texas is the wellspring for almost every western story that there is: the Cattle Kingdom, the Gunfighters, the Indian Wars, and so on. There's no better source material for western fiction than the history of Texas.

But other kinds of stories can take place here, too, as I demonstrated in *Texas Wind* and would again with another novel.

A couple of years ago I decided I wanted to write a crime novel. An idea for an opening had come to me, and as I started to develop it, I realized that the story had to be set in Texas. The novel opens in the Panhandle, and over the course of the story the action moves to the Dallas-Fort Worth area and then westward along Interstate 20 through Pecos before finally coming to its conclusion in the Davis Mountains of far West Texas. As with *Texas Wind* all those years ago, I was writing about places I've been, streets I've walked, sights I've seen. I know what the sky looks like and how the sun feels on your face and how the wind can whip up dust devils that swirl and dance across the landscape.

And so the book is called *Dust Devils.* It was published by Point Blank Press in 2007, and I'm very proud of it, just as I'm proud of all the other novels and stories I've written that are set in Texas. I remember thinking, back in the days when I was writing *Texas Wind,* that all the stereotypes, all the cultural baggage that goes with the state, aren't really accurate most of the time. Some of the myths have some truth to them, but Texas is so much more than that. One of my goals in writing *Texas Wind* was to write about Fort Worth, and Texas in general, as it really is. In all my work since that's set in Texas, I've tried to do the same, to present an honest, realistic picture of Texas, historically, geographically, and culturally.

It's important to me to get it right, and although I'm sure I fail at times, it's not for lack of trying.

Back to Robert E. Howard: he is probably the most important influence on my work not because of what he wrote but because of how he wrote, how he molded a career despite his surroundings. In a letter to H.P. Lovecraft, Howard wrote of his pride in the fact that he was the first person in his area to have a successful career as a writer, even though when he began he knew no one in the publishing business or even anyone who had written anything. He considered himself a true pioneer.

That attitude inspired me, and continues to inspire me. I am steeped in the history, the myths, the culture, the landscape of Texas. It's an inescapable, enduring part of me. I can write about other places, and have on many occasions in my career.

But whenever I can, I always come home.

Judy Reynolds

CLAY REYNOLDS

NATIVE TEXAN Clay Reynolds is the author of more than 800 publications ranging from critical studies to short fiction, nonfiction, poems, essays, reviews, and novels. He holds academic degrees from the University of Texas at Austin, Trinity University, and the University of Tulsa. Reynolds has won numerous awards for his work and is a National Endowment for the Arts Fellow, a member of the Texas Institute of Letters, and serves as professor of arts and humanities at the University of Texas at Dallas. His most recent work includes a collection of essays, *Of Snakes and Sex and Playing in the Rain,* and a collection of short fiction, *Sandhill County Lines.*

FROM WIT TO WISDOM: THE IRONY OF THE ARTISTIC JOURNEY

The original writer is not one who imitates, but one whom nobody can imitate.
François–René de Chateaubriand

UNREMARKABLY, I was born in a small town in Texas. It was fairly typical of hundreds of other small towns in Texas during the "boom years" following World War II, typical of tens of thousands of small towns across America in those days of "I Like Ike" and idyllic fictions of family and community. In most ways, I was an ordinary baby boomer. I wore baggy dungarees and ugly striped T-shirts, a flattop held up with butch wax, and had a passionate longing for a V-8 engine and a girl who looked like Annette Funicello or, later, Ann-Margret. My father was a blue-collar working stiff, a combat veteran of World War II who came home after trouncing Hitler and his minions to settle down and grow prosperous. He settled down, but he never grew prosperous, not in the way he planned. He always wanted to be a rancher and to raise horses, as his father had done. He wound up working for the railroad until they farmed him out with bad eyes and a bad heart, which were probably caused by trouncing Hitler and his minions when he should have been home becoming a rancher and raising horses. My mother was a typical small-town girl who married a likeable guy with a big heart and a good work ethic with whom she could have children and grandchildren and grow old and beam proudly whenever her progeny were on parade. She got most of that—the progeny, anyway—but my father died comparatively young, and her children moved away to hold their parades elsewhere.

I think that I began the "writing process" before I left home, but to realize it, I first had to go and find it. When the point of departure is West Texas, the trip is apt to be a long one. For me and my friends, the world ended at the county line. We knew there was something else out there, but we were afraid of it. Only a few of us would ever go there; almost none would return. I think we knew that would happen, and I think, for most, that was terrifying.

In an era when television had but three part-time channels, "out there" was a mystery. We weren't ignorant, backward, or poorly informed. We had AM radio beamed all night at us from KOMA, Oklahoma City, after all; through those static-filled airways, we heard of far off places such as Kansas City and Omaha, Chicago and St. Louis, of phenomena such as boardwalks and beaches, places we could only imagine. We marveled over the wonders of a "hemi under glass" and "double overhead cams" as they were detailed in the rapid-fire commercials for stock car races—interspersed between Gene Pitney and Buddy Holly and Elvis and Patsy Cline crooning about depths of pain and love we couldn't fathom. Cousins from Fort Worth and Dallas, from Atlanta and San Francisco and New Jersey visited and told us of a world of juvenile delinquents, beatniks, surfboards, then flower children and heavy-duty rock and roll. Our vocabularies expanded with words like "cool," "boss," and "far out," and we learned about sex and drugs and even met some kids who had seen Bob Dylan live, been to a Cowboys' game, or flown on an airliner. We heard there were places with rivers you couldn't walk across and trees so abundant you couldn't see the forest for them. We didn't believe it. We also heard that people were orbiting the earth, but I don't think we believed that, either. For us, West Texas, empty, vast, and hostile as it seemed, was vacuum enough. Who would blast off on a rocket merely to discover more?

Through these outsiders, though, and through grainy black-and-white television images that other world forced itself into our view. We imitated them and impossibly tried to make our place like theirs; meanwhile, we watched *The Andy Griffith Show* and desperately prayed that such hick towns as Mayberry weren't a reflection of our own rural reality, knowing all the while that they probably were. We wore the latest fashions, as observed on *American Bandstand* and the Sears catalogue, combed our hair in the style of our idols on record album and magazine covers, and talked with authority of the doings of faraway people and places most of us would never see. We sensed that somewhere out beyond the buttes and prairies there were places where people acted the way movie people acted, the way book people acted, and we wanted to know them, to be like them, to know what they knew about beauty and truth.

I left when I was seventeen, and I was bitter—angry over slights, real and imagined. I wanted to "show them"—although I wasn't sure, exactly, who "they" were, and I was insensible to the fact that "they" didn't care, that less than a decade later, most of "them" wouldn't recognize me on the street or have very much to say to me if they did. I didn't understand, then, that each individual has to find his own destiny, has to find his own stories to tell, and that geography doesn't really have much to do with it.

What I eventually learned, though, was that for a writer, it's necessary to leave a place—not merely physically or geographically, but spiritually—in order to come back to it, to understand it, and by all means, to write about it. But there are many ways of leaving, and it's not until you turn around and look that you can appreciate how far you've come. For a writer, it's often not very far. But it's the journey that's important, not the distance or the destination. That's where the first awareness of irony occurs.

It wasn't until I had been away for a decade that I found myself drawn back "home." At first, it was a kind of pedagogical thing. I found myself wanting to tell stories about where I was from, about the people I knew, about what I, like most writers, firmly believed to be the uniqueness of my life. Over the next several years, those stories coalesced into an idea, ultimately into a place that I eventually named "Sandhill County." As soon as I thought up the name, almost instantly, it became as real as the actual county in which I grew up.

I began writing because I wanted to tell some stories. It was as simple as that. I never expected the stories to be published, so I was honest in telling them. Although I'd never taken a creative writing course or known a writer, I followed the common advice of creative writing teachers everywhere —I "wrote what I knew." I didn't think what I knew was very interesting to anyone, having come from West Texas, a place that few people had ever heard of and even fewer ever wanted to. The idea that total strangers might want to visit a place in the pages of a book that they would not want to visit in person was absurd. That I never wanted to go back there made it even more absurd for me to write about it. But at bottom, the whole concept of writing is absurd; the one question that runs constantly through a writer's mind is, "Why would anyone ever want to read this?"

Many writers like to imagine that their primary concern is beauty and truth. I don't think so. I think the bridge between wit and wisdom can be found in the sublime appreciation of irony. Irony is the principal tool of the writer. Shelley reminds us in "A Defence of Poetry" that beauty and truth are inexorably linked, and his observation encompasses the by now over-labored definition coined in Keats' famous poetic line. Shelley, who had read that line, I'm sure—probably more often than he wished to—avers that poetry is "the record of the best and happiest moments of the happiest and best minds"; elsewhere, though, he notes that poetry differs from logic. We know from Aristotle that is as it should be, for logic has nothing to do with truth, and it has even less to do with wisdom. Logic, in sum, is witty. Poets, Shelley states, are naturally illogical. They are "teachers, who draw into a certain propinquity with the beautiful and the true that partial apprehension of the invisible world." This is the great equalizer between beauty and truth, the source of Keats' assertion that they are the same thing.

Writers are natural liars because fiction by its very definition is stuff we make up. It may be honest, but it's not real. Most of the time real life is too painful—and often too boring—to reveal in raw verity; it wants embellishment. Like a photographer working with a negative, a writer has to frame, isolate, filter, crop, dodge, and burn the subject a little, remove a blemish here, lighten a shadow there, tone down some distracting bright spot, or cut it out entirely to reveal something about the subject that might not be otherwise apparent.

In the darkroom of prose, writers seek to discover some deeper something—call it the heart, the soul, the psyche—inside the human spirit that might reveal some truth that clarifies Shelly's definition and Keats' tautology. This is an appropriate activity for writers, at least according to Pope, who dictates that "the proper study of mankind is man." Pope came before Shelley and Keats and may have been wiser. For sure, he was wittier, and, overall, he was a better liar. But since all writing is, ultimately, about character—about some person—then it makes sense that the proper subject of a writer's inquiry also is man.

The writer's renderings—his "findings," if you will—may reveal something about beauty and truth, anyway. It is the reader's obligation to admire that revelation, and that's not always easy; ultimately, it may not be that important. Poe averred that "the elevation of the soul" was the principal goal of art, but how? Aristotle taught us that all successful discourse both entertains and informs. Another way of saying that is that art must have wit as well as wisdom. Wit becomes the vehicle, in a metaphoric sense, that carries the tenor of wisdom. By analogy, the writer's job is to entice the reader through a witty portal where some wisdom may be found in the sharing of the universal nature of our common humanity, in those vital connections between one human spirit and another. This is where the notion of catharsis comes from.

What the reader experiences when he passes through the wit and discovers the wisdom isn't vicarious. It's empathetic. It's easily confused with the melding of beauty and truth, or with fear and pity, or with other raw emotions that actually were inside the reader all along. All that the writer does is expose them so the reader can feel them. But the experience has to be genuine, which means the writer has to feel them, too. "No tears in the writer, no tears in the reader," as Frost put it.

All of that sounds pretty high-minded, although I am certain that there are some writers who compose their fictions with that intent in mind. That is, they are trying to create beauty and truth in some pure, nonironic way. Their ambition wants admiration, but they are doomed to fail more often than not. That's because another irony is that art can't be deliberately created. It can be imitated, duplicated, translated from one form into another; but the creation of original art is as much an accident as the discovery of that gem of wisdom that writers always are seeking to expose. In short, developing a sharpness of wit is easy; it's the other part that's hard. It takes an abstract set of qualities to do it. Some writers have them; some don't. They're also unreliable; they may inexplicably disappear, never to return.

All art is synthetic. Whatever is observed and, one hopes, understood, passes through an interpretative filter that translates its original shape into something plastic. It appears to be true, but it cannot be; it appears to be beautiful, but it can only suggest beauty. Shelley was right on that point, for sure; but he stole the notion from Wordsworth, who taught us that the only authentic beauty lies in nature, and, ironically, only an innocent sensibility can fully appreciate it. Therefore, it's nature that's true, not its recreation or its shadow, for there is too much irony in art for it ever to be genuinely beautiful; and, as Juvenal pointed out, there's too much indignation for it to be true.

At the same time, irony also defines art, makes it appealing. It may be found in the complexities of personalities struggling on Troy's windy field or in the poetic protests of one of Shakespeare's hapless heroes; it may be observed in the simple mystery of Mozart's genius, in something as splendidly tragic as the *Pietà,* or in the quiet enigma of *Mona Lisa's* smile, the sublime sweetness of a ballet, or the towering grace of a modern skyscraper. But that's the wide-eyed wonder of it, for it can also be discovered in the contrived terror of a paperback horror novel or the clichéd thrill of a pulp western, the manipulated tension of a crime story or courtroom drama, or the predictable triumph of a war novel's hero or science fiction tale's alien invader. It can be found in the worst movie ever made or in the trite lyric of a country western cheating song. Whatever makes someone laugh out loud, weep bitter tears, shudder with fear, or cringe in pain offers it. The question is only how effective, how lasting the sensation may be.

All of these works, whether brilliant or banal, can attract us with their wit, then leave us breathless with their wisdom, emotionally awash in their combination of the abstract with the concrete in an exquisite aesthetic. Yet, if we dare stop and consider them objectively, we know that they are not real; they are imagined, created, wrought, shaped, and constructed. How can they be true? How, indeed, in the brighter light of the deeper probing of human experience, can they even be beautiful?

Actually, most of those who profess with the greatest authority about the "writing process" are not, themselves, writers. They generally are critics, and often they are very good readers. They spend a lot of time trying to find deep and sometimes "hidden" ideas in another's writing, trying to divine that famous secret everyone believes writers know but are too mean to share. They're sometimes correct. But sometimes, they're just plain wrong, even when the writers whose work they're analyzing agree with them, and especially when the writers are dead. Most writers, dead or alive, don't have any idea what their work "means." Most are just trying to tell a story the best way they know how.

But if they're careful writers, they never stay within the lines when they "color" their fiction. They may start with a form, a shape, a place, or a time that is well drawn, but most writers soon stray outside those boundaries. They have to create an imaginary world to contain their lies, a lie to surround their lies, as it were. In the process, the true shape changes; in their minds, it becomes more real than the original; if not more real, it certainly becomes more ironic.

This isn't such a problem when a writer is writing about New York City or Los Angeles, London or Tokyo, Dallas or Rome; those are large places in small areas, places where the manipulation of geography and even people can be done with reasonable ease. In a way, it's like looking through the wrong end of a telescope, something that produces a view focused on the wittiness of specific detail but hazy on the overall wisdom that may come to light. But when a writer is dealing with a very small place in a large area—such as a small town in Texas—then the telescope is right-side-around, and a great deal depends on the connections that may be drawn between the mundane and the archetypal. Lying about a small place is hard when the actuality is so handy for comparison. What writers have to do, then, is to step back and take a hard look at the whole context, not merely of the imaginary world that contains the lies they want to tell, but of the place where they are, of who they are, and where they came from. That, too, requires a context, and it's sometimes hard to find in a confusing depth of field.

As an academic and working critic of fiction, I read a great deal about "the writing process." To me, the phrase generally calls to mind my cluttered office and my rapidly aging self peering idiotically at the pixels of a computer screen while my fingers try desperately to tap out some meaningful sentence that will advance my characters and plot another page or two. My walls are lined with books I've not had time to read, which demand accusingly that I stop trying to add to their numbers, and my walls contain posters and photographs and other miscellany that I displayed at some point in the past so I could contemplate them in some future leisure that I never seem to find. Outside my window, the seasons inexorably march along, one after the other, while a wall calendar features gorgeous prints of faraway places I know I'll never have the time or money to visit.

That's hardly the glamorous view of "the writing process" that one usually imagines. In movies, authors all sip sherry and brandy and wear lots of expensive woolens and silks. They spend their time in oak-paneled bookshops signing mountains of copies for eager fans who jockey for a place in line. They never seem actually to write anything, but they often vacation in exotic places and are on intimate terms with the maître d's of five-star restaurants in famous cities. Such fantasies are powerful incentives, even though few writers ever realize them. When they finally abandon such pedestrian ambitions, they usually settle for seeking beauty and truth. Few ever realize those, either.

We have achieved so much in so little time that it's difficult to stop and consider what shreds of wisdom might have been lost in our self-congratulation of just how much wit we so readily display. Propelled with the symmetrical haste of an expanding mushroom cloud, we have moved in half a lifetime from an era when people plowed fields behind mules to a time when men walked on the moon. Disaster, deprivation, death, and disease, it would seem, are in full retreat from the power of our wit; but in our headlong rush to reach an apotheosis of human endeavor, where is the wisdom, where are beauty and truth?

This is the supreme irony; it's the writer's job to use it to remind us of who we are, from where we came in a fundamental rather than a scientific or anthropological sense, to urge us to pay less attention to the shadows and far more to the objects that block the light. Writers remind us that the abyss holds many mysteries, and that we aren't the most important one or even the most difficult to solve. Writers exist to remind us that while we can moo, we can never be cows, nor can we see the world with a cow's simple understanding; while we can fly, we can never soar with the freedom of will casually displayed by the common sparrow. In the final analysis, we are only what we are; our possibilities, however exciting to contemplate, are always bound by human limitations.

Ideas for writers' fictions come from such ironies. I think the mysteries of the past are the most powerful, and they provide some shape to the emptiness that so often threatens to smother us; they give veracity to the artistic lie we so need to define our present.

I find inspiration for character everywhere: in junkyards full of rusty automobiles, every one of which was once shiny new and probably the answer to some driver's dream; in the flyspecked windows of an old building's second story, where some business or service once found office space and the promise of prosperity; in an abandoned highway that once connected two places, the names of which have been lost to time. These are not the same as cemetery stones or other memorials designed to keep the past in living memory; these are accidental monuments, ironic testaments to the real connection between beauty and truth.

Sometimes, I look at an old photograph or, maybe, watch an old piece of film. Rather than focus on the subject of the picture, I like to pick some anonymous bystander, some curious and unidentified individual who might, for the briefest moment, peer into the lens and gape, grin, frown, or simply stare. Usually, he or she is quickly out of the frame or only a part of the background. But the image of that face, captured forever on grainy celluloid, fascinates me. I wonder what happened to that person, not years later when he or she was old and looking back on a long life; rather, I wonder about the next few moments after the camera was gone, when he turned his attention once more to his ordinary routine, when she retreated back into the anonymity of her personal history. I wonder, did he go back to work, stand behind a counter for the rest of the day, or perhaps exchange that jaunty boater for a welder's helmet, that snazzy suit for a barber's smock? Did she make that bonnet, and what caused the stain on her apron? Had he ever fired that pistol in his belt or blacken those scuffed shoes; did she truly love that child beside her, or did she wish her never born? What did he eat for supper that night? Was she in love that day? Was her shirtwaist too tight, or did his underwear bind? Had she seen a dentist lately, or ever? Did he smoke, drink to excess? Or was he a loyal temperance follower? Did she attend church regularly, or was she a prostitute off on a respectable lark? Did he, at that moment, have a tumor that was quietly killing him? Would she live long enough to vote? Was it hot on the street that day, did sweat run down into his eyes, did he have an odor about him? Was she married? What were his worries, her fears, their joys? Was he generally happy, a good man with a good life? Or did he harbor some deep, sinister secret beneath the mugging grin. Did she perhaps leave the street and murder someone for two dollars and an expired trolleycar pass? What did they see in the distance beyond the camera?

Such questions can be maddening if they become obsessive. But to me, it is the raw material of character, the fountainhead of fiction, for from looking into the smeared countenances and studying the vague details, I can often find all kinds of lies to tell, and if I can employ the right amount of wit in telling them, I might reveal some wisdom.

. . .

Sometimes, I pass a lone wanderer on the highway. Mindful of commonsense cautions, I never stop; but as I whiz by and spray them with heat and gravel, I catch a glimpse of their eyes, and I find myself wondering about them the same way I wonder about long-dead images in antique photographs, rusty cars, and crusty windows blinded by dust and age. Often these vagabonds are scraggly, dirty, overburdened with packs and possessions. Sometimes, they trudge along with no effort to find a ride; other times, they hold up hastily scrawled signs or the ever-ineffective thumb, seeking a quicker way to wherever they think they're going. They often look sad, weary, and worn. I know that somewhere they had a mother, a father, though they might never have known them. Somewhere at some time, someone must have cared about them, perhaps loved them, hated them, or at least known their names.

As I zoom past, I often wonder: Where have they been? What do they think they're running from? Why do they think that where they're going will be better, safer, more secure, or comfortable than anywhere else? Like Odysseus, they're bouncing from place to place, they think; like Oedipus, they're running from their fates, they think; like Huck, they've "lit out" for the territories, they think. They stare with contempt at those who pass them by, thinking they're ignored. But they're wrong about that. Although forever anonymous, they invade our consciousnesses, one way or another; and whether they know it or not, they're always going home.

In a way, that is the same impulse that draws me to the photographs, that notion of "coming home." And as a writer, coming home meant going back, over and over again, to Sandhill County.

. . .

"Sandhill County" is the background for my lies. I made up the name after checking an almanac and making sure that there really wasn't a "Sandhill County" anywhere in Texas. Writers have to be very careful about inadvertently telling the truth. The name was appropriate, because the county I was writing about was bordered on the north by the Prairie Dog Town Fork of the Red River, a sandy and treacherous waterway. It was bordered on the east and south by the Pease River, a smaller but no less sandy road that frequently flooded and washed out bridges and fields. Lining both steams were huge mounds of sand, diluvium hills covered with light vegetation at their crowns and descending into labyrinthine loblollies filled with dark and dank plants, thickets of thorns, and dens of coyotes, wild cats, and poisonous snakes.

Among the few more naturally appealing fauna farmers and ranchers hadn't hunted into extinction or merely slaughtered out of pure meanness, was the sandhill crane. These huge, graceless birds made an annual pilgrimage from points north each winter, camping out on their stork-like legs on the riverbeds, enticing the blood sportsmen among us to—what else?—kill them.

As a youngster, I tried to hunt sandhills along with quail, dove, and rabbits, but the birds were skittish and elusive. Their preference was the vast, gritty emptiness of the rivers' beds, which, when they weren't flooded, were truly just huge sandbars occasionally cut by shallow rivulets of briny water. To reach the browsing flock, I often crawled through a frozen swamp, a quarter mile of mud, mesquite, and plum thickets, and endured thick red goo and horsefly and mosquito bites, sharp thorns and stings from a variety of nasty, ugly plants. Finally, I and my stealthy companions would emerge onto the riverbed, wipe off the slime and ignore the pain, then tread our way around quicksand bogs. When at last nearly in shotgun range of the tall, gray birds, we would stand there helplessly in our frigid, wet misery and watch them rush in an awkward gait down an icy beach, spread their huge wings, and rise, slapping and honking, into the cloud-mottled blue West Texas autumn sky.

I think we tried to bag a sandhill crane maybe fifty or sixty times when I was young. We were assured they tasted "just like turkey" by old timers who said they knew. But we never found out. The closest we ever came to them was still too far away to identify their cockscombs' colors with the naked eye, and we never forgave them for waiting until we had labored so hard to come near them before taking off and beating, tantalizingly close, over our heads toward a safer haven.

So I named my imaginary county after those elusive birds, and after the hundreds of fields of dry-land cotton that were plowed and churned out of the loamy soil of the bottoms, farms that were mostly abandoned to the Dust Bowl and Great Depression before I was born. Those fields contributed to my motivation to take wing and leave that gritty, biting, stinging hell behind.

I remember one summer, hired at the exploitative rate of fifty cents per hour, I trudged row after row of cotton plants, officially charged to chop out the weeds that threatened them. Actually, we didn't need hoes. The weed of cotton field choice in that loosely packed soil was the "careless weed," a tube-rooted, fuzzy-shafted vegetable demon that thrust its sticky leaves upward toward the sun from the shadows of the tender cotton plants. A careless weed could not be hoed out. If chopped off, it would merely grow back—overnight, it seemed. It had to be pulled out. This meant stooping, grasping, and tugging, until the tip of the root came reluctantly from the dusty sand, where it could then be dropped, exposed to the harsh sun and utter aridity of West Texas' summer that would, in a day's time, shrivel it to virtually nothing. The thing about West Texas is that, fecund as it sometimes is, it often shrivels everything, particularly ambition and personal dreams, to virtually nothing.

After an hour of this labor, my hands stung from the sap of the plant and its pointy, tactile leaves, and my back ached from the effort of tugging them from the soil. It was July, which meant it was yellow-grass hot. At the end of each row, I turned and went back up the other. But alongside of the field at one end was a huge billboard designed to be seen from the highway some two miles away. Across the enormous blank white field of the sign swept a muscular fist that held a frothy stein of FALSTAFF BEER, or such was the red-lettered claim. The foamy head of the brew swept out behind it in an icy contrail that splashed the hairy, disembodied forearm that moved it as, I imagined, a bartender might sweep the beverage across a mahogany plain to sit in front of a thirsty customer. In the history of the world, no one has ever been thirstier than a kid chopping cotton in a sandy river bottom.

For half the time I trudged through the grasping, ankle-deep sand of those cotton furrows, I was confronted with that promise of permanently slaked thirst and icy, frothy wonder of pure refreshment. Although at that tender age, I had never tasted beer—never smelled it or been in the room where anyone had done so—I knew that people "out there" could have it, and at will. They could walk into any saloon or bar—dens of sin, from my mother's point of view—plunk down a few coins and be presented with this ambrosia, this golden liquid that I was sure had a bouquet and aroma that not even a Baptist god could resist.

I vowed that, once departed from that powder-house dry county, I would never again live where such liquid balm could not be had, even by a preteenager whose only barrier against grainy, gritty thirst was a tin-cooler of warm gyp water and a well-worn stick of Juicy Fruit.

Sand and West Texas, skin-scorching heat and bone-aching cold, then, were inscribed on my experience from my youth. I became familiar with the bitter disappointment of anyone who realizes that his entire life would be rooted in the loose and shifting soil of a county drawn out of the sand of West Texas. But I wasn't merely leaving to find a place where I could have a beer; I left to find a place where such a possibility wouldn't be a distracting consideration. I wasn't, in sum, either "the best or happiest mind" around, but I may well have been the most desperate.

It struck me later how much more ironic it would have been to accept that; for not every vagabond is an aimless wanderer, and not every writer has to leave his geography in order to find the wisdom it might have to offer. In many cases, people who spend their lives trying to avoid their fate often go nowhere. They remain where they always are and keep a wary eye on the horizon, fearful that any day, fate might come riding in on a horse—pale or otherwise—and bring with it some cosmic vengeance blown on an ill wind. The choices are not particularly appealing: Run and you rush toward it, stand where you are, and it will find you out.

My relationship with this place of my imagination was initially one of antipathy for its shifting and ephemeral but somehow always painful and torturous nature. Its clinging insistence vied with its centrifugal velocity. It had existed in reality, briefly, when I was a child in my own reality. But, when I finally decided to run, it quickly became memory, and as memory, it shaped itself into destiny; like a careless weed, plucked from the sand and left to rot in the sun, my destiny was ultimately mortified by the quest for wit and wisdom. At first, of course, such values somehow escaped me. Like most youngsters in their callow twenties, I was far more interested in outrage than in irony, more interested in causes than effects. But eventually I came to understand that both of those elements were a part of who I was and who everyone who had ever lived there was. If I was going to tell stories about it, about them, to find some wisdom in the wit, then that had to be my subject, and it had to reflect, however indirectly, the ironic relationship between beauty and truth in a place that ostensibly offered little of either.

Just as with old photographs and films, I also often find myself speculating about the myriad of small towns that dot the nation's landscape, especially those that scatter themselves across the vapid prairies of West Texas. When I have occasion to pass through one of those many fading hamlets and see the bricked-over windows and boarded-up doors facing cracked and abandoned sidewalks, I think, sometimes, if I squint just right, I can bring back a time when hope had promise to bolster it, when the ragged and deteriorating buildings lining a vacated Main Street were once teeming with life and commerce. I understand that the people who carved this place out of raw prairie or flatland plain believed in themselves, in the values and principles and dates of construction they stamped in mottos on the structures' capstones or carved into the bases of crumbling statues on the courthouse squares. They took pride in where they were, whence they'd come, and where they believed they were going. For them, it was a sufficiency of surplus.

In a way, the towns were constructed as bastions, fortresses to protect the people there from their collective fate. They were attempts to ward off the inevitable ends that would most certainly come if they ever let down their guard or failed to stand a vigilant watch. What they never understood was that no matter how strong their defenses or alert their pickets, the ends would manifest themselves anyway. In a tragic sense, then, they become heroic; but not all of life is tragic, much of it is comic, as well. And the essence of both forms is irony.

Such towns are very much like characters with whom I've populated my fictions. Each has a distinct personality; each has a particular point of view. Though small, virtual microcosms of human experience, they are complex and diverse, emotionally sensitive, ambitious, and self-deceiving. In that way, they're also archetypes. Like people, these towns were born, grew up, and then were obliged to seek their own destinies, in some cases, their own mythologies. Some died away quickly; others adapted and prospered. But some continue to rock along from year to year in abject denial that the world is changing around them and their time is limited. Clinging to prescribed and never-questioned values, they bask in the glow of self-gratification they hear preached from pulpit and political dais; they observe the outside world with a chary eye, hopelessly awaiting something supernatural to rise and save them from the inevitable.

These tiny towns call themselves "cities," replete with "municipal" cemeteries, buildings, and hospitals; but they usually devolve into parodies of what they imagine, lies incarnate to some extent. Insensitive to injustice and ignorant of their own faults, they mistake pity for compassion, indolence for pride. Substance eventually gives way to sensation, and nothing is concrete, nothing real. The fears and hatreds that once were honestly expressed and openly dealt with are eventually suppressed. Someday, they have to emerge, though, because, fate always catches up with small towns, just as it does with people. Sometimes, the confrontation is exquisitely painful.

Some readers and critics have made much of my using a small town in West Texas as the setting for my fictional lies. They enjoy pointing to Faulkner's Jefferson or even Larry McMutry's Thalia and say, "See? He's doing the same thing." And I guess I am, in a way. But what's annoying about this kind of comment is that those esteemed writers were doing the same thing writers—who are liars, remember—have always done. They've sought wit in choosing a setting that would be familiar to their audiences and would, at the same time, reflect the wisdom their stories hoped to reveal. Jefferson—the father of democracy and, not incidentally, of unacknowledged children; Thalia, a classical muse and, not incidentally, a ghost town in Foard County, Texas. Has McMurtry visited Foard County? Did Faulkner consider Monticello's hypocrisy?

I feel no propinquity with regard to my fiction. We don't know if Sophocles ever saw Thebes or if Homer dropped by Troy, if Shakespeare ever visited Padua, or Coleridge ever discovered Xanadu; but, they created them in their minds; I believe they created them out of their memories of places that they wanted to recreate in the lies of their fiction. The difference was that most of their audiences hadn't seen these places —the actual ones, anyway—either. And to them, it was unlikely that Trojans or Paduan readers would ever sit around saying, "Oh, that's not the correct location for that," or "They were nothing like that." These writers could lie with aplomb. They had the liberty of irony to insulate their imaginings with wit, so they cut directly to the wisdom. In such settings the power of their stories, of their people, and their places won't disappear, won't fall into the oblivion of actual places and people. They somehow endure. And unlike memory or geography, or beauty or truth, all of which are imperfect and temporary, the lies of fiction somehow endure.

It's as dangerous as it is boring for a writer to discuss philosophy or art, particularly with regard to his own work; and I don't want to imply that I am trying, somehow, to make more of my work than it is. I could claim, I suppose, that I've tried to adapt my small-town Texas fiction into a mythological framework and to give it some kind of universality, but that would be too big a lie even for a writer to tell. Still, just as we are products of all we've done, we are also products of all we know. I began to understand as I wove my lies that I wasn't so much adapting the mythology of the literary past to my own purpose; rather, I was trying to demonstrate that the place and people I wanted to reveal fit into that mythology almost too neatly. The trick was to show how they were all a part of the same thing and how the irony of that made it relevant.

Such pronouncements and evaluations are probably bogus. For sure, they seem self-serving; most anything writers say about their own work is bogus and self-serving. But, as I said, I've always been more interested in effects than in causes, so trying to come to terms with the reasons why things turn out the way they do tends to kill my enthusiasm for the examination. I write the same way I read: one page at a time. If I know how the story will turn out, I have no particular interest in finishing it. The best surprise is always the genuine one, that moment when you open the door to "the eternal footman" and decide that maybe things won't turn out so badly after all.

I do think my work is important. I'd be truly lying if I said otherwise, and I'd quit doing it, too. It may be self-gratifying to think that way, but I hope not. I hope that what I write provides at least some wit and reveals at least some wisdom. Some more forward-looking writers and critics have averred that the "myths" of the past are dead letters written by dead hands, that there is nothing left there of interest and nothing to learn. I don't agree. I think that in the greater scheme of things the dramatic moments of imagined lives caught in microcosm, as it were, and fretted by the significance of exposure provide a closer and more cogent look at the truth of the human experience, of the beauty of the human heart; time has even less to do with it than geography.

In the end, I have to admit, that I have no idea in the world how "fiction works"; I know nothing insightful about the "writing process." The only method I understand about writing fiction that makes sense to me is that I create a character or two, put them into situations that cause them to react in some human way. After that reaction, I think, the characters are on their own, just as, finally, we're all on our own, and it's the effects, not the causes that matter. As the writer, I can "nudge" them here and there, can throw more obstacles, opportunities, and situations in their paths; but how they find their way to some kind of resolution is up to them. I won't conclude their stories. They must do that. The writer really shouldn't—in my case can't—interfere with how things develop, with how the effects are assessed. To me, my characters are as real as my own life, my own memories; and, in many, many ways, they're more real than the actual county and town and the people, still living or long dead, who drift shadow-like in the gritty fog of the sandy past.

I probably will tell as many stories as publishers are pleased to put into print. I hasten to say, though, that I don't do this out of pure ego—although on at least one level, all writing is merely an exercise of nothing else—but rather because this is ultimately what I know, what I do. I am hopeful that by melding wit and wisdom and greasing the skids with irony, I can send a reader sliding into some unique perception of beauty and truth, however fleeting it may be. It's enough to ask for, more than enough; I can only hope that if it happens, it will bring me and my reader closer to a better understanding of what kind of creatures we are, and what kind we may become.

Arthur McWhirter

JOYCE GIBSON ROACH

JOYCE GIBSON ROACH holds BFA and MA degrees in English from TCU where she was adjunct professor from 1984 to 1997 specializing in the western novel and literature of the Southwest. She is a three-time Spur Award winner from the Western Writers of America, Inc. for both fiction and nonfiction. Along with co-author Ernestine Sewell Linck, she received the Carr P. Collins prize for nonfiction from the Texas Institute of Letters for *Eats: A Folk History of Texas Foods* (TCU Press). She is a fellow of the Texas Folklore society and the Texas State Historical Association and a member of the Texas Institute of Letters and the Philosophical Society of Texas.

SAVED TO THE UTTERMOST: THE LIFE AND TIMES OF A NAÏVE WEST TEXAS WRITER

I'M FROM Jacksboro, Texas, and have never gotten over it —and I'm not trying. I wear that corny phrase around my neck like an albatross, and, like the ancient mariner, am compelled to hold any and all with a glittering eye while explaining my rural, small-town West Texas background. The remark brings laughter and that's probably why I say it, but I learned the hard way in front of the wrong audience that it's an inside joke. If you aren't from West Texas or haven't spent some time there, you don't get it. Those who do get it understand that my beloved home town of Jacksboro stands for every small West Texas settlement from the Trinity to the Rio Grande, from the Panhandle to the Big Bend, from the Southern Plains to the Brush Country with a population hovering around 3,000, give or take 1,500 or 2,500. Small towns are alike in their differences; or different in their likenesses—something like that? But in West Texas the one constant was —is—never enough rain. If rain occasionally comes, can drought be far behind?

Crowded into that one sentence, folks understand that the place of my dry, rocky, thirsty, oak trees and grassland genesis and personal historical time frame of the 1930s through the 1960s, somewhere between the music of "The Old Chisholm Trail" and the "Dawning of Aquarius," free love and hippies, made all the difference in what I am and am not; has inspired, confused, helped and hindered me; given me great confidence and terrible insecurity, pushed me way ahead, and held me way back from all sorts of notions. It will surprise no one that I write from and about that West Texas background; can't get away from it; tried but failed. The stage and setting were provided, almost supernaturally it seems, appearing without my summons, and populated with all the supporting cast—pioneering ancestors who marched undiluted through generations, those at home in the kitchen (the most important room in a house), neighborhood, church, around the square of a county seat. You just can't trust a town that isn't built on a square—the countryside complete with an old military fort, Fort Richardson, ranches, a red brick school house, and a city set on a shining hill located a far piece away so that getting to go there was a big trip, an event. You can guess just how short the play and how small the stage, but understand, too, that exploring every trail, furrow, fork in the road, creek, and river, knowing intimately the land and the people, and yearning to tell about it all has been the ultimate for this writer and all I could write about with any authority or ownership. Sound naïve? Yes, indeed.

My babyhood took place during the Great Depression, my childhood encompassed World War II, and my coming of age embraced (and I do mean hugged it up tight) the world as it still was—mostly rural, patriotic, innocent, gullible, familial, optimistic, religious, honorable, decent, civil, and for me, wanting an education, to know and be known, all this right up to the edge of Integration-Bra Burning-Pill-Hippie-Cold War-Kennedy-Camelot era. There is suspicion that rural West Texas stayed twenty-five to fifty years behind the philosophical, political, and religious nonsensical fads. Yes, all were merely fads that would pass, leaving us with our good old ways intact, leaving us practiced in the arts of naiveté.

The Great Depression was instructional for me, even if

most of what I knew came from my parents and the citizens of Jacksboro. Everyone knew

> the year when the Great Depression began—1929. That's when the government, who was a great noticer of things after they happened, said it began. . . . While it sounds undemocratic, unpatriotic, and unrealistic to admit it, I loved the Depression. Nobody had anything, but we all had plenty of nothing together in the same proportions and at the same time so that no one felt inferior or left out. ("In Search of Uncle Freddie," *Texas and Christmas)*

The Depression segued nicely into war, at least for a time:

> For a while, war was entertaining, fun—parades, victory gardens, rolling bandages, saving tinfoil from gum wrappers, doing without some items we didn't need much of anyway, going to the movie to see news films about the war, or listening to the radio that gave word about the big battles on land and sea, and how many soldiers we were losing, but not their names. After awhile we weren't so jolly about it. The truth set in and we, at least the women, cried a lot. ("The Promised Land," *Collective Heart: Texans in World War II*)

War turned really dark when my Uncle Fred went into the navy, the ink on a bachelor's degree from Rice University barely dry and with an All-American football title to boot. He served aboard the *Blackhawk* in the Pacific, but also manned a PT boat that landed troops ashore on Iwo Jima. Fred came home only once just before the war ended, arriving in

Jacksboro after dark, appearing

> in the distant moonlight as the figure of a man wearing a dark navy uniform, the gold buttons plainly visible and the emblem on his hat shining. He was leaning on a cane. This was not my uncle. But something about the way he stood and held his shoulders told me that it was my uncle. There was never any need to think about exactly what kind of a man my uncle was until I saw the man he wasn't anymore. ("The Promised Land")

Except for depression and war, nothing much of national or international interest touched me. I was born in Cleburne at the very end of 1935 but came to Jacksboro in 1938 as a barely two-year-old with my parents, David Henry and Anna Pearl Hartman Gibson—Dave and Ann—where my daddy had a job as a butcher for Safeway Stores. Mother was at home with me, as were other mothers of that time. Neighboring, PTA, and church was the order of the day and the times. Daddy worked long hours and on Saturdays, too. Sometimes we'd go to the picture show on Saturday night after he got off work.

Movies were central to my education, teaching geography and the ways of the world, morality, and even confirming my religious beliefs. When I was old enough, I attended the picture show all day on Saturdays, seeing the same movies, serials, and cartoons about three times. From the B westerns starring Roy, Gene, Hoppy, and Dale, and later Randolph Scott, Gary Cooper, and John Wayne, I garnered information about how to dress, behave, women and children first, woman gets the last bullet for herself, not to swear or spit but to fistfight for what's right, and ride hell-bent for leather. I never did any of those things except ride like hell. A lady couldn't get away with the rest of that stuff. It was a man's world, but I wanted to fit in to it. Okay, so things were somewhat confused in my mind. I told you I was naïve. Oh yes, and I heard all the best cowboy songs, adding them to my religious repertoire of hymns.

Even the horses were moral and honorable, otherwise my heroes and heroines wouldn't have been riding them. When I heard that Roy had stuffed Trigger, I thought even more of him than I already did.

Outside B westerns, Tarzan movies were the most instructional, teaching about other races and cultures, and underscoring my religious responsibilities:

> What little we knew of geography or the larger world, we knew from mission study.
>
> God called upon missionaries and us to feed the hungry and to clothe the naked. I assumed from the movies that only Africans needed missionaries. Tarzan and Cheetah were already in service there. Clothing the naturally naked was the high aim of the missionary movement before 1950 and after. Such a work! I could help Tarzan and the missionaries civilize and robe them in a fashion worthy to be presented at the throne of God girded about the loins and covered with Fruit of the Loom, not merely a fig leaf. ("A High Toned Woman," *Hoein' the Short Rows*)

I saw the classics of black-and-white film with my parents, but they were not instructional or educational as were the B westerns. Another reason many of us treasured those respites from real life in the moving picture houses was that it was cool, air conditioned. And we didn't worry about needing rain.

Friday was always football game night, and sometimes the businesses closed down early because everybody was at the field anyway. Friday night lights were the Word—life is real, life is earnest, a thing of beauty and a joy forever—made flesh!

Interspersed between school, which I loved, church, which was the best, Girl Scout meetings, even better, was learning the basics of the out of doors—camping out "every night where the only law is right," building campfires, swimming, fishing, hiking, hunting, picking up pecans with my Uncle Fred and Mama Hartman. My grandmother was always the protector. Once while fishing she managed to hook a water moccasin. Before anyone knew what she was about, she hollered, "Look out! Duck!" "By the time she said, duck, she had jerked that viper out of the water, landed him, grabbed a loose fence post lying nearby and beat the bejesus out of that snake" ("Mama and the Box Top Christmas," *Grandmother Stories from the Heart of Texas*). Then she got me by the hand, saying "stay close to me, hear." Staying close was often where the real danger lay. It was from her I learned first hand about strong women—strong in the kitchen, powerful in church—a Fundamentalist Baptist, grown out of the old Primitive Baptist root; a J. Frank Norris Baptist—fearless in the natural world. She was also the one who taught me to study the clouds and hope for rain, not mercy drops but gully washer showers of blessing.

Out in the wilds of Jack County, I came upon the great love of my life, horses. The love was furthered by two friends—the Gustin boys, Lewis and Lloyd—one a year older and one a year younger than I. Their daddy, Harry, was foreman for the Coca Cola Ranch and spent his days on the back of a great stallion. We went to the same church, and lots of Sundays we'd go out to the Gustin's for Sunday dinner and an afternoon of "back in the saddle again, out where a friend is a friend, where the longhorn cattle feed on the lowly jimson weed," living the life portrayed in the Saturday afternoon movies, except that the cattle were Herefords. My mount was a steel-jawed, jug-headed, rough-gaited gelding by the name of Billy that knew only one pace—a hard trot. Harry had few rules: don't run the horses in the heat, stay away from the stallion, "take ceer, hear?" I did my best to take care in the wildest, roughest, rockiest land this side of hell, overpopulated with rattlers, coyotes, skunks, cactus, thorny brush, and harmless horny toads. Yes, I fell under the spell of both wicked horses and wickeder land. Every boy needs a dog. I needed a horse. Much later, I paid my debt to *Phrynosoma cornutom,* Texas horned lizards, with a children's book entitled *Horned Toad Canyon.*

Looking back on those halcyon days, a lot of it a-horseback, and the people and places that inspired me so, I notice not a pattern but certainly a path. Graduating in 1954 from Jacksboro High School, I headed for Texas Christian University in Fort Worth, the center of the universe. Fort Worth contained the most beautiful courthouse in the state, maybe the world, and culture was there in the form of the Fort Worth Cats that played at La Grave field and the Fort Worth Fat Stock Show and Rodeo at Will Rogers Coliseum. TCU was the only college I ever wanted to attend, and I was already in love with the grand scheme and the setting. My reasons for choosing TCU were not based entirely on lofty aspirations for learning but because their colors were purple and white, also my high school colors. The football coach, Abe Martin, was from Jacksboro, and horny toads, my childhood playmates, were the mascot. I have never found either Fort Worth or TCU wanting even to this very day:

> The city was the center of the universe for countless small towns in West Texas. Fort Worth was as far east as many ranchers were willing to send their children for culture or education or to come themselves to buy and sell. Fort Worth was the only proper place left in the state, at least as far as West Texas folks knew or cared. Its ways were not the strangers' ways. It was as friendly, inviting, well-mannered, good-humored, and high-toned as one ever needed to get, as quality without pretentiousness as anyone could stand. ("Fort Worth—Through the Storefront Windows," *Literary Fort Worth*)

My mother, Ann, went to work when I was in eighth grade in order to pay my way. It was a great sacrifice, great hardship to get me educated, but she always made me feel it was my due as her only, perfect child. She was, and still is at age ninety-one, more independent, strong, and even wiser than my grandmother. She appears in short stories, although she may not recognize herself. More than once "her tears covered me sweeter than a baptism." ("Just As I Am," *Women Who Made The West*)

At TCU I embraced education and campus life whole hog. I was in the band, joined the debate team but didn't last long—you weren't supposed to quote poetry or offer maxims and had to be able to concede there were two sides to any argument. Speech/Drama was my declared major. My freshman year I tried out and was cast as the aged English madam in "Ladies in Retirement." At the tryouts I was able to pull off a perfect upper crust Brit accent. During the run of the play, however, the accent disappeared (stage fright, probably) and the madam strode about the stage speaking some strange dialect, a combination of West Texas and English English—"Gawd! It's nun a' yore bloody bidness." The play called for the madam to get bumped off early and her body stuffed in a brick oven in the wall. The director, cast, and audience looked forward—even prayed—for my demise. I never tried out for another play, but it only took one to remain forever devoted to footlights.

English literature captivated me from the beginning. And I was an excellent reader of Shakespeare, although in Texas dialect. Called upon often to read by my favorite professor, Mabel Major, she seemed perplexed about my ability to get the phrasing right, the rhythms precise, and the expression and emphasis on the nose. Why? How?—especially when it became obvious from tests that I barely knew what was going on. Such matters as themes, literary devices, and meaning didn't mean a thing to me. This went on for some time until one day Miss Major asked me if I read the Bible much. Of course; I read it until I got most of the important parts memorized, feeling conscience stricken to do so as a fully immersed, born guilty, Southern Baptist Convention Baptist who read the Holy Baptist King James Bible. I had even heard Billy Graham, in person, for Jesus' sake. That King James, Shakespeare, and Jesus spoke the very same English was an epiphanistic moment for me! It will come as no surprise that Shakespeare, but also the Medieval period Arthurian legend and lore were my favorites, and, as I would discover later, the stuff of westerns and the foundations of more than just West Texas life. Hearing that it rained in England all the time caused me to long to visit someday. I did and it did—rain all the time. Loverly!

About the time I was really getting good at research, figured out the Dewey Decimal system in the library and wrote in an acceptable footnoted style, the same professor who asked me to read Shakespeare as an undergraduate asked me to take her class entitled Life and Literature of the Southwest and if I and my by-then husband, Claude (we married in 1957 just before I completed a BFA in 1958), would like to be guests and give her a ride to a meeting of the Texas Institute of Letters. There I met the triumvirate—Walter Prescott Webb, J. Frank Dobie, and Roy Bedichek—and we later accompanied Mabel to a meeting of the Texas Folklore Society. The rest may not be history, but for the purpose of my life as a Texas writer, it's the most important part.

Mabel Major made one other illuminating suggestion to me as I was writing my thesis in Chaucer studies (MA, 1965). "Why don't you turn away from England and look in your own backyard when you want to write again?" Frankly, it was a relief. Training to be a scholar was instructional and much needed, but confining, fenced in. She had also discovered that I yearned to write, trying short stories, poetry, and personal narratives to enter in TCU's creative writing contests, which she helped found and organize. Subject matter for these entries was always the same—life and times in small town West Texas. Mabel was the first to let the gap down, rescue me from myself, and save England from me.

The year 1965 was important to my writing passion. I became a member of the Texas Folklore Society, and to that group, various and sundry particular members, I owe much. Full participation in the folklore society meant giving papers—a chance to speak, to render with feeling, expound on topics. In the beginning I went at it in true scholarly form, footnotes, outline, and such, but always the topics leant themselves to a popular style. I was caught between, and the writing was a peculiar mix, but the voice came through in ways that covered my lack of skill on paper. I learned that a speaker does not a writer make, but finding one's voice can help. And the voice? Speech patterns, gospel songs, scripture, maxims, jokes, tales, religiosity, and philosophy of dry, rain-starved West Texas.

By then, however, I was not so wet behind the ears but beginning to look at West Texas nouns—persons, places, things and events—with new eyes and able to poke a little fun, discovering the truth pointed out in a Chaucer class taught by Troy Crenshaw that human nature does not change, regardless of the periods in human history or the humans who inhabit the earth. That piece of information set me free!

Another important figure entered my writing life in 1971—C. L. Sonnichsen. It was he who rescued a writing damsel in distress, often. Hadn't heard of him at that time, but James Ward Lee, whose acquaintance was made through the Texas Folklore Society, asked me to interview Sonnichsen, read his prolific output, and write a monograph for Steck-Vaughn's Southwest Writers Series for which Lee was editor. Steck-Vaughn broke contract and cancelled the series, but the piece was later published by Boise State Press's Western Writers Series. By that time, I had two children, Darrell and Delight, and was at home on a very small piece of range along with a few cows and horses near Keller.

Continuing my acquaintance with Sonnichsen—he taught at the University of Texas at El Paso for forty-one years and served another fifteen as editor of the Arizona Historical Society publications—led him to ask me what my next project was. I told him it was about cowgirls, ranch women, and others of their ilk. Why? he wanted to know. Because I'd grown up observing and admiring at a distance the Worthington sisters of Jack County, who lived life on horseback, roping, riding, working cattle, and rodeoing for entertainment. They didn't seem to be cut out of the same piece of cloth as pioneer women who got by, made do, walked behind a plow, and such. These cowgirls rode everywhere—they didn't walk—worked just as hard as men, talked tough, acted tough, were tough, but had an air of confidence about them that was hard not to notice, if not admire. Discovering stories about other like-minded females from the frontier to the then present made me want to write a book detailing characteristics that noticed an authentic American folk heroine. Sonnichsen predicted, "You're on to something." He insisted, "Let me see an outline, look at chapters, give you some advice." He did. The first two chapters appeared as western magazine articles, and the rest of the book followed.

The western novel was still in vogue, in fact riding high in 1975 when *The Cowgirls* first started making the rounds. Nonfiction wasn't. But still I sent the manuscript to Doubleday. We all want New York to tell us no first. The editor was a man known to like westerns a lot, but this wasn't fiction. It took a long time for the rejection to come back, but the editor said something important: "If your work had been written by someone with a 'name' we'd take it in a minute. But you're an unknown. Sorry." Yes, I was disappointed and didn't waste any more postage east of the Mississippi but approached Bob Gray, editor of *Horseman Magazine,* having heard they sometimes published longer works about western subjects. They took the manuscript and published it without changing a word or a footnote! For that I will ever be grateful but at the same time wished for a good editing and some rewriting. The book stayed in print with some five printings from 1977 until 1988, but it couldn't be bought in bookstores. It had to be ordered from

Cordovan Press through half-page ads and blurbs in *Horseman Magazine*. Then in 1991, Fran Vick at the University of North Texas Press took the book, cleaned it up, put footnotes as chapter notes, added an index and bibliography, put a smashing color cover on it, and it's still in print—at a time when the world wanted to know about women called cowgirls. A few lines have been quoted often and are now emblazoned on the wall of the National Cowgirl Museum and Hall of Fame, which beats a lot of other walls words have been written on:

> Emancipation of women began well before Susan B. Anthony marched and carried signs declaring that women, too, were created equal. I'm certain that real freedom began when some unnamed, obscure woman of the Border regions looked at the world from the back of a horse and realized how different and fine the view, how far she could go, who she might become.

Fran was new at publishing in 1991, taking on the job as founder and director of the UNT Press. She took a chance on the book and therefore me. Once again I was rescued, and other books were possible because of her. After that there were lots of articles, essays, and short pieces published in newspapers, western magazines, historical and literary journals, and books such as Texas Folklore Society publications. Oh yes, and speeches, talks, at symposiums, panel discussions, and conferences of historical or literary groups. Talking, and listening to others, at such events led me to try being humorous at a time when neither western history or literature groups had much humor. I didn't have to try very hard; it was, and still is, impossible not to notice the foibles of southwestern types, folk, characters of the past. All that's needed is the voice.

Two men entered my life somewhere along the line, thus

saving me from being a spinster speaker, if not writer. Robert Flynn, whose wife, Jean, had already rescued him, and James Ward Lee allowed me to be doubly funny but never as witty or skilled as they. From time to time, we did speaking duets wherein Bob and I traded insults about our hometowns and religion, and Jim and I swapped creative stories about characters. Jim has edited many of my pieces over the years, thereby saving me yet again from myself.

Reading Sonnichsen's forty plus books and scores of articles confirmed how I wanted to write. He was as familiar with the Bible as I was and put it to use by quoting, misquoting, misapplying the scripture, knowing how to bend it to humorous use. He was familiar as well with literature, which he also quoted and bent. He wrote history in a creative, readable, unbiased way, perhaps because he was an English professor and not a history scholar. If there was more than one way to interpret the facts, he did. During the years between the 1950s and 1980s, Sonnichsen was often out of favor with the "pure" historians who put down his work. He often went back over subjects the historians had already passed judgments on. Sonnichsen's response was that scholars didn't like another rooster crowing on their dung heap. He also knew his own importance as a writer. He was, by his own definition, a grassroots historian, and played second fiddle in the orchestra. Yet, he knew he was still necessary to the whole orchestra—or that while he sat at the king's table, he was a little below the salt. Sonnichsen became my best friend, sternest critic, and guide, teaching me more about myself as person and writer. Our subject matter was much the same, he said—characters living in the land of *poco tiempo* and the land of little rain; my West Texas Jacksboro was descant to his El Paso borderlands. One of his favorite hymns, which we were never reluctant to share as duets anywhere, anytime, was "Throw out the lifeline, throw out the lifeline; someone is drifting away"—appropriate for our relationship.

Because almost every work of non-fiction, papers given at various conferences, and later, personal narrative, humorous prose, a play or two, a little music, and, eventually, short fiction was connected in one way or another to my time and place, I felt the need to invent a town and county—Horned Toad, Texas, in Caballo County.

Toad, for short, is one of those plain, no-nonsense names such as Texas is full of: Muleshoe, Levelland, Hereford, Prairie View, and Plainview. Such places

> are marked by aberrant weather, hard-nosed religion, peculiar politics, curious customs, clubs and rituals, some of them having to do with games on horseback. It is ranch country, dry-land farming country, oil country, King James Bible country. West Texans compare their place favorably with the Wilderness of Zion that Moses knew for sure wasn't the Promised Land. The characters, male and female, have their crosses to bear and gospels to proclaim, are various mixtures of saints and sons-of-bitches. They take God's name in vain, swear expertly, quote the scriptures, Edgar A. Guest, and Shakespeare in the same breath, pray mighty prayers, and sing gospel tunes at the drop of a stained Stetson. The litany of brown places is always supplication for rain and their colloquy of praise is ever for it. ("The Chronicles of Toad," *Writing On The Wind*)

There are heroes and heroines among the males and females of Toad. Real heroes in West Texas are mostly football players who've gone on to great college careers or even to the pro ranks. Writers, scientists, politicians, entrepreneurs, even gangsters, hucksters, and crooks, had to move on to a larger arena if they were ever going to get ahead. Schoolteachers occasionally qualified as heroines. Most never wanted or needed to be important people in any of the aforementioned categories. Such people were heroes and heroines to me because they didn't or couldn't go anywhere else, stayed put and made the most of life on earth as it is, not as it is in heaven. One hero, Joe Don Wheelright, and heroine, Annie Laurie Rogers, are typical of mine. Jesse Earl is short, fat, sloppy—"I swear his momma must'a put a nipple on the ketchup bottle when he's a baby"—has a college degree, and is the smartest man in town. He is also kin to the meanest and most dangerous man in town who is running unopposed for the sheriff's office. Annie Laurie is six feet in her stockings. "She was nice enough, but you know, typical ranch woman—bronc buster, roper, shrewd cattle dealer—even rodeoed some. She didn't put a rifle in her pickup. She kept it about her at all times. Talked Spanish real good and hired mostly Mexicans." The unlikely pair team up to elect a write-in candidate and end up falling in love in the process. The narrator muses at their wedding, that he couldn't "understand how such as them two could have married one another. But my wife said at the wedding in her sentimental voice that she figured they both fell in love with the better parts of each other that nobody else could see." ("In Broad Daylight," *Texas Short Stories*).

The one matter not mentioned, for a good reason, is racial prejudice in small-town Texas against African Americans and Mexican Americans. I never write about it because I'm not qualified to do so. Yes, I heard the "N-word" all the time but didn't use it, knowing it was something awful, terrible. Many of the Negroes were descendants of soldiers connected with Fort Richardson in one way or another—may even have been parts of Buffalo Soldier units that were garrisoned there for certain times when they weren't at Fort Concho. All this information was part of the county's history lesson. Everything else was hearsay. I learned soon enough about reality, but was blind to it.

Yes, in the fifties I worried more about needing rain than I did about segregation. The closest thing to a racial joke was from a Jacksboro native who recounted a tale of two local, colorful citizens, John Moore, a lawyer, and Roy Cherryhomes, a land and oilman, whose ancestors helped found Jacksboro. The story goes that John came in Eckman's Café—the only place to eat besides the legendary Green Frog Café—saying that integration was now a legislated fact and blacks could now come in and sit down and eat with "us." Without missing a bite, Roy's reply was, "Yes, and it will serve them right, too."

As to Mexicans—the term "Hispanics" was not even a word then—I knew only one and not personally. The moving picture show portrayed them as fabulous swordsmen and horsemen, even if they were bandits. Who could resist the Cisco Kid—"Ah, Cisco! Ah, Pancho!" The one known to me was the handsomest man I ever saw and had blue eyes. Such a character appears under the nickname of Fudge, a little boy who comes to live with his daddy, a ranch cowboy. In true cowboy tradition, nobody asks anything, certainly not who his mother was—nothing. It's obvious that the little boy is Mexican but has blue, blue eyes—his daddy's eyes. Ma'am, the owner's wife, takes the child under her wing, and it is she who must teach him how to shoot her small pistols. One night Fudge gets her guns off a peg on the wall, goes outside in the dark, practices the draw, fires by mistake and kills Ma'am's cat; then the rest of the ranch is shot up pretty bad by cowboys firing back—at someone:

Gathering back the horses, digging bullets out of the

> bull, mending the corral, scalding dead chickens for plucking and cooking, repairing Manuel's wagon, cleaning the chicken yard off Fudge, ordering more glass for the house windows, and scraping what was left of the cat off the outhouse wall took . . . time. ("A Two-Gun Man," *New Trails: 23 Original Stories of the West*)

Although there was limited practice of personal racial prejudice, I didn't hold back from religious prejudice against any denomination that wasn't mine. There were excellent reasons for not liking other denominations, having to do with serious matters such as hymns, length of sermons, preachers, their wives, who could take the Lord's Supper, when and where, baptism (infant, immersed, or sprinkled); the plan of salvation, once saved always saved, backsliding, falling from grace, the essentials. Two groups, not even classified as denominations, were the Catholics, who had too many children, drank wine instead of Welch's grape juice as God intended, and had services in a foreign language, and the Pentecostals. Both were considered secret organizations. Nobody would have visited either church, although the invitation was always open. The rest of us were in one accord on that matter. We were Christians! The Pentecostals, however, caught the worst of it. There was a negative feeling that amounted to discrimination. For one thing, they didn't look like us—women wore their hair different, and the skirts and sleeves on their dresses were too long. Their services were mysterious: glorious music in four-part harmony that echoed all over town, fiery sermons that caused the congregants to shout in some other foreign language—tongues, they called it. I lived not two blocks from the church and sort of had a front row seat. I longed to go to that church. It was mostly because of the music and their prayers for rain. Their religion was stubborn, hard-headed. They believed in some God that seemed stronger than mine, more demanding. When the Pentecostals prayed for rain, as did every church in the summer, our supplications were weak compared to theirs. A short story, "Won't Somebody Shout Amen?" *(Texas Short Stories II)* pays homage to a group who, like trees planted by the water, shall not be moved.

One more savior entered my later life, a lad from New York City, David Lieber, who is the finest columnist ever to grace the pages of the *Fort Worth Star-Telegram*. He ranks with Molly Ivins. I'm old enough to be his mother, but because of his influence, I wrote folklore columns for the paper for a few years. From that I developed audio columns wherein a person could call a number and hear some news from Horned Toad, Texas—about life in a West Texas town. All of it was fictional truth, of course, based on the characters I'd already written about in other forms, but a few e-mails arrived asking where Horned Toad was on the map and for directions. Every time I tried to write like a journalist, Lieber jerked me back. "Keep being your West Texas self. Nobody likes the other you."

And so I am a West Texas writer successful in a very small puddle, a dried up puddle at that, in the state of Texas. It's all I've ever aspired to, to know and be known here. My work is nothing more than voices speaking maxims, platitudes, scriptures, singing hymns and country songs, quoting and misquoting lines from many sources—naïve voices in the first person often failing to recognize the truth they speak, and always, forever, thirsty for rain and its metaphor. As for me, I am fortunate to know exactly who I am, just as I am, as a writer—once saved, always saved!

Skeeter Hagler

RED STEAGALL

RED STEAGALL is an author, songwriter, poet, recording artist, and radio personality. For over forty years, Steagall has entertained around the globe. In 2006, he was named the Poet Laureate of Texas.

The author of three books of poetry as well as a collection of interviews, Steagall has won five awards from the National Cowboy and Western Heritage Museum in Oklahoma City for his music. In 2003, he was inducted into the museum's Hall of Great Westerners. In 2004, he was inducted into the Texas Cowboy Hall of Fame, and in 2006 was awarded the prestigious Charles Goodnight Award.

Steagall's syndicated radio program, *Cowboy Corner,* is heard in 158 markets in forty-three states and is in its fourteenth year of broadcast.

DRAWING INSPIRATION

I GREW UP in an idyllic setting for a boy who was and is crazy about the history of the cowboys and Indians. The little town of Sanford, Texas, lies about one-half mile south of the Canadian River in the Panhandle of Texas. I spent every hour that I could on that river. I remember sitting on my favorite rock at the top of the river bluff and letting my imagination run away. One day I would go up the trail with Goodnight and the next day I'd fight the "white eyes" with Quanah Parker.

In our little town lived a man named Lou Steen. Lou built a cabin in the area of Sanford before Sanford was a town. He was a government wolf trapper and knew that country like the back of his hand. He taught me how to set coyote traps and how to identify Indian campgrounds by the terrain, the shelter factor, and the availability of fresh water. He already knew where most of the campgrounds were, but with his guidance I found some new ones on my own in later years. I still very much like to hunt for arrowheads and other Indian artifacts.

During the time that I was taking classes at West Texas State College in Canyon, Texas, I spent all of my free weekends in the Palo Duro Canyon looking for fossils and Indian campgrounds. I had neither car nor money to take a girl on a date, and I didn't want to sit around the campus by myself all weekend, so on Friday afternoons I would pay a friend to take me to the south side of the canyon, let me out, and then pick me up on Sunday evening. Gasoline was eleven cents a gallon so I usually paid him a quarter. I bought a mummy sleeping bag, a pack, and a tote bag from an army surplus outlet. The sleeping bag cost a dollar, the pack fifty cents, and the tote bag a quarter. I would get a supply of fresh water in my Boy Scout canteen, fill my pack full of saltine crackers, cheddar cheese, and summer sausage, and I was fixed for a weekend of adventure. I treasure the memories of those weekends alone in the vastness and grandeur of the Palo Duro Canyon. That canyon is a very spiritual place to me. I can still feel the presence of all the people who have lived there for the past 12,000 years.

Sanford, Texas, is located inside the boundaries of the Sanford Ranch. I used to stare in awe of the cowboys who came over from headquarters to work the river country. I wanted so desperately to saddle up and ride with them. Of course I didn't own a saddle or a horse to put it on, but in my mind, I could have been as good a cowboy as any of them. I learned later that you just can't want to be a cowboy without first learning the skills necessary to do the work properly. It made all of the boys in town, all twenty of us, so proud to help fight grass fires, pull a cow out of a quicksand bog, or repair a fence where someone had driven a car through it. In addition to closing gates that someone had left open, we did these things without question. After all, that was our ranch too. The foreman of the Sanford Ranch, Mr. Leonard Whiteside, was our hero and friend. He allowed us to camp anywhere on the ranch as well as hunt rabbits, raccoons, and coyotes. This was his way of saying thanks for all of the extra eyes in our small group of boys.

My mother was a schoolteacher and a really good one. It's amazing how many people I meet who were her students and will take the time to tell me how much my mother's teachings mean to them. She has six offspring, five boys and one beautiful girl. Every one of us knows that she has a favorite, and each of us thinks we're it. It was very important to her for her children to speak and spell properly. What a gift to give to your children. These lessons of self-discipline have been the most beneficial gifts each of us can imagine. I was three when mother taught me my first song. It was "When The Work's All Done This Fall." I fell head over heels in love with storyline songs about the cowboy, and to this day, those songs are still my favorites. I entered my first talent contest at the age of five. I recited a poem mother had taught me entitled "Me and Ma Kilt a Bear." I didn't win, but at that point I was hooked on show business.

I learned to read at an early age. I fell in love with all of the images that came into my mind's eye when I scanned the printed word. Books transported me to places I never dreamed that I would one day see in person. The same thing happened with radio. I would sit enraptured with the scenes I conjured up in my mind by listening to shows like *The Lone Ranger, Fibber McGee and Molly, The Great Gildersleeve,* and most of all, *The Grand Ol' Opry.* When the cloud cover was right, we could get a signal from WSM in Nashville, Tennessee. We had a small Arvin radio that sat on top of a white Servel gas refrigerator. I would sit in a cane-bottom chair on that cold linoleum floor and watch that radio as if it were alive. I envisioned myself a performer on the Grand Ol' Opry stage, never allowing myself to imagine that one day I would be introduced to the audience in that revered hall by my hero, Ernest Tubb. Gosh, how life takes strange turns!

Then, on a Thursday in 1952 Marvin Neely, Gene Packenbush, and I were sitting cross-legged in the middle of Marvin's living room staring at an eleven-inch round Sylvania TV set watching the test pattern. All of a sudden KGNC television in Amarillo went on the air. Our first television experience was to watch Lou Thez whip Wild Red Berry for the West Texas wrestling championship. We became rabid wrestling fans with each of us identifying our own heroes in the wrestling ring.

Another big deal in my life was to play football for the Phillips Blackhawks. I envisioned being good enough to win a scholarship so I could go to college. I wanted desperately to go to Texas A&M University to earn a degree in veterinary medicine. I thought that would give me something to fall back on just in case I couldn't make it in show business. However, in the fall of my junior year in high school, I contracted polio and lost partial use of my left arm. At that time the hand was also useless. There went my football scholarship, so I realized my life would have to take a different direction, and I would have to find another way to go to college. I never doubted that I would find a way to finish school. A college degree was the foremost thing in my life, and for four years, I worked day and night to put myself through college doing everything from shucking feed to breaking horses to running a pool hall. I finally made it in 1960.

Mrs. Harry Miller lived about three miles from town, and she gave the kids of Sanford music lessons. From her, Mother bought a mandolin for ten dollars. I would ride my bike over to her house to take lessons. It took several months to strengthen my fingers to the point that I could make a two or three-finger chord. Soon I could use my entire hand. For my high school senior year graduation, mother bought me a Guild guitar, and I continued to learn more chords. Then that guitar and I went off to college. My freshman year was spent at Frank Phillips Junior College in Borger, Texas. As a sophomore, I transferred to West Texas State College in Canyon where I earned a Bachelor of Science Degree in Animal Husbandry. While at West Texas I joined four other guys in a band, and we played dances on Friday and Saturday nights at the VFW hall. We earned five dollars for the whole band per night. That was a dollar apiece, and in 1957 and 1958, a dollar was as big as a wagon wheel to us. The night we got $150 for a dance in Miami, Texas, we thought we had hit the big time! We thought we were stealing 'em blind and that we would never see a poor day.

It was around that time I started writing songs. They weren't very good, but my roommate thought they were. A childhood friend, Don Lanier, had joined Buddy Knox and Jimmy Bowen to form the group called The Rhythm Orchids. They went on to stardom and actually are credited for inventing rockabilly music. All of West Texas was blooming musically at that time, and everyone who had any talent at all had role models from right there at home. Of course, all of us thought we would be the next Buddy Holly, Jimmy Gilmer, Buddy Knox, the Fireballs, or the next internationally recognized songwriter. In later years, I joined Lanier and Bowen in Hollywood, and Don and I wrote "Here We Go Again" for Ray Charles. Since Ray's recording in 1966, folks like Nancy Sinatra, Dean Martin, Glen Campbell, George Strait, Billy Vaughn, and a host of others have done us the honor of recording that song. We were so happy when Ray Charles and Norah Jones recorded "Here We Go Again" on Ray's last album in 2005. That one's been really good to us.

"Here We Go Again" came about in a very unusual manner and very quickly. When I moved to Hollywood, I knew nothing about the entertainment business, but I did have a background in chemical sales. I got a job with a chemical company. Don Lanier and I had an apartment in north Hollywood. Donny was a session contractor for Jimmy Bowen, and he stayed on the phone a lot. He hated that phone! My office was on the east side of Los Angeles, so I got home late in the afternoon. I stopped by the mailbox and picked up the mail. When I walked into the apartment, Donny was in his bedroom sitting on the edge of the bed playing his guitar. He said, "I've got a little piece of melody that's been floatin' around in my mind." And he played me the lick. About that time the phone rang and he said, "Ah, hell, here we go again." He looked at me and said, "Let 'er ring." He sang the first line, "Here we go again." I immediately sang, "She's back in town again." Then he sang, "I'll take her back again." And I said, "One more time." We finished the song in about ten minutes, showed it to Jimmy Bowen, cut a demo on it that night, and after presenting the song to several people, I took it to Ray Charles, and he recorded it. This was in 1966.

Between 1965 and 1969 approximately sixty of my songs were recorded by other artists. I cut my first chart record in 1969 and have had a marvelous career in country music that has taken me from the White House to the Middle East, Europe, Australia, South America, and the Pacific Rim. Music has allowed me to make friends in places I never dreamed I'd ever see. I am the luckiest guy on this planet.

By 1974 I had put a band together and bought a bus. We traveled 250 days per year from border to border and from coast to coast across this great land of ours. Many nights I couldn't sleep. I would take my guitar to the front of the bus and write songs from the jump seat of that Silver Eagle. I would write about a person I had met, a place that I had seen, or just make up scenes and circumstances. My brother, Danny, would often join me in the front of the bus, and we would write together. Going down the road we started or finished several hundred songs.

In 1975 I went to Nashville to record a new album. My producer was my dear friend Glen Sutton. When I got to Glen's office, he played me a group of songs. I didn't like any of them. Glen got mad and said, "Well, what do you want?" I said, "I want a beer-drinkin', western swing song that the folks in West Texas can appreciate and dance to." Glen said, "Well, how 'bout 'Lone Star Beer and Bob Wills Music'?" I said, "That's exactly what I want." We wrote "Lone Star Beer and Bob Wills Music" in about ten minutes. That was at 4:00 P.M., and we recorded the song at 6:00 P.M.

Another time we were out on the road trying to think of song ideas for a new album, and we were staying in the Rodeway Inn in El Paso, Texas. Danny and I were talking about ideas and the kind of songs we wanted to write. I said, "Danny, we need a plain ol' three-chord country song." Shortly thereafter we had finished "Three Chord Country Song." It became one of our most requested songs, and even today, it's still one of our best dance tunes. By 1983, over 200 of my songs had been recorded by myself and others, and twenty-six of these had reached a national chart position.

By 1985 the world of country music had changed drastically, and I was no longer in the middle of the industry. I was on the fringe and very disappointed. In January of that year, Waddie Mitchell, Hal Cannon, and a group of other poets and folklorists staged the first National Cowboy Poetry Gathering in Elko, Nevada. Danny and I went out to see what it was all about. I was overwhelmed. All of a sudden I found a creative place that not only fascinated and intrigued me but also made me feel at home and introduced me to a group of like-minded people who have become a major force in my life. For twenty-five years, I had not allowed myself to spend creative energies on a piece of work that did not have value in the commercial market. But for the next five years, I wrote nothing but poetry. It was as if all of those ideas had been stored up in my mind since my youth. I had always been especially fond of poetry, especially the works of Robert W. Service, but I had never allowed myself to try to write poetry. After all, I was a hit songwriter.

The National Cowboy Poetry Gathering in Elko has changed the lives of a multitude of people, myself included. All of a sudden we recognized the fact that a large number of people love cowboy poetry and cowboy music. It certainly changed my life and took my career in a different direction. It has also created a world of international recognition for a great number of my friends like Don Edwards, Michael Martin Murphey, Waddie Mitchell, R. W. Hampton, and Baxter Black, just to name a few.

I started writing poetry like I wrote songs, using sympathetic rhymes. One day in Goodwell, Oklahoma, my good friend, the great Montana poet Wallace McRae, insisted that I attend a poetry workshop that he was presenting. After the workshop we went over to Phil Martin's house, and Wallace and my dear compadre Baxter Black got me off to the side. Here's what they told me: "Red, you write well-crafted poems, but your rhyme scheme is not strict, and some of your meter is off." They explained to me that the three most important things about writing poetry are:

1. Original Thought. Try to write something that no one else has said or say it in a unique way.

2. Perfect Rhyme. Don't use a rhyme scheme that is sympathetic.
3. Perfect Meter.

They explained, "You can continue to write as you do now and a lot of people will appreciate what you have to say. Wouldn't it be nice to know that perhaps fifty years from now an English teacher will present your work to her students as a classic example of poetry written during the time that you lived?"

What a forceful and short lesson! I immediately rewrote all of my poems and applied the discipline necessary to write poems from the proper form and perspective. I continue to use that discipline in everything that I do, and it has made a dramatic difference in the pride that I feel about my endeavors and myself.

Ten years before the first Elko gathering, Mrs. Ann Marion and J. J. Gibson invited me to the spring works on the famed 6666 Ranch at Guthrie, Texas. Now, twenty-nine years later, I have not missed the opportunity to ride for a few days with the cowboys. There is no way to explain how much those experiences have meant to my writing and me. I have been able to use the proper lingo in my poems and songs as well as feel confident that I am constructing a realistic portrayal of the life of the West Texas cowboy. I only write about the people that I know and work with because it is so important to me that these hard-working people are recorded in a reverent and realistic light.

In 1994 Nina Ritchie, her son Andrew Bivens, and their ranch manager, Jay O'Brien, first allowed me to bring a group of friends to the JA Ranch in the Palo Duro Canyon of Texas, where we spent a week at the chuck wagon working with the cowboys. It is truly a western experience, and for the past twelve years, we have returned with the feeling that we have, indeed, lived the life of a cowboy. However, the most important thing we do is stay out of the way and have a good time. For me it is simply another window of opportunity to watch people at work doing something that they love and that I admire so much.

I don't write poetry specifically based on personal experience, but I do draw inspiration from events, people, and history. I always try to write in first person because I believe people place themselves in the role of the storyteller. The storyteller then takes them on an adventure. "Ride for the Brand" was written on a cold December night at the old Cedar Top Lodge on the Waggoner Ranch in Wilbarger County, Texas. A group of us were there to hunt and spend time together. A fellow named Paul Whitley had lived in that old lodge by himself for forty-one years. I got to thinking that if anyone ever "rode for the brand," it was Paul Whitley. On Saturday night the cowboys came by to eat with us and play penny ante poker. In their conversations, they mentioned "the brand this" and "the brand that." Then the wagon boss said, "You know, those are our cattle. We calve them out, we feed 'em, we doctor 'em, and make sure they're safe. The family gets the money, but they're our cattle." I looked at the cowboys and at Paul, then stepped outside in the cold night air and wrote "Ride for the Brand" in honor of those dedicated men.

One day I was riding horseback with my friends Don Malone, Virgil Johnson, Virgil's son Duane, and Duane's fourteen-year-old son Doug. Watching Doug, I realized that the ranching industry would not die with Duane's generation. Doug was a cowboy through and through. Today, he runs the family ranch. I turned to Virgil and asked, "How long has your family been on this place?" He said, "My grandfather homesteaded that patch of ground where the house is. When he died, my dad took over. But he was killed in the war, and I took over when I was quite young." He gigged his old horse and rode off. He had said all he had wanted to say about that. As soon as I got to my pickup, I wrote the poem "Born to this Land."

I spent five summers during my youth on my uncle's farm in northwestern Iowa. I probably learned more in those five summers than in the rest of my life put together. One day we were going to work in a field about a mile and a half from headquarters. My uncle looked out his side of the pickup and said, sorta to himself, "I'd give anything in the world if Mr. Cornwall would have those boys plow the rows straight."

I looked out his side of the pickup and all I could see was the next stalk. I looked out our side, and I could see all the way through to the end of the field between each row. I very foolishly said, "Uncle Floyd, what difference does it make? The corn's in the ground, and it's going to grow anyway."

He looked at me and, as the color started rising in his face, he said, "It makes a difference to me. I want to know that I'm the best farmer I can possibly be."

I never forgot that because, at that moment, I realized that I am the captain of my ship. I alone decide my destiny, not my uncle, not my parents, not my teachers, and not the government. I am in charge. Then several years later I read what John Deere said in 1856: "I will never put my name on something that's not as good as the best in me." That experience was the inspiration for "The Fence that Me and Shorty Built."

Throughout my entire career, I had written cowboy songs and tried to include one on each western swing album. However, after I started writing poetry, I just naturally starting using some of those cowboy ideas to write songs for my western albums. Some of the first ones that I wrote were rodeo songs because I was associated with rodeo as an entertainer. For about seventeen years, we performed at thirty-five to forty rodeos a year.

The world of rodeo became my extended family, and I wrote songs about my friends and things that I saw in the rodeo arena. For example, "The Ballad of Freckles Brown" was inspired by Freckles himself. He was a wonderful person, very engaging and everyone had nothing but good things to say about him. He was every bull rider's hero. In December of 1974, I made a trip to the National Finals Rodeo in Oklahoma City. It was there that I met Freckles and was privileged to watch a tape of his historic ride on Jim Shoulder's bull, Tornado. The story of his ride on this bull was legendary long before 1974. By 1967 the bull had never been ridden after being bucked out over 200 times. Freckles was the first person to ride him a full eight seconds. The night that he qualified on Tornado was December 1, 1967, at the National Finals Rodeo in Oklahoma City. That night the average age of the bull rider in the arena was nineteen-and-a-half- years old. Freckles was forty-six. I was hooked on the idea of writing a song about this legendary bull rider and his night of fame on an unrideable bull. I couldn't wait to get on a plane back to Nashville and write that song. I had it finished by the time we landed. The rest of that rodeo album is a tribute to all of my rodeo competitor friends. It is still in release and is a very popular album among rodeo contestants young and old.

Some of the first songs that I wrote about the West and ranch people were "The Wagon Tongue" and "When The Cimarron Was Red and on the Rise." To date we have recorded eight cowboy albums. Although we still play a few western swing dances a year, the majority of my time is spent performing for audiences who love and appreciate the songs of the West and the working cowboy. As a result of my involvement in the cowboy music genre, I started a radio show in 1994 called *Cowboy Corner.* Today we are in over 160 markets in forty-three states and have a loyal and dedicated audience. It is so rewarding to play cowboy music and recite poetry to my audience and to interview people who continue to have a dramatic influence on the image of our beloved western way of life.

Throughout my life, I have drawn my inspiration from these men and women of the soil and have learned invaluable lessons about the handling of cattle, horses, and the environment. However, I attribute whatever success I have had in the world of music and poetry to those childhood experiences that let my imagination run wild and prepared me to write about the people who I admire the most. I would never have been able to express myself properly without the guidance and love of my wonderful, exceptional mother, Ruth. I still live the majority of my life through the written word. It takes me to places that I would otherwise never be able to visit and introduces me to people that it would have been impossible to meet in this lifetime. I feel that from my experiences and my rock solid upbringing, I have lived six lifetimes, and I know that I am greatly blessed and extremely fortunate.

For all of these gifts I am eternally grateful and deeply honored.

Pat Stowers

CARLTON STOWERS

AMONG THE MORE than two dozen books authored by Carlton Stowers are *To the Last Breath* and *Careless Whispers,* both winners of the Mystery Writers of America's Edgar Allen Poe Award for the Best Fact Crime Book of the Year. Stowers' books have been selections of the Book of the Month Club, Literary Guild, Mystery Book Club, and others. Five of his books have been optioned by motion picture/television production companies. *Careless Whispers* inspired the CBS Movie of the Week *Sworn to Vengeance,* and *Open Secrets* was the basis for the ABC mini-series *Telling Secrets.* Stowers' writings have been translated into German,

French, Japanese, Swedish, Dutch, Afrikaans, and Spanish. He has won numerous state, regional, and national awards.

UNIVERSAL TRUTHS IN YOUR OWN BACK YARD

SOME YEARS AGO I read a quote from famed Texas novelist Larry McMurtry in which he boldly described himself as a Minor Regional Novelist, even posing in a T-shirt with the title proudly stenciled across its front. This, of course, was in his younger days, long before he'd won a Pulitzer Prize, had written an Academy Award-winning screenplay, and regularly climbed to lofty spots on bestseller lists. Yet, despite late-arriving prosperity and star status, little seems to have changed as the one-time literary prodigy from Archer City has advanced well into his AARP days.

Talent and riches aside, the thing I most admire about the man is his stubborn insistence that the best of his subject matter is still found in his own back yard, that he still holds firmly to a belief that he need not travel east, west or abroad to seek out the universal truths that could be better told by his neighbors.

That awareness, frankly, is the only kinship Mr. McMurtry and I enjoy. Before you bother reading further, consider yourself duly warned that my own successes are light years removed from *Lonesome Dove* territory, that I've never paraded along red carpets, and I no longer even bother to check the *New York Times* bestseller lists for my name.

Yet as I've pursued a career as a journalist and author of nonfiction books, I too have been reluctant to stray too far. I am, by determined dedication, a regional writer, a literary homebody. Send me on an assignment beyond the Texas borders and my confidence and interest decline with equal speed. Only when writing about my native state, speaking its language, describing its landscape, sharing its mores and history, do I feel I'm giving the reader a fair shake for his investment in time and cover price.

Maybe I should get a T-shirt.

And before you question the judgment of such self-imposed tethering, consider that the well I've regularly visited for lo these many years is deep; the boundaries I've limited myself to stretch farther than the eye could ever hope to see.

Once, while residing in the picturesque Texas Hill Country, attempting to jump-start a self-employed career by hacking out endless articles for newspaper Sunday supplements and magazines you've never heard of, I received an urgent call from an editor in Chicago, desperately in need of some story being played out in Texarkana, on the state's far northeastern border. While the subject now escapes me, I do recall him repeatedly insisting that time was of the essence. Could I drive there quickly and get the story to him in forty-eight hours? Physically impossible, I replied. He seemed more than a little nonplussed and no doubt viewed me as something of a country bumpkin smart-ass when I went on to point out that he was actually closer to Texarkana than I was and suggested he just high-tail it there himself if he was in such an almighty hurry.

What he had no grasp of was the fact that Texas is, pardon my French, a big-ass place: urban and rural, deserts to dense forests, sweeping plains to sandy coastal beaches; inhabited by filthy rich and dirt poor, famous and infamous, saints and sinners. We don't find it unusual that we've got our hustlers and con men living next door to the hard-working, God-fearing Joneses or that one man's nutty religious zealot is another's Heaven-bound role model. It's all here: the good, the bad and downright ugly. So far, we can still brag that the latter remain in the minority (though, having not yet read today's newspaper, I cannot swear that statistic still holds). Our football teams have won Super Bowls, we've sent men off to the White House to rule over the western world, have damn good chili and chicken fried steak, and ample quantities of Shiner beer. Too, country music icon Willie Nelson is ours, born and bred, and is, for my money, the best wordsmith the state has ever produced. What more to ask for?

As a writer, I can think of nothing.

Usually within a quick car drive or short plane ride, I can sit down with an incredible variety of people in equally fascinating places, gathering information that allows me to introduce the reader to something new and, hopefully, of interest.

Still, the battle to earn a living in a confined space, however far-reaching, goes on. New York publishers, many of them still convinced that fiddlin' contests and horse operas are the only thing playing down here in the Lone Star State, remain a hard sell. If I had a buck for every book proposal or story suggestion I've had turned down because some tweedy, pipe-smoking easterner viewed it as "too regional," I'd be loaning McMurtry money.

For example: It was back in the early eighties when, following a lengthy career in newspaper journalism, I decided the time had come to devote more effort to book-length projects. I knew only that I wanted to tell nonfiction stories that offered the widest range of human emotion possible. I hadn't a clue what that meant or where it might lead me—until an old high school and college buddy dropped by for a visit. Ned Butler was then a prosecutor in the McLennan County District Attorney's office, preparing for the trial of a Waco man accused of the murder of three teenagers. As he sat on my patio that summer evening telling the nightmarish story, it was not the foul deeds of the murderer that particularly interested me. Rather, I was far more engrossed by his remarks about the shortened lives of the innocent victims, how their devastated parents had dealt with the evil forces and unanswered questions that had invaded their once-normal lives, the effect on law enforcement officers duty-bound to involve themselves in such an evil and troubling tale, investigating and seeking resolve and justice.

The story being told me had all the dramatic and emotional elements I was looking for. And New York editors could not have cared less. Almost without exception their turndowns included the polite but tired litany, "too regional." Finally, having grown weary of the same refrain, I fired off a response to the latest nay-sayer, summoning the same smartmouth wit I'd used on the Chicago editor years earlier: "I wonder," I wrote, "just how many people in New York had heard of Holcomb, Kansas, before Truman Capote traveled there to gather material for his legendary and award-winning crime book, *In Cold Blood*?"

Of course, I got no reply. But eventually I did get a contract—with Taylor Publishing, a small Texas publisher based in Dallas that offered encouragement, a measure of enthusiasm and even a small amount of advance money to get me through what would be a two-year project. I snapped it up and went to work. And in 1985 the hardback edition of

Careless Whispers was published. It is appropriate, I suppose, that it was initially distributed primarily to Texas book stores. But the sales were good, most reviews warm, and, lo and behold, it was honored by the New York-based Mystery Writers of America as the year's Best Fact Crime Book (the same award, incidentally, that had been presented several years earlier to the urbane Capote and his *In Cold Blood*). Suddenly, one of the same big city publishing houses that had viewed the book as "too regional" was making a substantial offer to publish it in paperback. West Coast moviemakers were calling. Foreign rights were being purchased. As this is written, two decades after its initial publication, the book remains in print both domestically and in faraway outposts like Germany to Japan, and if you are prone to insomnia you can still catch the occasional rerun of the TV movie it spawned.

In darker moments I like to refer to it as my Revenge of the Regional Writer. In kinder days I see it only as a simple reminder that a good story, fiction or fact, told as best a writer can tell it, can leap beyond all geographic boundaries. Ask far better craftsmen than I'll ever be: bestselling novelists like Texas' own Cormac McCarthy and Elmer Kelton.

You'll not likely find the description in any literary text, but simply put, I am a matchmaker. I seek out people and places, situations, and circumstances that interest me to a degree that I feel duty bound to share them with others. Whether it is internationally famous Houston attorney Richard (Racehorse) Haynes, spinning colorful tales of headline-making cases, a quiet Brownwood florist named Ed Devery reflecting on his New Rochelle, New York, childhood when he posed for many of those nostalgic *Saturday Evening Post* covers drawn by next-door neighbor Norman Rockwell, or accused rapist Donald Wayne Good, telling the heartbreaking story of how DNA testing done two decades after his conviction proved him innocent of the crime, their unique stories are prime grist for a writer's mill. And I'm delighted to serve as the middleman. *Mr. and Mrs. Reader, please allow me to introduce you to...*

And while, admittedly, I've sometimes tended the mortgage and made the car payment by accepting travel fare to faraway places, there to interview celebrities ranging from self-important movie stars to stuffy politicians and business world wheelers and dealers, rarely do I recall them as moments of any great achievement and will mention them no further. I've dutifully recorded and written all the clever-but-well-worn phrases and talking points others before me have heard and reported. As I've mentioned, it helps pay the bills, even if one is occasionally forced to type with one hand while holding his nose with the other. It is what you do if you aren't Stephen King or haven't experienced the good fortune to have a Rich Aunt Sally pass along that small fortune she'd secretly rat-holed through all those scrimp-and-save years down at the Old Folks Home.

Truth is, however, financial reward seldom enters the picture when one stumbles upon the magical subject that begs to be written, the one nobody else has discovered or, had they, somehow failed to see its true merit. If I have a valid talent to claim, it is in the recognition of (and appreciation for) stories that lend themselves to a broader readership than one might at first expect. They are out there, along the back roads, off the interstate, in the big city back alleys, and I have long been their happy hunter.

Give me the little no-stoplight community of Hye, Texas, where, back in the long ago days of town baseball, the team was made up of nine brothers and I'm on the phone to *Sports Illustrated*. Did you know that the second largest meteor crater in the United States can be found just a few miles outside of Odessa? Pull up a chair and let me tell you about it. Rich and varied, there are Texas yarns to be spun in every direction. And I've got the odometer to prove it. I've spent time out west in the Big Bend, gathering material for a book on a teacher in the state's last one-room school, traveled up into the Panhandle to sit at the kitchen table with a couple of Wicca devotees, then to Texarkana to write about the legendary and never apprehended Phantom Killer. With an apology to my fiction-writing friends, you can't make this stuff up.

This begs the question I've routinely heard when invited to speak at the Blue-Haired Babes Book Club or noon gatherings of fun-loving Rotarians: "Where do you get your ideas?"

I'd dearly love to brag that it is some degree of crafty investigative know-how, maybe even direction divinely sent. Alas, it is far simpler. Stir in equal parts dumb luck, friendly phone calls, and a large dose of garden-variety curiosity and you've got all one needs—that and a keen awareness that Texas is brim-full of serial killers and millionaires, brilliant lawyers and crooked politicians, great educators and superb athletes, musicians, and actors and, most important, ordinary people with extraordinary stories to tell.

Truth is, they're not hard to find; you just need to know where to look.

Some time back I was reading a small sports page item announcing the fact that the Asherton High School Trojans had, after several futile seasons, finally won a basketball game. No big deal, really, until I got to the final throw-away sentence which informed the reader that the Trojans' hapless football team had already established a national record for consecutive losses. That one line set off an explosion of questions: How, in a state where high school football success is legendary, could any team be so bad? Why did they continue such an exercise in embarrassing futility? How did the surely embarrassed townspeople show their faces on Friday nights? And, where in the hell was Asherton anyway?

I found it deep in South Texas, a dot-on-the-map migrant worker community where there were no paved streets, all save one student qualified for the government-sponsored free lunch program, and where the two-dollar woes of daily living abounded. That the school board and townspeople saw the worth in fielding a team, however unsuccessful, was pretty damn remarkable. A kind editor at *Parade* magazine agreed its millions of readers might be interested.

The story was published, and the reading public was not only taken by Asherton's woes but was moved to respond. Small donations rolled in as encouraging mail postmarked from sea to shining sea arrived in Asherton High's mailbox. A Catholic grade school in Pittsburgh adopted the Trojans as "their team"; so did the inmates of the Atlanta, Georgia, Federal Penitentiary. Several college graduates phoned to offer their services as pro bono assistant coaches. An NFL team donated new equipment.

Asherton's story was there, hidden and waiting to be told. I simply had the pleasure of driving the getaway car, making the introduction.

Visits to such aforementioned people and places have, in recent years, served as brief and welcomed escape from more lengthy and demanding writing tasks. With not the slightest intent, I became, in the wake of the minor success of *Careless Whispers*, a true crime writer. While not even looking for a genre pigeonhole to climb into, I found myself fitted into one. Not, understand, that I'm either complaining or apologizing. We regional writers can't be choosy.

For the better part of two decades, when my agent and/or editor would ask what I planned my next book project to be, they already had the answer in mind. It did me absolutely no good to suggest the definitive biography of Robert E. Howard, one-time Cross Plains resident and the creator of adventure tale hero Conan the Barbarian, or the *Hundred Best Recipes for Chuck Wagon Cooking*. Their response was predictable: Why not write another true crime book?

Which I did at eighteen-month to two-year intervals, always careful to pick Texas settings. In the small town of Midlothian I wrote of a young undercover police officer who, while posing as a high school student in an effort to ferret out the teenaged drug dealers, was shot and killed by the sixteen-year-old son of a Dallas police officer. The crime and all of the tragic irony in *Innocence Lost,* however, played second chair to the story of the devastation it rained on the once-quiet community. When, after five years of futile investigation, the Richardson police finally determined that a wealthy socialite had orchestrated the hired killing of her husband's girlfriend, I chose to write *Open Secrets,* in which I chased a serpentine and bizarre case from Texas to France and back. After spending considerable time in little Alvin, south of Houston, *To The Last Breath* resulted, telling of three remarkable women—a private investigator/grandmother, a police detective, and an assistant district attorney—who combined efforts to prove that a ne'er-do-well father was, in fact, responsible for the death of his two-year-old daughter.

Along the way I detoured briefly to help a colorful FBI agent tell his war stories, co-authored the recollections of a Texas prison chaplain whose job it was to keep men bound for the death chamber company in their final hours, and was the ghostwriter for a Texas private eye with an uncanny ability to solve the unsolvable. When it occurred to me that so many people had openly and candidly confided how their once private lives had been battered and bruised by unspeakable crime, I realized I could do no less. After long consideration and numerous starts and stops, I finished *Sins of the Son,* an autobiographical reflection on the troubled relation between me and my long imprisoned firstborn.

And while I had always attempted to choose my subject matter carefully, making a concentrated effort to make each book in some way unique, I began to feel the walls of my pigeonhole closing in. Even the magazine editors who called had begun increasingly to request crime stories. *People* wanted one on an East Texas funeral home attendant and church choir member who, after killing his aging and contrary female benefactor, neatly hid her body away in a freezer. Others wanted profiles of forensic specialists, jury selection experts, or haunting tales like the one played out in tiny Bangs, Texas, where a family, remodeling the attic of their rural home, discovered in a crawl space a throw-away sack that contained the mummified remains of three tiny infants.

Not to say there weren't lighter moments. My favorite came from an editor at *Texas Parks & Wildlife* magazine eager for a story on a midnight bulldozing of a bird sanctuary that had defied several city ordinances and enraged naturalists. "We'd like for you to write it," the editor suggested, "like one of your true crime stories." I didn't know whether to be flattered or amused.

Still, the fact of the matter was I had begun to feel I had spent about all the time on the dark side that I wanted and began to look to some way to reinvent myself professionally. More and more I found myself longing to write about subjects that were alive, well, and reasonably carefree.

Breaking away, however, wasn't easy.

One evening a long-distance call came from a young Wichita Falls woman named Catie Reid, asking in a pleasant voice if I was the person who had written *Careless Whispers.*

No sooner had I acknowledged authorship, than she began to spin a remarkable tale: Her older sister and one of the Waco victims I'd written about years earlier had, for a time, been best friends. And, she went on to say, her sister had also been the victim of a homicide just months after the Waco murders were making headlines. Small world, Texas.

There had, in fact, been a series of killings that had occurred in Wichita Falls, beginning in the winter of 1984. Three unsolved cases—the murders of her sister and two other young women—had languished for fifteen years before a bricklayer-turned-district attorney's office investigator had determined that one man had committed the crimes. An arrest, I was told, had finally been made. The long and tragic saga now had a beginning, a middle, and, at long last, an ending, she quietly explained, and she felt the complex tragedy should be told.

It didn't take me long to agree. The story presented a new challenge, that of weaving several stories into one, providing the reader some insight into how families, none known to the other, had negotiated through a decade and a half of not knowing who had taken the lives of their children. Once again the research process put me into the company of a remarkable cast of characters and in a vast and stark part of Texas about which I'd never before written.

No one I encountered was more interesting than the thirty-year-old woman who had first alerted me to the story. Catie Reid, just thirteen years old at the time of her sister's death, had for years been the family rock, never faltering in her determination that justice would one day be done. In the acknowledgments of *Scream at the Sky*, written two years after our first telephone conversation, I noted that if I'd had a daughter I would have hoped her to be just like Reid.

When the book was published I followed my traditional

routine of sending copies out to those whose lives I'd been allowed to chronicle so they might have the opportunity to read the book before it appeared in the stores. It is always an anxious time, filled with sleep-robbing concern that those who had so willingly confided in me might somehow feel betrayed, however unintentional.

Catie Reid, as I'd expected, was the first to respond. "I've just finished your book," she told me late one evening, "and I'm so very proud of it."

It was far and away the best review I'd ever received. She suggested I drive up the following week for lunch with her, her sister, and an aunt who would be visiting from San Diego. Not to rehash troubled times or discuss the book but, rather, just a friendly get-together. I wasted no time accepting the invitation.

Thus, on an early Thursday afternoon I sat in the company of the three women I'd not known until interviews and trials and repeated checking of facts had brought us together. It was one of those clear, cloudless days when all about the world seems right. I remember there being a great deal of laughter and Catie talking of plans she and her husband had to build a lakeside home nearby. She drove me to the hillside lot they had purchased and proudly pointed out where the house she had helped design would soon be under construction.

I returned home through the suddenly more attractive North Texas landscape in high spirits. I rolled down my windows to breathe in the sweet smell of an early evening breeze. Not only had my book been well received by all, but for the first time since I'd known Catie Reid she seemed genuinely happy, looking eagerly forward instead of into the dark and angry past. There was about her a calm that only new-found resolve and answered questions can offer. Finally, a bright and welcomed future loomed ahead.

Then, just two days later, a call came from her aunt. Her voice was fragile and she was crying as she spoke. Catie, she informed me, had died in an automobile accident just hours earlier.

In the days leading up to the funeral, I found myself asking questions for which there were no satisfactory answers, trying vainly to make sense of the senseless. How could something like this happen to someone so young and with such promise, a vibrant young woman who had experienced a lifetime of doubt and despair, followed by only a brief moment of relief and optimism?

As I grieved her loss, it occurred to me that I could not explain such an unwarranted tragedy any better than I had the cruel and senseless murders I'd written about for too many years. The world, however warm and bright it might seem, is filled with heartbreaks I shall never fully comprehend.

And if I don't understand them, what right do I have to write about them?

So, even as my mother's time-worn warning to "never say never" loudly echoed, I knew I was done with another stage of my career. If not forever, at least for a lengthy respite. Someone else could be the true crime writer. I would look to greener literary pastures.

My next stop, then, would not be a crime scene or a courtroom but, rather, tiny Penelope, Texas, population 211. There a rich and almost magical story awaited telling (though convincing the good folks on Publishers' Row was, again, no easy matter). Within the down-at-the-heels city limits of this rural community were people I felt the outside world should know, pursuing a lifestyle so quiet and ordinary as to be both foreign and fascinating to those who populate today's clock-racing world. I chose to focus *Where Dreams Die Hard* on the town's small school, its struggling six-man football team and its people, young and old. In Penelope, the most serious crime I encountered occurred when a farmer's cattle broke through a fence to dine on the freshly-mown grass of the football field the night before a big game.

In the hardscrabble Central Texas community, I once asked who the richest man in town was and was quickly told, "We don't have one." Theirs is a paycheck-to-paycheck world where the coin of the realm is a simple act of caring and kindness, a hand outstretched to help a neighbor.

Though the book peaked light years removed from blockbuster status, it made it from hardback to paperback, and last word I heard, the publisher had recently ordered a new printing. The old regional writer was still alive and well.

Thus, I will continue to wander my neighborhood, knowing full well there are untold stories there, in my heart and homeland, somewhere just over the next rise, beyond the distant stand of cedars, waiting along some windswept back road; in my Texas' storied past, fascinating present, and God willing, its future.

Julie Metteaur Vick

FRANCES BRANNEN VICK

FRAN VICK is the retired director and co-founder of the University of North Texas Press and founder and president of E-Heart Press, Inc. She holds BA and MA degrees in English from the University of Texas at Austin and Stephen F. Austin State University, respectively, and a Doctor of Humane Letters (*honoris causa*) from the University of North Texas. As a press director, she has published more than 200 books, with topics ranging from folklore, history, literary criticism, science, biography, poetry, novels, short stories, and creative nonfiction.

Vick has served as president of the Texas Institute of Letters and vice president of the Texas State Historical

Association. She is a Fellow of the Texas Folklore Society, member of the Philosophical Society of Texas, and Life Member of the Texas State Historical Association and the East Texas Historical Association.

CONFESSIONS OF A TEXAS PUBLISHER / WRITER

I KNOW THIS WILL come as a shock to those of you who have heard me speak with my East Texas twang, but I am terribly provincial. It is embarrassing to be so provincial, but there it is. Furthermore, I come by it naturally, even genetically, perhaps, from deep in my family DNA. My brother and I have often discussed the year we spent during World War II in Laguna Beach, California, while our father was stationed at El Toro Marine Base. Having spent all our lives in East Texas, we thought we were in the most glamorous place in the world. And we may have been. After all, Mother sold Bing Crosby some shoelaces at the local store where she was working. Our mother loved California and the artist colony she found herself in, but when our father left the marines he headed back to Texas, bringing the rest of us with him, of course. He had been gone more than long enough to suit him. My brother laments the fortune we missed by not selling East Texas land and buying land around Laguna Beach and thus becoming part of the boom in southern California after the war. I have always doubted that myself. For one thing I doubt that the $10 to $25 an acre to be gotten for East Texas farm land at that time would have bought much around Laguna Beach. For another, fortunes do not seem to come easily to this family.

But back to this DNA business. My father's people swam the Sabine ten years before the Civil War and Mother's family came in 1824 and helped start the Fredonian Rebellion, being people who were ahead of their time since the real revolution was some ten years off. So of course I am so Texan that it is ridiculous, thus making me provincial in many ways.

How can it but help affect my interest in Texas writing? I love this state. I love the people. I love the writers and the publishers. I love its history and its characters. I love the state even when I hate what is happening here on occasion. I even love the crazy climate. This past week it went in a three-day span from spring with temperatures in the 80s to winter and freezing with snow flying, then to a lovely fall day. Somehow we missed a summer day, unless you want to count that 80-degree day as early summer—*very* early summer, before the 100 degree plus hits. Next to lamenting losing football games, Texans love to complain about and make observations about the weather.

Deep down in that DNA there is always a Texan. So how does this affect me? It doesn't prevent me from exploring new places intellectually and even literally, but I do seem to inspect and even compare what I find to that Texan DNA. As an East Texan there may be southern roots in there, but there is also something that always pulls me west to the wide-open spaces of West Texas and beyond, so that southernness is very much tempered by the pull of the West, perhaps inspired by that golden year in Laguna Beach. Or perhaps I am inspired by the openness of the terrain, the big sky—not closed in as is East

Texas with its tall pines and forests. Perhaps the personalities of the people seem a bit like that, too.

On the other hand, the only poetry (if it can be called poetry) I have ever written, which I would be embarrassed to show anyone, was on a trip to New York City, but who knows? If I had found a life there I could perhaps have become a poet. I doubt that, though. My poetry never sounded like a Naomi Nye or a St. Germain or a Jan Seale or a Walt McDonald or a William Barney or any of the poets I ended up publishing at one time or another. Not anywhere close to it. What I became instead was a publisher of those poets and other writers, with particular emphasis on Texas writers. I was learning and absorbing all the time I was publishing.

First I published from my own press, E-Heart Press, named after my father's old family cattle brand—those Sabine swimmers. I began, it seems to me in my arrogance, very close to the top with a Texas Folklore Society publication—*Built in Texas,* edited by the best of the best, F. E. Abernethy. Ab became my mentor in publishing, as J. Frank Dobie had been to Bill Wittliff. I was never a designer as was Bill, who, in addition to being a publisher, was also a writer, screenwriter, and photographer. No way to follow that act. Wittliff produced striking books out of Encino Press for the Texas Folklore Society and others, and many of them are collector's items today. When Bill basically stopped publishing I stepped in with E-Heart Press to take up some of the slack with the Texas Folklore Society publications. I was learning from the bottom up since I knew nothing about publishing. I had been teaching English all those years before, so it was a fast learning curve. I had lots of help—from F. E. Abernethy, Bill Shearer and many others. I published and/or reprinted some twenty books with F. E. Abernethy.

The Texas Folklore Society Publications were the hook on which I hung my entire publishing career, both E-Heart Press and the University of North Texas Press. There is no way to discount their importance to me and to the presses I was involved with. It brought me many writers who were members of the society, such as Jim Lee with his *Classics of Texas Fiction* and later *Texas, My Texas.* He was also a friend who was instrumental in getting me to help found the University of North Texas Press. Other folklorists were Joe Graham with his work on the ranches and people and folklore of South Texas. Alan Govenar and Jay Brakefield brought their work on Deep Ellum in Dallas. Roy Bedichek's letters to his family kept me laughing when I wasn't musing about his observations. Ken Davis just kept me laughing with his *Black Cats, Hoot Owls and Water Witches.* The title alone gives pause, you have to admit. Those early years were full of diverse publications, such as Jim Hoggard's take on the Bobby Johnson story, the man who faked his death in the Gulf.

Archie MacDonald called on me one day, and I was sure he would be giving me some treatise on Texas history. What he brought me was *Helpful Cooking Hints for House-husbands of Uppity Women,* which took him to the *Today* show because of his title. Lou Rodenberger and Sylvia Grider, with their interest in *Texas Women Writers* (with a book by that title) gave me a slot in the book. Lou then allowed me to keep her classic *Her Work* in print.

As I published and read Texas writers, I learned from their writings and from them. What I learned is that they are all as different as they can be and yet Texan to the core. Elmer Kelton is always at home in his part of the state in West Texas, and he makes his reader comfortable there, too. Although I never published Elmer, except in Texas Folklore

Society books, perhaps, I published Judy Alter's critical biography of him. Earlier my good friend Ellen of Ellen Temple Publishing and E-Heart Press co-published Judy's *Maggie* books. John Erickson delighted us with the antics of his cowdog, Hank, who was in charge of security on the ranch in the Panhandle, which I did not publish. However, he also wrote of his own adventures cowboying and his observations of the people of the Panhandle, and I was lucky enough to publish those. Joyce Roach is most comfortable in her *Cross Timbers,* sometimes getting the rest of us tickled with her escapades at revivals and other places but also informing us of the cowgirls of the state and the region. She, on occasion, fights it out with Robert Flynn on who has the best hometown—Chillicothe or Jacksboro. Flynn, with his Baptist boots firmly planted in the West, keeps us entertained, but he also makes us think about the travails as well as joys of the old folks who went before.

A.C. Greene, who never forgot the Abilene he came from, moved easily into Dallas life and literature, although some of the books from his West Texas days are hard to forget—*The Santa Claus Bank Robbery* being one of them, as is his classic *A Personal Country.* However, he also gave us *The Highland Park Woman*. East Texan Jane Roberts Wood went west as a child and was forever marked by it, although she occasionally travels back east to her first roots in her novels. Her first *Lucy* book, published by Ellen Temple, took us west in her classic *The Train to Estelline* but brought us back east for *A Place Called Sweet Shrub* and then back out west again for the third book in the *Lucy* trilogy—*Dance A Little Longer.* We kept the books in print as a trilogy, as they had been planned to be.

My Cajun buddy, Gary Lavergne, explores the minds of the murderers he comes across or hears about and seems to be happiest lost in the minds of killers whose evil and horrifying deeds have changed our criminal justice system. He explores Charles Whitman and his tower murders that brought us SWAT teams and a diabolical serial killer from Rosebud, Texas, who changed the pardon process, among others. How this happy Cajun got into this remains a mystery to me.

I was lucky enough to run across Evelyn Oppenheimer, Jean Andrews, and Madge Roberts, all of whom fulfilled some dreams of mine. Evelyn's agenting brought me Stanley Marcus's work and an added bonus was her own memoir of her years in books. She enriched me in many other ways, including telling me when I was wrong and always being totally honest with me. That unusual and recognizable voice of hers giving book reviews was one that radio listeners recognized and listened to for decades. It always brought me up short. I wasn't going to argue with her and that marvelous voice. Not for a minute. It is a rare gift to have such a friend.

Jean Andrews, with her impeccable scholarship, her exquisite art, and her dry wit was always a joy to work with. Her *American Wildflower Florilegium* allowed me to publish a four-color book in a stunning presentation that contained both her art and her scholarship. She followed that with *Pepper Trail* and her research that makes her The Pepper Lady.

Madge Roberts brought me Sam Houston and the letters he had written to his family. What a treat that was, coming from a descendant of the man himself. The letters were contained in four volumes and could not have been done without Madge because she knew where all the bones were buried, so to speak. Following on the heels of Sam Houston came Jane Monday and Patricia Smith with Sam Houston's servant, Joshua Houston. Jane would later lead me into the world of South Texas, inviting me to co-author a book with her on

Petra Kenedy, *Petra's Legacy.*

Evelyn bringing Stanley Marcus to the press was a great honor and pleasure. He was one of my heroes and role models. I have hanging on my wall a letter Mr. Stanley wrote lauding me as a publisher. I treasure it because it is from him, about me. He writes that publishing his books with me "was a delightful experience because she performed for me, and for others I know, better than anyone in the publishing field with whom I've had experience. She not only kept her word, but she delivered far more than she promised. She was a delight to work with at all times and if anyone in her industry has given publishing a polished-eye instead of a black-eye, it would have to be Frances Vick." I can die happy now. I have been handed kudos by my hero.

Some of the other major male writers I was lucky enough to publish were David Westheimer with his *Death is Lighter Than a Feather,* the story of what might have happened if we had been forced to invade Japan to win World War II; Marshall Terry with *Land of Hope and Glory;* Bryan Woolley and other writers from the *Dallas Morning News* with *Final Destinations;* Rod Davis with *American Voodoo;* Pete Gunter with *The Big Thicket,* a cause he has championed for years and continues to do so. Kent Biffle brought his *A Month of Sundays,* collected columns of his work in the *Dallas Morning News.*

Lynn Cuny made me fall in love with buzzards because of her wonderful stories from her wildlife sanctuary, one of them being about a heroic buzzard with a wounded wing making it impossible for her to fly. She walked back no one knows how many miles to the sanctuary after being blown away by a storm. I will never look at buzzards with the same eyes again, nor most wild animals, thanks to Lynn's observations in *Through Animals' Eyes.*

I was lucky to be able to publish some of my heroes. Stanley Marcus, as already mentioned, and Helen Corbitt. How could I have started out my adult life without her cookbook firmly tucked under my arm? I read Helen's cookbooks the way one reads a novel. And I still do. Robert Asprey's *At Belleau Wood* had been a book my father read, which, since he participated in that battle in World War I, was of great interest to me. It was like touching my father again to meet Asprey and keep that book in print.

Because Chancellor Al Hurley of the University of North Texas led one of the most famous and intellectually stimulating seminars on military history in the country, I began publishing military history. That brought to me the delightful Frank "Foo" Fujita, a Japanese American from Abilene, Texas, of all places, with his inspiring story of capture by the Japanese in World War II. Foo was one in a million, along with Cal Chrisman who brought me *Lost in the Victory,* observations of the children of the men who were killed in World War II, stories that had not been told before of the effect of war on the families of the men killed in the war. There were books by a naval intelligence officer behind Japanese lines in China, *Wenbon,* Mexican War letters of a young lieutenant, and letters of an army doctor from the 56th Evac hospital in Italy, among many others. I have always been fond of letters and diaries. Could be snoopiness or something akin to it that finds these writings so interesting, but also it is a first person observation of a life, an intriguing thing to explore. It has a tendency to put me "right there" in the moment with the writer of the letter or the diary.

The joy of putting people in print who had been ignored, such as James Thomas Jackson and his revealing *Waiting in Line at the Drugstore,* Eddie Stimpson and his memoir of being raised in Plano in *My Remembers* are two that come to mind. G. William Jones brought me *Black Cinema Treasures Lost and Found,* about the cache of films he found in a Tyler warehouse. Those films and the knowledge of them would have been lost without Bill Jones. A. C. Greene reminded me that the *WPA Guide to Dallas* was languishing in the Dallas Public Library and had been there since the 1930s, waiting to be published, so together with the library we brought that out.

Jay Milner brought his often hilarious *The Confessions of a Maddog, A Romp through the High-flying Texas Music and Literary Era of the Fifties to the Seventies.* What a hoot that was to read and to publish. Who could forget the wild flaming ride with the legendary newspaperman Stanley Walker riding shotgun in Jay's William Randolph Hearst, being pulled through Lampasas by a dilapidated green pickup truck? Walker had written Jay that he had better hurry on his visit as, Walker writes, "I think I am entering my THIRD childhood and there are weevils in my cortex." It turned out to be throat cancer in his cortex, unfortunately. Or Jay's experiences with Billy Lee Brammer of *The Gay Place* fame or any of the other Mad Dogs: Bud Shrake, Dan Jenkins, Gary Cartwright, Larry L. King, Jerry Jeff Walker, Willie Nelson, among others.

Then there was that dear, dear man, Donald Vogel, whose artistry and gallery were known nationally, even internationally, particularly when he uncovered the art fraud played upon Algur Meadows by being sold fakes. Donald also was a writer as well as a man who had had many experiences with the art scene in north Texas, particularly Dallas. It was always a treat to meet with him in his studio/home at Valley House Gallery. He gave me the most marvelous gift upon my retirement from publishing from the University of North Texas—a portrait of a woman reading a book. Fran Vick? I think so. I hope so. It is a treasure, too.

All of this aside, I have to be frank with you—publishing was a lot easier for me than writing. I published some 200 books in the twenty years I was a publisher. Maybe I will get the hang of writing one of these days if I live long enough to write that many books, but at the moment I have nothing but the highest admiration for the writers I have published. I have been influenced by them all, in one way or another. My hat is off to all the Texas writers and Texas publishers. They all deserve medals.

Texas is so big and has such a colorful history that it is nigh impossible to know it all intimately. It is an incredibly rich field to mine. We can skim over the top of all of it and carry on conversations to some extent about it, but to write about it is another matter entirely. You have to start digging into the matter. That is where the work comes in. In publishing, one learns a lot about a variety of things, but you are not digging into the subject. You are editing or proofreading or approving designs and all the other details that go into producing a book, and you are learning about the subject as you do all of these things, but you are not doing that digging. The digging encompasses either research or digging in your own mind if you happen to be working on fiction. Fiction, some folks are surprised to discover, also involves research, of course. But the underlying base on all of the digging is that Texan DNA.

J. Frank Dobie once made a pitch in 1936 for Texas writers to write about their own spot in the universe. His exact words were, "great literature transcends its native land but there is no one that I know of that ignores its own soil." No problem for me to follow his edict, although I will never produce the great literature he is referring to. For me it would be impossible to ignore my native soil. Other than that one year in California as a child, I've never lived anywhere but on my native soil.

Texas has defined my whole life as it did my parents' and grandparents' and those on back down the line. My earliest memories are of climbing in my father's lap and begging him to "tell me some more bull," my mother's opinion of the family stories he spun for me. Those stories formed a basis of how I would understand myself and where I came from. How my ancestors responded to events would influence my own actions and my understanding of my DNA and what I owed it. Later it would help me understand my mispronunciations of words and my East Texas twang and yes, my provincialism.

So there it is, my friends—my confession and my truth as a Texas publisher/writer—all laid out in a not-so-neat package.

INDEX

Notes from Texas

ISBN 978-0-87565-358-7
Cloth. $27.95